"So you would've sat at home all by yourself today—as usual—Mr. Cool Lone Wolf," Bailey said

Trent grunted. "So that's what you think of me, huh?"

Bailey pursed her lips and nodded. "Pretty much."

"Humph."

"Don't tell me you're going to deny it."

"I don't deny it, Bailey, and I don't make excuses for it, either. It's simply the way I like my life."

"Really?" Irritation bubbled within her. "You're going to stand there and tell me you prefer being alone and lonely to being here with me and these kids, having a good time?"

"That's right," he said stubbornly.

"You know what?" She glared at him. "You're hopeless."

He shrugged nonchalantly. "Probably."

"I ought to stop wasting my time with you."

"Maybe so."

Then why didn't she?

D0366270

Dear Reader,

I first began writing romance in 1986. Fifteen years later, with more rejection slips than I can count, I finally got "The Call" from Paula Eykelhof, senior editor for Superromance. I'm sure you can imagine my excitement!

Sarah's Legacy came straight from the heart. I was in the middle of writing this book when my seventeen-year-old nephew was killed in a snowmobile accident. It took months for me to be able to go back to the book, but when I did, the writing became a way to pour out the grief that threatened to drown me. There is nothing more devastating than the loss of a child. Trent Murdock must find a way to get past that pain. But I promise you, this book doesn't need to come shrink-wrapped with a bottle of antidepressants! After all, the reason I write romance and love this genre so much is that the reader is always guaranteed a happy ending.

Just how *does* a city-woman-turned-country-girl manage to get a stubborn cowboy to love and laugh again, especially when she's never had a family of her own? Come with me on Trent and Bailey's journey and find out. I hope you enjoy their story, and that you never ever give up on your own goals and dreams. I'm living proof that if you keep at it, your dreams will happen.

I'd love to hear from you. My e-mail is BrendaMott@hotmail.com. Please reference the book on the subject line. Thank you and happy reading.

Sincerely,

Brenda Mott

Sarah's Legacy
Brenda Mott

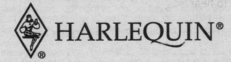

HARLEQUIN®

TORONTO • NEW YORK • LONDON
AMSTERDAM • PARIS • SYDNEY • HAMBURG
STOCKHOLM • ATHENS • TOKYO • MILAN • MADRID
PRAGUE • WARSAW • BUDAPEST • AUCKLAND

ISBN 0-373-71037-2

SARAH'S LEGACY

Copyright © 2002 by Brenda Mott.

This edition published by arrangement with Harlequin Books S.A.

® and TM are trademarks of the publisher. Trademarks indicated with ® are registered in the United States Patent and Trademark Office, the Canadian Trade Marks Office and in other countries.

Visit us at www.eHarlequin.com

Printed in U.S.A.

This book is dedicated with love to the memory
of my nephew, Steven Dale Springer,
who left this world much too soon—I miss you, bud

CHAPTER ONE

BAILEY CHANCELLOR slowed her Ford Mustang, looking out through the car's open window. The little Christmas tree seemed so out of place fully decorated in the month of August, yet there it stood, its red and green ornaments and shiny tinsel reflecting the summer sun.

Curious, she forged ahead on the gravel road until she spotted the entrance to the Roth Hill Cemetery. Putting on her blinker, she turned into the driveway, parked and got out of the car.

The Christmas tree rested beside a marble headstone, the blue-green branches sweetly fragrant. Flipping her braid over one shoulder, Bailey crouched in front of the stone. *Sarah Adelle Murdock.* A cowboy hat and boots were etched into the marble above the name.

Bailey's throat thickened, making it difficult for her to swallow, as she read the dates and the words below the name:

> Daddy's little cowgirl. Gone from this earth,
> but not from our hearts.

From the dates on the headstone, Sarah had been just seven years old when her life ended a year ago…on this very day. Knowing that today was the anniversary of the little girl's death made Bailey all the more sad. That a child's life should be cut short seemed so unfair. Whose little girl was she? How had she died?

Bailey's eyes burned with unshed tears. How many times had she wished for a child of her own? With no family, she often felt lonely. She traced the engraving with her fingertips, and her gaze strayed once more to the little blue spruce.

A porcelain angel, cheeks rosy, hands folded in prayer, topped the tree. The satin bulbs hung in the company of plastic reindeer, elves and teddy bears in Santa hats. The wind that must have blown through the night had scattered tinsel all about. Slivers of gold lay caught in the neatly clipped grass, and two of the ornaments had fallen to the ground at the base of the tree. Bailey picked them up.

The satin felt smooth against her palm, the ornaments weighing almost nothing. Carefully, she lifted one by its metal hook and placed it on the tree. As she hung the second bulb, she sensed someone behind her. Even so, the gruff voice startled her.

"What are you doing?"

Stifling a gasp, Bailey swung around and rose to her feet. Gray eyes as cool as the marble stones in Roth Hill glared back at her. At five foot nine, she had never been accused of being short, yet the stranger before her made her feel small. He topped six feet by a good three inches and had the muscles of someone well acquainted with physical labor. A black T-shirt stretched across his chest and was tucked into faded jeans, and he wore scuffed cowboy boots.

Bailey felt like an intruder. "I'm sorry." She studied him. His face wasn't movie-star handsome, but it was a face that would make a woman look twice. His dark blond hair, just long enough to brush the neckline of his T-shirt, made him seem like the type of guy a mother would warn her daughter to steer clear of. He clutched a paper sack in one hand; the other he held fisted at his side, not threateningly, but defensively.

"I saw the tree from the road," Bailey went on, "and I was curious about it, so I stopped. I didn't mean to intrude."

His expression remained sullen. "It's not meant as a curiosity."

Her face warmed beneath his accusing glare. "Of course not." She felt the need to say something further, but what? "I really *am* sorry." She gave him a look of sympathy, sure he would soften. His expression changed not one little bit.

"Excuse me." Bailey walked away, still feeling his gaze on her. Human nature had compelled her to stop, and she shouldn't feel awkward that she had. But she did.

Reaching her car, she opened the door and slid inside. The hot upholstery burned her skin through her T-shirt. She cranked the engine and flicked on the air-conditioning. As she pressed the button to roll up her window, she couldn't resist another glance at the stranger. He knelt in front of the grave and withdrew something from the paper sack.

Bailey watched him take an ornament and hang it on the tree.

Her heart ached for him and for the little girl who'd died at the age of seven.

She slammed her car door shut and drove from the cemetery.

BAILEY FOLLOWED the curves in the road, doing her best to shake the memory of the cowboy from her mind. He must be Sarah's father. The way he'd stared her down left no other explanation. He didn't want a stranger at his little girl's grave, and she didn't blame him. She reminded herself that small-town life was different from life in the city. A curious passerby in a cemetery in Denver might get overlooked. One here in the Colorado mountain town of Ferguson obviously wouldn't. But then, that was the sort of thing that had first attracted her to this town. Its old-fashioned charm and laid-back ways were exactly what she wanted.

The road twisted in an S-shape, and as she rounded the curve and headed out on the straight-away, her house came into view.

Her house.

Not an apartment she'd rented for an obscene amount of money, where pets weren't allowed and children were frowned upon.

The white-frame, two-story farmhouse sat on eighty acres. A white picket fence surrounded the front yard, with massive cottonwood trees offering shade. The backyard stretched in an expanse of long thick grass, bordered by shrubs of lilac and honey-suckle. The clothesline—a wire strung between two poles—was a place to hang sheets so the sun and wind would dry them and leave behind a touch of the outdoors. A swing on the porch provided the perfect spot for a mother to sit and watch her chil-dren play on a Saturday morning, a dog curled at her feet and Randy Travis singing on the kitchen radio.

Her own little corner of paradise.

She couldn't wait to move in. Her furniture would arrive tomorrow, and though she'd had fun staying at the little bed-and-breakfast in town for the past two weeks while she cleaned up the farmhouse, set-tling into her own home would be nice.

For the first time in her thirty-three years, she had a home where she could put down roots.

It was something she'd never let anyone take away from her again.

TRENT MURDOCK HOPPED UP on the bed of his truck and cut the bright orange twine around the bale of alfalfa with his pocketknife. The herd of Arabian mares quickly gathered around the truck, bickering to establish pecking order. The closest ones thrust their heads eagerly over the top of the truck bed and tried to snatch a bite of hay.

"Get back!" Trent waved his arms at them, and they scattered to a respectable distance for all of thirty seconds before returning. He threw hay to them as the pickup rolled slowly along, driverless and in neutral gear, on the downward incline of the pasture.

He would have to move the mares to the upper field soon, but enough grass remained to hold them for another two or three weeks, anyway. They really didn't need the hay he now tossed to them—though one would think so from their greedy antics—but he liked to baby them. He threw the last of it, then swung down from the pickup bed and slipped into the driver's seat. Pressing his foot on the clutch, he put the truck in gear once more and drove toward the gate.

His mind wandered to the anniversary of his daughter's death. It had been tough, and he'd fought the urge to get drunk the way he had a year ago. Instead, he had gone to the cemetery.

Everyone in Ferguson knew about Sarah and her battle with cancer. They'd paid their respects at her funeral but now stayed away. They'd given him plenty of space to grieve in the last year, plenty of time to be left alone. Though some of the ladies from the Baptist church occasionally put flowers on Sarah's gravc, no one else ever went there. Only him.

So he'd been surprised to find the woman there, crouched beside the tree, holding one of Sarah's ornaments. He'd seen tears in her eyes when she'd spun around to face him. For the past year, he'd closed his heart to all emotion save his grief for his daughter. Nothing had touched him; nothing had penetrated the emptiness inside him. He didn't like the fact that the woman in the cemetery had stirred something deep within him. Why should her tears bother him? He didn't even know her.

He'd gruffly dismissed her, not wanting to learn so much as her name, but now her face preyed on his mind. Who was she? He didn't remember ever having seen her around town. Not that it mattered. Hc had no interest in anyone or anything outside Windsong Ranch. The ranch was all he had left. It was all he needed.

Trent drove from the pasture, stopped and climbed out of the truck, then walked over to shut the gate. He dusted the chaff from his jeans, then climbed back into the pickup. He had errands to run, and no time to waste entertaining thoughts of a woman he didn't even want to know.

The bank was the first stop on his list. A check for the sale of a yearling filly he'd shipped to Dallas was in his wallet and had been for a week now. Money meant little to him, just so long as he had enough to take care of the horses. Still, he should deposit the check in his account.

He saw her the minute he stepped through the doors of Colorado Western National Bank. He would scarcely have recognized her, if not for her eyes. Long-lashed, violet blue, they were the eyes behind the tears that haunted his memory. But the rest of her looked far different from what he recalled. Gone were her faded jeans and pink T-shirt, and her golden-brown hair was no longer confined to a braid. Instead, it fell in silky waves well past her shoulders. She wore a skirt and suit jacket, and sensible low-heeled pumps.

His gaze strayed down the length of her legs, long legs that went on forever, and back up to her face. She'd barely missed a beat in talking to the man who stood in the middle of the lobby with her, dressed in jeans, a tool belt slung low on his hips. Still, Trent knew he'd caught her attention. She glanced his way, then continued her conversation with the man, whose shirtsleeves were rolled up over tanned biceps and who kept flashing a tooth-paste-commercial smile at her.

Trent couldn't help wondering if the guy was business or pleasure. The woman's persona hardly fit with Mr. Tool Belt's, but then the image of her in the cemetery returned, and he realized there just might be two sides to her. It piqued his curiosity all the more.

Irritated that he was even taking time to think about her, or to care one way or the other whom she did or didn't talk to, Trent strode past the two of them.

"Excuse me. Mr. Murdock?" Her voice curled around him like warm whiskey, and he tensed.

He wanted to ignore her. But he had a feeling she wouldn't disappear that easily. Sighing, he faced her. She tucked the clipboard she held underneath one elbow and offered her hand. Reluctantly, he took it.

"I'm Bailey Chancellor."

"It's Trent, and I'm pleased to meet you." His words were a formality only. He didn't want to make small talk; he wanted to finish his business and leave. That she knew his name made him wonder if she'd asked someone. Or had she simply assumed he was Sarah's father, having seen the last name on the headstone?

Her touch, her perfume, stirred something in him

that he didn't care to deal with. He released her hand and let his arm drop back to his side.

Bailey cleared her throat. ''Look, I'm sorry about yesterday.'' She hesitated, as though searching for the right words. ''I want you to know I really mean that.''

He held her gaze, unable to turn away, and shrugged dismissively. ''I guess I was a little uptight yesterday. It wasn't a good day.'' This was as close as he could bring himself to apologizing. She really hadn't done anything, and he shouldn't have snapped at her. But Sarah's Christmas tree was a private thing.

Bailey lowered her voice. ''We got off on the wrong foot. Neighbors in a small town shouldn't do that.''

As her words sank in, he put the obvious together. His former neighbors, the ones who'd owned the eighty acres behind Windsong, had sold their place to the new president of Colorado Western National Bank, but he hadn't realized that anyone was living there yet. So *she* was the woman who'd been the center of Ferguson gossip the past few weeks. *Terrific.*

''I suppose not,'' he said grudgingly in response to her comment.

''Good. I'm glad you feel that way.'' She smiled again. ''Maybe you wouldn't mind showing me your horses sometime. My secretary, Jenny, told me you own Windsong.''

Trent bristled. The last thing he needed was Bailey Chancellor coming to his ranch. He had no inclination to entertain a city woman with big ideas. Especially one who had his libido awakening for the first time in over a year. "I'm sorry." He took a step backward. "I really can't entertain visitors right now. I'm too busy preparing this year's crop of weanlings for sale.''

She pursed her lips in apparent amusement and once more tucked the clipboard under her elbow. "I see. You don't think a woman like me might actually want to *buy* a horse.''

He raised his eyebrows. "Do you?" His face warmed at the look she gave him.

"You figured I wanted to come pet them, is that it?" Her eyes sparked with something between amusement and irritation.

Trent cleared his throat. "Something like that." He folded his arms in front of his chest. "If you're serious about buying, then I'd be more than happy to show you what I have for sale.''

"Wonderful. When's a good time?"

Never. The uncharitable thought startled him, yet he couldn't help it. Something about Bailey Chancellor set his nerves on edge. Not in a bad way, but in a way he certainly didn't like. The prospect of her coming to his ranch displeased him, but he could hardly tell her no. His horses were for sale to anyone who would provide them with a good home and proper care. As long as Bailey qualified, there was no reason to turn her down. "This weekend would be fine, if that suits your schedule."

"Perfect. Tomorrow, two o'clock?"

He nodded.

"Great." She gave a little wave. "See you then." She walked away, her hips swaying just the slightest as she headed back to resume her conversation with Mr. Tool Belt.

Just the slightest was enough to rouse more than his mind.

"Mr. Murdock?" The voice calling him didn't register at first.

He blinked at the teller on the other side of the counter. "Hmm?"

"May I help you?" She stared politely at him.

Where was his mind?

Forcing a smile, he stepped up to the window and handed the teller the check and deposit slip. He half listened as she counted bills into his hand for the return cash he'd requested, along with a receipt that read: Colorado Western National. Your Hometown Friendly Bank.

His gaze had strayed to the woman with the golden-brown hair, long curvy legs and a name that rolled off his tongue like cream over strawberries. *Bailey Chancellor.*

She caught him staring and flashed him a smile. He swallowed hard and turned away.

Your hometown friendly bank.

The only one he had any thoughts about getting hometown friendly with was Bailey.

A woman with violet eyes.

A woman who scared the hell out of him.

"DO YOU HAVE a headache, Bailey? Can I get you some aspirin?"

Bailey looked up into the concerned face of her young secretary. Quickly, she unfolded her hands and lowered them from her forehead. "No, Jenny, thanks. I was just thinking."

"All right." Jenny started to leave.

"Uh, Jenny?"

"Yes?"

"I was wondering something. You mentioned my neighbor this morning, Trent Murdock?"

Jenny nodded.

In the two weeks since she'd hired her, Bailey had quickly discovered that her secretary was a font of information. Jenny had lived in Ferguson all her twenty-five years, and knew everything about everybody. She loved to talk, and when Bailey had said this morning that she was in search of a good horse, Jenny had told her about Windsong. Jenny had bought a horse from Windsong two years ago, and gave the ranch and its owner, Trent Murdock, a good recommendation.

As soon as Jenny had called Trent by name, Bailey realized he was probably the man she'd seen at the cemetery, since Murdock was the name on the little girl's headstone. Normally she wasn't the nosy type, but she couldn't seem to get Trent Murdock off her mind, especially since he'd walked into the bank an hour ago.

"What happened to Trent's little girl?" Bailey asked.

Jenny's pretty face clouded over, and she stepped closer to Bailey's desk, her long blond ponytail swishing. "She had stomach cancer. It was so sad. And that Christmas tree on her grave…have you seen it? God, it just tears your heart out. No one knows why Trent put it there, but he did it the day after she was buried, and he hangs a new ornament on it every now and then."

She shuddered and leaned on the desk. "I can hardly bear to talk about it. No one does. Trent's wife left him after little Sarah died. She just couldn't take it, I guess. It was really awful, though—him grieving and then Amy leaving him that way. A lot of ladies around here tried to comfort him, if you know what I mean, but he wasn't having any part of it. Guess he just wants to be left alone in his grief.

"Those horses are his whole life, and the only time a person can get him to open up is when he's discussing them. You really ought to go see them. I'm sure you'll find one you like. But don't mention Sarah. Her death's just too much for him to cope with. Like I said, no one talks about it.''

Jenny paused for air and Bailey blinked. For a subject that was allegedly taboo, her secretary certainly hadn't held back much. But then, that was Jenny, and Bailey was quickly learning that in a small town gossiping was highly rated.

''Thank you, Jenny. I'll keep that in mind.''

BAILEY WORKED through her lunch hour and left the bank at two o'clock. Her furniture and other belongings were due to arrive at her house at two-thirty. She drove to the bed-and-breakfast where she'd been staying, changed into jeans and a T-shirt then headed for the farm. As she passed the cemetery, she glanced over at Sarah's tree.

Why had Trent put a Christmas tree on his little girl's grave in the middle of August? And why did he continue to keep it decorated? She couldn't shake the picture of him kneeling beside the grave yesterday, hanging a new ornament. Maybe he'd done it because yesterday had been the one-year anniversary of Sarah's death. Jenny had said he hung a new one from time to time. It tugged at Bailey's heart to ponder what occasions made him do so. The remembrance of a special day once shared with Sarah? Her birthday? The day she took her first step? God, how it must hurt to lose a child.

She couldn't begin to imagine the pain Trent suffered. She wished she could have somehow comforted him. Until yesterday morning when Camille Kendall, the owner of the bed-and-breakfast, had told her about the shortcut road that ran past Roth Hill Cemetery, she'd taken the long way around to get to her farm. That was why she hadn't seen the cemetery and the tree sooner. Odd that she'd happened by on the day Trent visited Sarah's grave—a day that surely caused him great sorrow.

Maybe fate had thrown him in her path.

Bailey shook off the thought. It was ridiculous. When she got involved with a man, it wouldn't be Trent Murdock. Clearly, he carried a lot of baggage. She didn't need that, no matter how much she sympathized with his loss. And he most certainly didn't need her to comfort him. He obviously was a loner, just the type of man she'd vowed to avoid. She'd seen enough of men focused on their careers, men who didn't want children. From what Jenny had said, the loss of his daughter had made Trent into just that kind of man.

No, Bailey couldn't let her feelings override good sense. The only thing Trent had to offer her was a horse, and she'd do well to remember that.

She pulled onto County Road 311 and minutes later turned into her driveway. The farmhouse had been remodeled in years past and was in good shape for the most part, but it still needed a few little repairs here and there, some paint, a loving touch. She had nearly finished painting the inside. The repair work would come as she made time for it.

The moving van arrived punctually, and Bailey spent the remainder of the afternoon directing the movers where to put the heaviest pieces of furniture. By six o'clock, she was hot, dusty and tired. But she was happy. She wandered from room to room, through rows of boxes, loving the way her furniture looked in the place. The big house seemed to swallow her possessions. She would have to accumulate things to fill it. The four bedrooms, living room, family room, dining room and spacious kitchen were a far cry from the two-bedroom apartment she'd rented in Denver.

One day, Bailey promised herself, all the rooms would be filled, not just with furniture but with her family. She planned to have it all. The house with the white picket fence, a dog, a cat, a horse…and kids. Lots of kids. Whether she could find the right man to share her dream had yet to be seen. That was where her version of the all-American family often fell apart. She'd witnessed so many empty marriages, met so many shallow men, that she'd begun to wonder if real love and romance existed. The businesswoman in her said no. But that didn't stop her from wanting children.

Growing up, she'd lived in enough foster homes to know that thousands of kids out there needed parents and didn't have them. She'd been one, and she longed to give a child what she'd never had, to complete the circle she'd traveled and close the empty space that had claimed a part of her life for so long. If she never found the right guy to marry, she would simply adopt children and raise them on her own. Her kids would never lack for love or for a true parent. They would have roots, and this wonderful farmhouse to call home.

Bailey's stomach growled, reminding her she'd skipped lunch. She ambled to the kitchen, where she grabbed a sandwich, then headed for the porch swing.

The sound of hoofbeats reached her ears as she pushed open the screen door. Her mouth dropped at the sight of half a dozen horses galloping across her pasture. Heads held high, necks arched, they raced in a semicircle. Hot on their heels was the stray dog she'd been feeding for the past two weeks, and right behind the dog ran a figure in a ball cap and faded jeans.

Quickly, Bailey set her sandwich plate on the porch railing and rushed down the steps. A jumble of thoughts filled her mind as she pushed through the pasture gate. From their dished faces, fine-boned heads and flowing tails lifted high in the air, she could tell the horses were Arabians, which could mean only one thing. The man in the ball cap, who continued to let out a steady stream of curses at the blue heeler-mix, could be none other than Trent Murdock.

Her experience with horses went no further than the research she'd done in preparing to buy one. Still, it seemed to her that the most sensible thing to do to get the Arabians calmed down and under control was to first contain the dog.

Considering that the animal was leery of humans and had yet to let her close enough to touch him, the task might be easier said than done. How could she get a dog that had obviously been abused, and therefore trusted no one, to come to her? Especially when he didn't even have a name. Rolling her eyes, Bailey headed toward the barn. The bag of dog food she'd stored in the feed room stood against one wall. She scooped some into a stainless-steel dish and hurried outside.

Putting her fingers to her lips, she let out a shrill whistle that immediately snagged the attention of both man and dog. Bailey ignored Trent and focused on the dog. "Here, boy!" She rattled the food inside the dish. "Come and get it." The dog had slowed his step and now glanced from the horses, which still raced in circles, to her, then back to the horses. He gave chase once more, and Bailey moved toward him, willing herself to walk. She didn't want to scare him, yet the angry posture of Trent's shoulders warned her she'd better reach the dog before he did.

She called to the animal again. This time he looked warily over his shoulder at Trent and immediately made a beeline for her. "That's it! Come on." She rattled the food, and the dog slowed to a trot and halted several feet away, tongue lolling over black lips. He pinned his upright ears, the black-and-white speckled tip of his tail drooping behind him, his stance indicating that he was ready to bolt at the first sign of a suspicious move on her part. She crooned reassuringly to him, and he flicked his ears forward and cocked his head.

Bailey bent over at the waist, trying to make herself appear smaller and less threatening. "Here, boy. I've got some dinner for you." The dog took a hesitant step forward. "That's right. Come on." Walking half backward, she began a slow retreat toward the barn, holding the dish out before her. "It's okay."

The dog shot Trent another glance and seemed to decide his best option was the safety of Bailey's company. He loped after her, and she walked a little faster. Reaching the open doorway of the barn, she set the food dish down in the aisle. The dog stopped and stared at her. His ribs showed through his black coat, and her heart went out to him. She couldn't stand to see an animal hungry. "Go on, boy. Dinner's waiting."

He edged toward the doorway, nose quivering as he sniffed the air. Scenting the food, he darted inside and thrust his muzzle into the dish. Bailey crept forward, whispering an apology to the animal. She'd planned to tame him gradually, and had tried not to do anything to scare him or betray his trust. But shutting him in the barn seemed to be in his best interest at the moment. After sliding the heavy door closed on its track, she slipped the latch into place, heaved a sigh of relief and turned around.

Trent Murdock stood behind her, so close she could make out every murderous frown line that creased his forehead.

"Lady," he snapped, "if that's your dog, you're in more trouble than you ever bargained for."

Bailey set her jaw.

She didn't doubt it for a minute.

But if Trent wanted to fight, she was game.

CHAPTER TWO

TRENT FOUGHT the urge to throttle both the dog and the woman. He pushed his cap back on his head, crossed his arms over his chest and glared at Bailey Chancellor.

"He's not my dog," she said. "Well—not exactly. But anyway, he didn't hurt anything." She folded her arms and stared defiantly at him.

Trent stared back, unable to believe his ears. "He ran my horses through the fence!"

The expression in Bailey's violet eyes flickered, and Trent's heart gave the smallest jump—just enough to make him wary. He was furious with her. He refused to feel anything else.

"They didn't get cut, did they?" Bailey asked uncertainly. "They seem all right—the way they're running around." She looked at the horses, and Trent did, too. They'd calmed down some, now that the dog was out of sight, and moved in slower circles around the pasture.

"I don't know," he said. "I'll have to catch them and see."

"All right, then." Bailey unfolded her arms and

walked away, looking at him over her shoulder. "Coming?"

Surely she didn't mean to help him. But that was exactly her intention. "I don't have a halter yet," she said. "We'll have to get a couple from your place." She paused long enough to grace him with a firm stare. "Well, don't just stand there with your mouth open. We've got horses to catch."

Trent shook his head, not sure what to make of Bailey Chancellor. Maybe he'd misjudged her. She hadn't struck him as the type to know a damn thing about horses. President of the bank, here from Denver, she'd caused a stir of gossip in town not matched since Jed Sanders had shot his brother in the leg for sleeping with Jed's girlfriend. Rumor had it she planned to create a day care right at Colorado Western National for the children of the bank's employees. Rumor also had it that the tough-as-nails woman just about everyone in town resented was behind the bank's new policy that had led to the rejection of more than one farmer's loan.

But Trent had seen a different Bailey Chancellor. The woman in a pink T-shirt and faded jeans, with tears in her eyes.

Shaking off the memory of Bailey in the cemetery, he followed her. She strode across the pasture, speaking soothingly to the horses, and headed for the downed fence. There she stopped, hands on hips, to survey the damage. "I'm glad to see it's barbless wire,'' she said. ''Otherwise your horses could've been cut to ribbons.''

Temper bubbled anew within Trent as he halted beside her. Resting one hand on his hip, he gave her a humorless smile. ''Really? Why, thanks for sharing that information with me, Ms. Chancellor. I'm much obliged.''

She frowned at him. ''Don't be sarcastic. I'm trying to help.''

''By telling me how to fence in my horses as though I don't have a clue?''

She raised an eyebrow. ''I was merely making an observation.'' Coolly, she brushed his attitude aside. ''So, where are the halters?''

''In the tack room.'' He enunciated each word, stating the obvious. ''I'll get them. Think you can make sure those mares don't run back through the downed wire?''

Bailey's slight hesitation made Trent wonder if his original instincts were right. She appeared confident, yet something about her demeanor left him thinking she was a little wary of the horses.

''Fine,'' Bailey said, turning to watch the mares. They now trotted around the pasture, ears alert, nostrils flared as they snorted loudly.

''You sure?'' Trent asked.

''Yes, I'm sure.''

Trent decided to give her the benefit of the doubt. ''Okay, then. Be right back.'' From the tack room in his barn, he took two halters and lead ropes, then returned to where Bailey waited.

He handed her a purple halter and rope, and for some stupid reason noted that it was damn near the same color as her eyes. Maybe his cap was on too tight. Bailey held the halter a bit awkwardly and fumbled with the buckle.

Amused, Trent watched. "You've got it backward," he said, not sure what to make of the entire situation. Did she or did she not know how to handle a horse?

Bailey flushed and promptly turned the halter around, this time opening the buckle and holding it in the proper position. "I see that now," she said. "Which horse do you want me to catch?"

"Dokina and Shafana are both alpha mares," he said. "If we get them, the others should follow." He produced a pair of wire cutters from his back pocket and snipped the downed strands of wire from the wooden post they'd been stapled to. Removing the wire was the only way to bring the horses safely back through the fence, since there was no gate in this section.

With Bailey's help, Trent set aside the wire, disgusted that he'd have to restring it, thanks to the dog.

As though reading his mind, Bailey spoke. "I'll help you put the fence back up later."

"That's not necessary."

"Yes, it is. My dog caused this." With a sweep of her hand, she indicated the downed wire and the loose horses.

"I thought you said he wasn't your dog."

"He's not exactly, but I hope he will be sooner or later. He's a stray," she clarified when he looked at her, curious. "I've been feeding him."

"No wonder he seems familiar," Trent said. "I've seen him around here before, several weeks ago, as a matter of fact, though he's never chased my horses until now. I'm pretty sure he was dumped."

"I can relate," Bailey mumbled.

"How's that?"

"Nothing. Which one is Dokina?" She walked toward the horses.

He followed. "The chestnut with the blaze and no stockings." He fumbled in his pocket. "Here. You'll need these."

Bailey faced him, and he placed four horse cookies in her hand, trying not to notice how soft her skin was as his fingers brushed her palm. Come to think of it, she smelled good, too. She'd caught her hair up in a ponytail, and golden-brown wisps strayed around her face as the hint of a breeze stirred the air. Today, she wore a yellow T-shirt with her jeans, and the same sneakers she'd had on yesterday. She reminded him of sunshine and a fresh breath of air.

He didn't want to notice that about her, didn't want to experience the desire to touch her. Amy had left him, Sarah was gone, and he didn't plan on feeling anything for anyone ever again.

"They're cookies," Trent said as Bailey stared down at the flat, rectangular alfalfa pellets.

"Not chocolate chip, I'd wager," Bailey quipped.

He fought a smile. "Some people call them cake. Take your pick, but you'll need them to get close enough to catch any of the horses."

Bailey crooked her mouth and arched one eyebrow. "Spoiled, huh?" Her words should have sounded accusatory, but somehow they didn't. Her whiskey voice seemed to carry indulgence.

"No," Trent said defensively. Then he lost his battle with the smile that kept tugging at his mouth. "Well, maybe just a little."

Bailey drew back and gazed solidly at him. Then her own lips curved. "You should do that more often. Smile, I mean. Looks better on you than that scowl you usually wear."

Trent grunted and let the smile disappear. "I thought we were catching horses."

"Okay, okay." Bailey shook her head and gave her attention to Dokina once more. Trent watched as she crooned to the little mare and held out a cookie. Dokina perked her ears and stretched out her neck to investigate, taking a tentative step in Bailey's direction. Two other mares came forward in response to the proffered treat. Immediately, Dokina pinned her ears and drove them away, teeth bared. The mares parted company with a volley of squeals and a show of back hooves, and all the while, Bailey stood her ground.

Trent shook his head and haltered Shafana, his favorite gray. He would have expected Bailey to run at the possibility of being smack-dab in the middle of a horse fight. But she only took a cautious step out of the way, then held the horse cookie out to Dokina once more. Though she fumbled with the halter a bit, she managed to slip it over the mare's head and get it buckled into place.

Bailey looked at him, a triumphant grin spreading across her pretty face, and Trent's heart did more than give a little jump. It was the first time he'd seen her smile with anything other than polite reserve, the first time he'd seen such an expression of pure, childlike joy on her face. He liked it, and that bothered him.

"Nothing to it," Bailey said, walking toward him, leading Dokina.

Trent fell into step beside her with Shafana. The other mares followed, as he'd known they would. Some had marks from the wire on their legs and chests, but fortunately none was hurt beyond those few minor scrapes, which hadn't done more than skin off small spots of hair and hide. A little nitrofurazone ointment would have them good as new.

Bailey's eyes sparkled. "They're beautiful." She nodded toward a golden-red chestnut with flaxen mane and tail. "I love that one. What's her name?"

"Bint Sihanna Bronnz."

"Quite a mouthful," Bailey said. "Is she for sale?"

He shook his head. "No. These are some of my broodmares. I raise and sell foals. I also travel around the show circuit, pick up horses here and there, then resell them."

"I see. Well, I hadn't planned on looking at your horses this way, but since I'm already here..."

He was quiet for a moment. And he hadn't planned on being with her this way. Hell, he hadn't really wanted to hang around her at all. Business was business and he'd agreed to show her what he had for sale, but he'd had every intention of doing so on his own terms, in his own time. Now, with Bailey walking toward the barn, leading Dokina and chatting with him as though she belonged right here, he felt confused and off balance. He'd tried hard to keep everything in his life orderly and mapped out since Amy had left him—since he'd lost Sarah. It was the only way he could deal with his emotions, the only way he seemed able to get through each day.

Bailey and her damn stray dog had upset all that.

"I've got time to show them to you now if you want," he heard himself saying.

She turned that blasted heart-stopping smile on him once more. "That would be wonderful. Where would you like Dokina?"

AFTER HELPING TRENT put ointment on the mares that had gotten scraped, Bailey assisted him in turning them out in a paddock behind the barn and tried to pretend he had no effect on her whatsoever. It had to be the horses that had her stomach in knots...that was it. She hadn't been around them much, and finding herself right in the middle of the group of mares was a little more than she'd bargained for, especially when they started to squabble over the horse cookies.

She hoped Trent hadn't noticed the momentary scare Dokina gave her when the mare pinned her ears, bared her teeth and charged. But then Bailey realized the horse wasn't after her at all—she was simply defending what she felt belonged to her. *That* Bailey could also relate to, and she'd immediately felt calm.

Now her heart was doing a little skip-hop. Damn it, why did Trent have to look so much better in blue jeans than any man she'd seen lately?

"So, are you ready for the grand tour?" Trent asked, pulling her from her musings.

"Sure." She handed him the purple halter and lead rope, and he hung it on the fence and shouldered the one he'd removed from the gray mare.

"The saddle horses I have for sale are in the upper pasture," he said.

"You've got a beautiful place here." Bailey's gaze swept Windsong Ranch. An adobe-style house, looking like something from a western movie, sprawled not far from the barn, beneath the shade of massive cottonwoods that circled the well-kept lawn. The pasture, fenced in either wire or white rail, stretched as far as the eye could see. The scent of horses, hay and wildflowers caught on the breeze and surrounded her, leaving Bailey with the impression that everything was neat, clean and in its proper place.

She wondered if that was the way Trent laid out his life day by day—nothing out of place, most especially his emotions. Telling herself she had no business analyzing the man, she turned her thoughts back to the ranch. "How many acres do you have here, if you don't mind my asking?"

"Two hundred and fifty."

"Wow. And I thought eighty was a lot." She smiled. "It's nice the way you put your house at the very back. Gives you some privacy."

Trent didn't smile. He shot her a funny look, then clamped his mouth shut as though he'd been going to say something but had decided not to at the last minute.

What *was* his problem?

He closed up more and more as they walked

along, restricting his comments to information about the horses he had for sale. Bailey felt that he'd suddenly thrown a wall up between them, and she wondered why. Sure, he'd been angry at what the dog had done, and she'd acted a little defensive in return. But he'd seemed to warm to her while they worked to bring the horses in.

It was just as well that she keep her distance from him, Bailey decided as she followed Trent into the pasture, where a dozen-odd horses grazed.

"How experienced a rider are you?" Trent asked.

"Not very," Bailey admitted. "I've taken some riding lessons, and I've been reading up on owning a horse."

He grunted. "So that explains it."

"Explains what?"

"Why you seem to know something about horses, yet don't appear totally comfortable around them."

She bristled. "I've learned a lot over the past few months, Mr. Murdock. I can assure you I plan to continue that route."

"No need to get your back up," he said. "I was just making an observation. And like I said at the bank, it's Trent. Mr. Murdock is my father."

"Only if you call me Bailey," she said. Just because they kept their distance didn't mean they had to be formal. After all, they were neighbors.

"Okay, Bailey. Let me tell you a little more about these horses."

She walked beside him, listening as he went into detail about the good points—and bad—of each horse. His knowledge impressed her and his honesty took her by surprise. "I thought people who sold horses were only supposed to mention their good qualities and hide their bad," she said. She'd recently read an article in *Western Horseman* entitled "Buyer Beware."

"There are a lot of disreputable people in the horse business," Trent agreed, "just as there are in any business. But I don't work that way, Bailey. I want my customers to be satisfied and my horses to have a good home. They can't have that unless I'm up-front in the first place."

"Good point."

"Not to say any of these horses are bad animals," he went on. "I wouldn't have them for sale if that was the case. But no horse is perfect."

In her experience, animals were usually far more perfect than people, but she didn't argue. "So, the little gray mare is hard to catch," Bailey said. "But she's a good solid riding mount."

"The best," Trent said. "She's bombproof."

"What does that mean?"

"She doesn't spook at anything. And she can cover ground all day long and be ready for more." He ran his hand over the shoulder of a dark bay gelding. "This is Mirage, a son of my stallion Alysana. He's one of the few foals I kept because he has such a great personality, but when he was a two-year-old he had an accident. Fell off a cliff and got pretty banged up. His foreleg took the worst of it.'' Trent indicated a scar on the gelding's right foreleg that ran the length of the cannon bone. "He's sound, but only for light trail riding. You couldn't work him hard or use him for endurance riding or anything like that. Still, he's got a willing heart and he's real easy to catch.''

Unlike his owner.

Bailey chuckled. "I can see that," she said as the horse nudged Trent's shoulder affectionately, looking for a treat. Trent pulled a horse cookie from his pocket and the gelding took it with a soft smack of his lips. He chewed with eyes half-closed, as though savoring the alfalfa cube. Several other horses made their way over to see what was going on.

Trent offered each of them cookies, then held up his empty palms. "I'm all out," he said, rubbing the forehead of a black mare. "That's it.''

Bailey smiled to herself. A man who talked to horses couldn't be all bad. "They're nice horses," she said. "It's going to be hard to choose one.''

"They're a pretty good bunch," Trent said, patting the black mare's shoulder.

"What about that one?" Bailey pointed to a gray whose coat was flecked with red markings. The horse kept to the rear of the group. As the animal turned his head, she noted his left eye appeared cloudy, and the skin around it was heavily scarred. "Oh! What happened to his eye?"

"He had it all but poked out by a tree branch when a pack of dogs ran him into the woods three years ago." Trent frowned pointedly at her and Bailey cringed inwardly.

No wonder he'd been so upset when her stray dog had chased his horses. "Can he see out of it?" she asked, ignoring Trent's underlying reprimand.

"No. I don't even know why I keep him in here with the others that are for sale. If he were a mare, I'd just put her with the other broodmares, but what am I going to do with a gelding? Most people turn away from him the minute they see his eye."

"Why? Just because he isn't perfect doesn't mean he isn't a good horse, does it?" Bailey moved toward the gelding. "Hey, there, pretty baby," she crooned. The gelding stretched his neck inquisitively and gently lipped Bailey's hand as she drew close to him. Bailey smiled, warming immediately to the horse that no one wanted. "I'm sorry. I'm all out of cookies." She stroked the gray's muzzle. "What's his name?"

"Star."

"Star?" Bailey gave him an amused smile. "No fancy Arab name?"

Trent shrugged. "He has some fancy stuff tacked onto it."

Bailey rubbed the gelding's forehead. "It fits him.

I like it, and I love his coloring. It looks like he has freckles.''

"He's a flea-bitten gray."

She glared at him. "How can you insult such a pretty horse?"

He laughed. "It's not an insult. That freckled pattern is called flea-bitten gray."

Bailey flushed. "Oh. Guess I need to read up on my colors a little more." She continued to stroke the horse, and Star responded by closing his eyes and nudging her with his head. "I think he likes me, too. So, is he for sale?"

Trent looked at her with surprise. "He's blind in one eye. You wouldn't really want him, would you?"

"Why not?" Bailey challenged. "Is he ridable?"

"Yes. He's a little shy on his near side, but as long as he trusts his rider, there's nothing he won't do for you. I guess that's why I've kept him. He's a good horse."

"Well, then, I'll have to try him out later." She gave the gelding one last pat, then walked back to stand beside Trent. "But for now we've got a fence to fix."

"I told you, I can take care of it."

"I wouldn't feel right not helping," Bailey said firmly.

"All right, if that's what you want," he said. "But it's too late to get started now. Come back in the morning. Then, if you like, you can ride any of the horses you're interested in.''

For a minute, she wondered if he was simply putting her off, not wanting her help, but the look in his eyes seemed genuine. ''Okay. I'll see you tomorrow. And thanks for showing your horses to me.''

''No problem.''

Bailey walked across the pasture toward the downed wire that separated her ranch from his, furious with herself at the disappointment that welled inside her. Surely she hadn't been enjoying Trent's company that much. Yet the prospect of going back to her empty house didn't hold quite the appeal now as it had when she'd driven home from work a short while ago.

Bailey gave herself a mental shake. What was wrong with her?

She reached her front porch just in time to see a huge gray cat leap onto the railing, snatch her forgotten sandwich from the plate where she'd left it and sprint across the lawn into the bushes bordering the yard. At the same time, a mournful howl from the barn split the air. Bailey sighed and placed her hands on her hips, rolling her eyes heavenward.

Why was it she always seemed to attract—and be attracted to—strays and misfits?

She knew the answer. She just wasn't sure she liked it. Years spent convincing herself she'd left her past behind hadn't really changed anything. Her whole life she'd felt unwanted, unloved; a misfit that people simply passed off whenever they could.

It didn't matter. She had a chance for a brand-new start here in Ferguson. She just had to remember that taking in strays and misfits was okay…as long as she drew the line where it needed to be drawn. She couldn't let Trent Murdock step across that line, nor could she let herself. Keeping her distance shouldn't be a problem. It was obvious from the time she'd just spent with him that Trent didn't want pity. He was far too strong for that.

Yet when she'd looked deep into his eyes, she'd seen a haunting pain that she could relate to.

Relate to or not, he doesn't want you getting close. Bailey's inner voice spoke sensibly. He wasn't one of her misfits to be taken in and watched over.

Which was a good thing, since she had no intention of doing so anyway.

Stray dogs were one thing.

Cowboys with haunting eyes were quite another.

CHAPTER THREE

TRENT COULD NOT SLEEP. What was it about a woman who took in stray dogs and stood up for the rights of a blind horse that had him tossing and turning all night? He neither needed nor wanted a woman in his life, much less Bailey Chancellor, yet he still couldn't stop thinking about her. She fascinated him.

She'd tried to seem nonchalant, but she was obviously drawn to the animals she perceived as needy. She'd taken a harder look at Star than any of the other horses he'd shown her; and most people would've called animal control and let them deal with a dog like the blue heeler-mix rather than feed it and lock it in the barn to save its sorry hide.

Trent shook his head. As much as he loved dogs, he'd come close to phoning animal control himself when he'd first noticed the heeler, for the dog's sake if nothing else. A stray could get into all kinds of trouble, not to mention that the animal had no way to fend for itself. He'd never understood why people thought they could simply turn an animal loose in the country and it would be okay.

He might have left food out for the dog if it hadn't looked so much like Jax. He'd brought Jax home to Sarah just before they found out she had cancer. The blue heeler–border collie cross had become her constant companion. Amy had taken the dog with her when she left, and Trent hadn't bothered to get another one.

But somehow Bailey had managed to distract him from all that with her unplanned visit to Windsong. Hell, he'd talked more to her than he had to anyone in a long while, other than the buyers who came to see his Arabians. He'd tried to tell himself that Bailey, too, was simply a potential buyer. But he knew better. Deep down, he had to admit he'd enjoyed her company far more than he wanted to. Why, he wasn't sure, and that disturbed him more than anything.

Trent got out of bed at six, ready for his morning routine: feed and water the horses, check the foals, have some coffee, then head back outside to work on halter-training the colts and fillies, which varied in age and in stages of learning. He didn't know what time Bailey planned to come over, but he was fairly certain it wouldn't be any time too soon. City people generally started their days when business hours began. They had no concept of rising with the chickens, so to speak.

As he went outside, a sharp ringing, like something striking the ground repeatedly, came from Bai-

ley's place, the sound carrying easily on the clear
mountain air. Curious, Trent walked to a high point
of ground where he was able to look down on the
small valley in which Bailey's ranch nestled. He
could just make out the woman who'd kept him
awake much of the night. She was in the backyard,
and from the looks of it, she was wielding a posthole
digger. Surely not. What on earth was she doing?

There was only one way to find out.

Rationalizing that he was being neighborly not
nosy, he headed across the pasture, through the gap
in the fence, onto Bailey's property. As he drew
near, he saw the blue heeler-mix tethered to a rope
tied to a tree not far from where Bailey was digging.
The dog acted like someone had just kicked the day-
lights out of him. A mournful expression on his face,
he crouched on his belly, ears flat, tail tucked, the
rope pulled as taut as it could possibly get without
choking him. Trent doubted Bailey had done anything to him. He was probably just afraid of the
rope.

Trent turned his attention to Bailey. She was indeed digging a hole, a pair of gardening gloves pro-
tecting her hands, her hair in a French braid. She
wore cutoff jeans, and a white tank top that showed
off a tan he wondered how she'd had time to acquire, given that her job kept her indoors all day.
Probably a tanning salon. But as Bailey glanced over
her shoulder and smiled at him, she somehow

seemed at home gripping the posthole digger, more than a city woman should have. More like a woman who'd come by her tan honestly.

"Good morning," she said, blowing out a puff of air and sweeping her damp bangs out of her eyes with the back of one hand. She leaned against the posthole digger, and the morning sun silhouetted her every curve.

Trent sucked in his breath. "'Morning," he said gruffly. "You're up awfully early."

"I had to be," Bailey said. "I'm building a fence. For him." She nodded toward the dog. "The one around the front yard won't hold him. He jumps it."

"I see." Trent fought a smile. "Do you have any idea how much work that entails?"

Bailey quirked one corner of her mouth. "I'm beginning to see," she admitted. She scowled at the posthole digger. "The man who sold this to me didn't mention that it's harder to use than it looks. But I'll get it. Just might take me a while."

To say the least. Trent eyed the hole Bailey had dug. It was no more than four inches deep. At this rate, the dog would die of old age before Bailey could fence in the yard.

"Why don't you hire someone to do the job for you?"

"Oh, no." She waved the thought aside. "I can do it."

Why don't you offer to do it for her? The inner

voice that prodded him was perfectly logical, he told himself. After all, the woman was obviously too stubborn to hire someone, though he had to admire her determination. And what could it hurt to be nice? Besides, he didn't need the dog running his horses through the fence again.

"I can't take a chance on him chasing your horses," Bailey said as though reading his mind. "And you can see he's terrified of that rope. Poor thing. I'm sure someone has beaten him."

"More than likely," Trent agreed. "I'll tell you what. Since you're going to help me restring my fence, why don't you let me return the favor and help you dig the holes for yours." He knew she'd be too proud to accept his help if it sounded like charity.

"Oh, I couldn't possibly—"

"I won't take no for an answer," he interrupted. "Like you said, you can't leave him on the rope, and I sure don't want him going after my horses. The sooner the holes are dug, the sooner you can put the fence up and turn him out in the yard. It would be in his best interest."

"Well, I suppose you've got a point there." She shrugged. "All right. I'll dig one hole—you dig the next."

He had his doubts she could finish the one she'd started. "Okay." Enjoying himself, Trent leaned against the tree the dog was tied to and watched.

Bailey gave it a hell of a shot, he'd grant her that. But the ground was hard, and operating a posthole digger took a lot of muscle—more muscle than Bailey had, though there was nothing wrong with the shape she was in. Nothing wrong at all.

He couldn't help but let his gaze travel her curves as she worked. Her breasts jiggled beneath the sports bra she wore under her tank top, and he felt the blood stir in his veins—and someplace else. Swallowing, Trent shifted his gaze elsewhere.

Bailey's arms were firm, her long legs trim beneath her cutoffs.

This wasn't getting him anywhere.

"Let me see that thing." He pushed away from the porch and reached for the posthole digger.

"But I'm not finished," Bailey protested as he pulled it out of her hands.

"At the rate you're going, it'll be dark out before you get so much as one hole dug." He realized he sounded rude, but he didn't care. Irritation filled him: he knew he was attracted to Bailey. He'd help her dig her blessed holes, but that was all.

"I didn't ask for your help," she reminded him.

He glanced up long enough to wish he hadn't. Anger rode high on her cheekbones in a soft blush that did everything to complement her complexion and nothing to help his frame of mind. On top of that, the flash of fire he saw in those violet eyes began to give him a picture of the formidable figure she must make at the bank; a glimpse of the woman who turned down farmers' loans and wreaked havoc on small-town tradition with her big-city ideas. Bailey obviously wasn't a woman to tangle with.

The challenge drew him like a bug to a zapper.

"And I never asked for yours, either, but didn't you say that's what neighbors do? Help one another?" He returned his attention to digging but stole a glance at Bailey from the corner of his eye.

She bristled anew at his words, and he nearly smiled as he scored himself one point.

"I suppose I did." She folded her arms across her chest. "But that doesn't mean you need to dig all the holes for me."

Pausing, Trent leaned on the posthole digger. "Do you have any idea how many holes you'll need to fence in a yard this size?" He gestured at the huge backyard.

Bailey chewed her bottom lip. "Quite a few."

"Exactly. What type of fence are you planning to put up?"

"Chain-link."

"You'll have to set the posts in cement if you want to make it sturdy."

"I realize that," Bailey said. "I just thought I might as well get the holes dug first." She let her breath out on a sigh. "Fine. Dig them all, then, but if you're going to go to so much trouble, I insist on paying you for your time."

"Tell you what," Trent said. "If you want to pay me, do it by fixing me some breakfast. I'll have to have some fuel to run on if I plan to be out here building fence all morning."

Bailey eyed him as though he'd just suggested she put on a hula skirt and dance for him. "Breakfast? You want me to *cook* for you?"

"Yeah. You do know how, don't you?"

"Of course I do." The spark was back in her eyes.

"Good." He jabbed the posthole digger into the ground and left it there. "I'll go feed my animals and get my gloves, then be right back." He turned away, hiding a smile.

"I have to run to the store first," Bailey called after him. "To buy a few things."

"Fine. See you in a bit." Without looking back, he waved over his shoulder, then chuckled.

Bailey Chancellor was obviously a smart woman and a real go-getter, but she was a terrible liar.

From the look on her face, he'd safely bet his best horse she couldn't boil water.

BAILEY DROVE to town mumbling curses all the way. How had she managed to get herself into this? She couldn't cook. She didn't have time to bother with it, and the fact that she lived alone made learning seem like a waste of time. Frozen dinners and takeout were her staples, as were cereal, fruit and yogurt. Why she hadn't just admitted that to Trent, she had no idea, but for some stupid reason she couldn't bring herself to.

Not that there was anything wrong with being overly domestic. She had a desire for home and hearth, but she'd centered most of her life on her career. It wasn't a crime. Men did it all the time. She wondered if Trent could cook a decent meal. Probably not. It was likely the reason he'd turned down money in lieu of food. She'd bet he hadn't eaten a decent bite of home cooking since his wife left him, and Jenny had said he kept to himself, didn't date, didn't seem to care about anything except his horses. Odd that he was suddenly spending time with her.

Of course, the way things had happened, it wasn't as if he'd planned it. His being at her house wasn't anything personal. He was helping with the fence just as he'd said—to be neighborly and to keep the dog in and the horses safe.

Ignoring the voice that told her he could just as easily have left her to deal with her own problems, Bailey focused on her dilemma. What the hell could she cook that she wouldn't ruin? She could simply purchase a variety of fruits and arrange them attractively on a platter, but she doubted Trent was the sort of man who'd call that breakfast. He seemed more like a bacon, eggs and hash browns type of guy. Visions of scorched scrambled eggs and bacon blackened beyond crisp tormented her.

She needed help. If anyone could rescue her from the corner she'd painted herself into, Camille could.

When she'd first arrived in Ferguson and spotted Bea's Bed-and-Breakfast, the name had automatically brought to mind a picture of Aunt Bee from *The Andy Griffith Show*. So she'd half expected a plump, grandmotherly woman to answer her knock at the door. She had been more than a little surprised when a young African-American woman greeted her with a welcoming smile.

Bailey hit it off with Camille right away. With her almond-colored, almond-shaped eyes, tiny waist and hair that flowed in soft waves past the belt loops of her Levi's, Camille was like a porcelain doll. Yet she was anything but fragile. She'd lost her husband, who'd been a bullfighting clown, to a rodeo accident two years ago. They'd been newlyweds. A lot of women would have curled in around themselves and let grief consume them, but not Camille. She'd worked two jobs until she'd saved enough money to buy the bed-and-breakfast, determined to get on with her life, unwilling to let her sorrow interfere with her dreams. She'd named the place Bea's in honor of her grandmother, the strong-willed woman who had raised her.

Bailey strode up the walkway to the back door of the B&B. A group of cats had gathered on the back stoop, some sitting, some sprawled contentedly. A yellow one got up, greeted her with a meow and laced itself around her ankles. Like Bailey, Camille had a soft spot for animals, cats in particular. Every stray in the neighborhood seemed to find its way to Camille's back door. She fed them, loved them and spent her money to get them neutered. Many got homes; the rest just stayed at Camille's.

Bailey paused to give the cats a little attention, then went inside. Camille was in the kitchen.

"Hey, stranger." A smile lit her face. "How goes the move?"

"Not bad, but I'm in a jam."

"Already?" Camille shot a faux glance at her watch. "And here I'd allowed you at least a few more hours before you got yourself into trouble. Whose loan did you turn down this time?"

Bailey laughed. "No one's. I need some cooking tips."

Camille stared at her as though she'd just announced she'd like to run naked across the town square. "What—did the grocery store run out of frozen dinners?"

Bailey explained her dilemma. "I should've just admitted I can't cook, but damn it, Trent was looking at me so smugly. There's got to be something I can make that's not too difficult."

"Mmm-hmm." Camille nodded. "Something like cold cereal."

"Cute." Bailey graced her with a mock scowl. "Come on, Camille, I'm desperate."

"In that case, you're in luck." Camille pointed one perfectly shaped nail at her. "But this is going to cost you. I may want to refinance my loan sometime."

"No problem," Bailey said.

"Trent Murdock, huh?" She pursed her lips and made an appreciative noise as she moved toward the kitchen counter. "He's a tasty dish himself. Did you say you were having him *for* breakfast, or *over* for breakfast?"

"Camille!"

"Just asking." She held up one hand in a gesture of peace and with the other flipped a dish towel away from a huge cutting board to reveal what was underneath. Two dozen, made-from-scratch, perfectly formed, raw-dough cinnamon rolls lay curled there. "Will these work? Trent doesn't have to know you didn't make them."

Bailey groaned. "You know I love your cinnamon rolls. But I'm not so sure I'd feel right telling him I baked them myself."

Camille shrugged. "You *will* be baking them yourself. Don't lie. Just don't tell him I made the dough."

Bailey quirked her mouth. "That's treading the line of truth a little on the thin side."

"Suit yourself. You can always fry him a couple of eggs."

She rolled her eyes. "What if I burn the rolls?"

"You won't. All you have to do is set the oven temperature and keep an eye on them. Nothing to it."

"That's easy for you to say."

BAILEY DROVE to the grocery store while Camille prepared her homemade rolls for travel. She couldn't very well claim to have bought groceries if she didn't have any bags to carry in from the car. She purchased orange and grape juice, milk and instant coffee, not sure what Trent liked to drink with his breakfast. She also bought a few other items, including more sandwich fixings in case he decided to stay for lunch. The way he'd talked, building a fence could take a while.

The thought of spending the day with Trent gave her shivers. He was far too appealing. It would be easy to get herself into trouble with a man like that, but as long as she was aware of the potential for disaster, surely she could avoid it. She wanted no part of any man who preferred being a loner. The man she hoped to find would have to be outgoing, with a strong desire for a family. A lone wolf like Trent Murdock hardly fit that bill.

After thanking Camille profusely for the cinnamon rolls and placing them carefully inside a paper grocery sack, Bailey headed home. Trent did little more than glance up and wave as she pulled into the driveway and made her way into the house. He looked hot—in more ways than one. He'd taken off his shirt, and his muscles bulged as he worked the posthole digger. Bailey tore her eyes from him and told herself the roiling in her stomach came from having had only a cup of yogurt before working on the fence this morning.

In the kitchen, she placed the half-dozen cinnamon rolls on a baking sheet Camille had loaned her and slid them into the oven. Now, if she could only manage not to burn them. She put away her meager groceries while the rolls baked, and to her delight, they had turned a perfect golden brown by the time she pulled them from the oven. So what was that smell?

Frowning, Bailey gripped the tray with one oven-mitted hand and slid a spatula under one of the rolls. Terrific. In spite of the top looking fine, the bottom was scorched and appeared decidedly crispy. She'd watched Camille bake everything from rolls to pie to homemade bread, and she always made it seem so easy. What on earth had gone wrong?

Bailey flicked on the ventilation fan over the stove and slid the rolls onto a platter. Okay, so she wasn't Martha Stewart. She'd just have to slice the bottoms off and call it good. Maybe Trent wouldn't notice.

A short while later, the rolls were slightly cooled, frosted with the glaze Camille had put in a plastic container. Standing back, Bailey admired her hand-iwork. They looked pretty good, and the fan over the stove had done its job. The aroma of cinnamon prevailed over the odor of burned dough. She should be able to pass off the rolls just fine.

Bailey nearly jumped at the rap on the door. Trent opened the screen and poked his head in. "What does a guy have to do to get a glass of water around here?" he asked. Then he inhaled deeply. "Mmm, something smells good."

"I'm sorry. Come in." Bailey moved toward the refrigerator. "I meant to bring you a glass of water. You looked really hot when I drove up. I mean…"

He cast her an amused glance as he pulled off his gloves and tucked them in his back pocket. "I know what you mean."

Bailey poured cold water from a pitcher over a tall glass of ice cubes. Trent raised the glass to his mouth. She watched his throat move as he swallowed, her gaze drifting over his tanned skin, slick with perspi-ration, across his broad smooth chest…and lower. A single drop of moisture slid down his washboard stomach and disappeared beneath the waistband of his jeans.

She licked her lips just as Trent lowered the glass and met her eyes. He rolled his tongue against the inside of his cheek and gave her a look that said she was busted. Starting guiltily, Bailey moved toward the kitchen counter. "I hope you like cinnamon rolls," she said, pulling two plates from the cupboard.

"Sounds good," he said, setting his empty glass in the sink. He helped himself to the bottle of dish soap on the counter and washed his hands. They were strong hands, with long fingers and wide palms. And she'd bet Trent knew just the right way to run them over a woman's body.

Bailey jerked her gaze away. "Would you like milk, juice or coffee? I don't drink coffee, but I've got instant if that will do."

"Milk will be fine, thanks." Seemingly unaware that she'd been staring at him like some sex-starved maniac, Trent turned his back on her and dried his hands on a paper towel. She held her breath when he tossed it in the trash can, hoping he wouldn't notice the blackened bottoms of the cinnamon rolls she'd thrown away. He didn't, and mentally Bailey heaved a sigh of relief as she set the platter of rolls in the middle of the table.

"Be right back." Trent went outside and returned wearing his shirt once more. Though she appreciated his good manners, she couldn't help but feel a tug of disappointment that he hadn't come to her table bare-chested. Trent might be all wrong for her, but she'd still enjoyed the view.

He sat down across from her and slid a cinnamon

roll from the plate. ''I love homemade rolls,'' he said, looking at her.

She looked right back and smiled. ''I do, too, though I usually try to stick with something healthier.''

''A little indulgence now and then never hurt anyone,'' he said.

She wasn't so sure about that.

Bailey reminded herself that fantasizing about Trent Murdock was not in her best interest. But her mind kept wandering back to Trent—shirtless. Come to think of it, there was absolutely nothing wrong with how he looked in his shirt, either. The faded denim fit snugly across his biceps, and the partially rolled sleeves revealed his tanned forearms.

Bailey focused her attention on her cinnamon roll.

Trent's moan a second later had her toes curling. She jerked her focus back to him. He'd closed his eyes, savoring Camille's homemade roll with obvious pleasure.

''Man, this is great.'' He opened his eyes, and she could've sworn she saw a twinkle in them. He tilted the cinnamon roll slightly to glance at the bottom but made no comment about her having cut anything away. ''Do you bake very often?''

''No, actually, I don't.'' Bailey felt her face warm. ''I really don't have much time for things like that.''

Trent grunted. ''Too busy making sure farmers'

loans get turned down, or are you just all tied up thinking of new ways to make the folks in town crazy?''

Though Trent's tone was teasing, the words stung. Bailey set her cinnamon roll on her plate. "Is that really the way everyone sees me—as the mean old banker? Is that what you think of me?" If so, why had he even bothered to be nice?

Trent surprised her by reaching across the table to enfold her hand in his. "Hey, I was just razzing you.''

A shiver started at the base of her spine and crept up to her neck. His touch was gentle and reassuring. It felt far too good. Far better than her fantasies. As though thinking the same thing, Trent glanced down at their hands, then quickly removed his.

Bailey cleared her throat. "Hey, it's no big deal. There are aspects to my job that aren't always pleasant.'' She picked up her roll once more. "For the record, I don't enjoy seeing anyone turned down for a loan.''

"Like I said, I was just razzing you.'' Trent took a swallow of milk, leaving behind a trace of mustache that made her recall a recent commercial that sometimes featured sexy men.

Got milk indeed.

Mmm-mmm.

Bailey pictured him shirtless again and mentally kicked herself.

"But people in town do talk about me," she said, her words more statement than question.

"Sure they do," he admitted without hesitation. "You've created quite a stir, coming in here with ways of doing things that aren't typically small-town. That day care, for instance. And you're holding a job position that traditionally has been male since Ferguson opened its very first bank. The old-timers, who've done the same things the same way their entire lives, are shook up."

Bailey picked up her glass of milk. "I can assure you that accepting the position of bank president at Colorado Western National had absolutely nothing to do with wanting to create a stir in this town. If something happens to the economy, given the crises the majority of family-owned and -operated farms and ranches face these days, then the bank could go under and take the town with it. I'm trying to help by making money available to new businesses. This will benefit the town by keeping more young people here, rather than forcing them to find work else-where. That's why I was brought to Ferguson."

Trent lifted a shoulder. "I suppose. Folks just need a while to get used to it, to realize that things change."

He grew silent, and Bailey wondered if he was thinking about the changes that had occurred in his life the past year. She wanted to offer him a shoulder to lean on. But Jenny had said he didn't like to talk about his daughter's death, and Bailey had her own reservations in this regard.

Trent saved her from her troubled thoughts with a crooked grin. "Hey, I wouldn't let it bother me if I were you. Besides, a woman who bakes homemade cinnamon rolls can't be all bad, even if she does own a rogue dog."

"He's not a rogue," Bailey said. "He just needs a little love, that's all." She finished the last bite of her roll. "What kind of dog do you figure he is?"

A shadow passed over Trent's features and was gone so quickly Bailey wondered if she'd imagined it. "I'd say he's a blue heeler-mix," he said. "Maybe part Border collie. They're both herding breeds, which would explain why he chased my horses."

"You said you first saw him some time ago," Bailey remarked. "Do you suppose he ran away from somebody during the Fourth of July weekend? I've heard that a lot of dogs get scared of the fireworks and take off."

"I guess he could've, but I don't recognize him as belonging to anyone around here."

"Do they have a fireworks display in Ferguson?" Bailey asked. "He might have gotten away from someone who was just passing through and stopped to see the show."

Trent finished his milk and set down the glass. "I

didn't pay any attention, Bailey. I'm not much on holidays.''.

''Boy, I am. I go all out for every one of them, especially Christmas.''

Trent's expression went completely dark, then his face paled beneath his tan. Bailey could have kicked herself.

Christmas. Trees. Duh.

But before she could say a word, he pushed away from the table and put his dishes in the sink—a little too hard. ''I'd best get back to work.'' He strode from the kitchen and left her sitting there, feeling like a complete idiot.

CHAPTER FOUR

TRENT DROVE the posthole digger into the ground, furious with himself for letting his emotions show. Bailey's comment had been totally innocent. She couldn't have known. Still, the words burned inside him.

He hadn't celebrated a single holiday since Sarah died. Unless one counted his hanging an ornament on her grave on Christmas, as he had on her birthday and other special occasions…as he'd done the other day on the anniversary of her death.

He gripped the double handles of the tool and let the blades bite furiously into the earth, venting his pain. A part of him wanted to block the memory of his daughter's voice from his mind, and another part wanted never to forget it.

I wish every day could be Christmas, Daddy….

The back of his throat swelled, and he swallowed hard and blinked. He hadn't ever viewed a Christmas tree—or a holiday—in the same way after planting the blue spruce on Sarah's grave. He'd decorated it by himself. Amy hadn't wanted any part of that.

Pushing the thought from his mind, he continued to dig. He had all but two of the holes finished by the time the screen door creaked open a couple of hours later. Though he knew Bailey had come outside, he ignored her. He heard her footsteps on the porch, then in the grass as she walked up behind him.

"I thought you might like some iced tea."

Damn it. He shoved the posthole digger into the ground and faced her, then wished he hadn't.

Bailey looked good standing there in her tank top and cutoffs, holding a glass out to him. Her well-manicured fingernails, painted with clear polish, weren't overly long. She had pretty hands and a great smile, and he was sorry to see he'd made that smile vanish.

He accepted the tea and gritted his teeth when his fingers brushed hers. "Thanks." He took a drink. The tea had lemon, no sugar, just the way he liked it.

"I'm sorry, I don't keep sugar in the house," Bailey said. "I seldom use it."

His gaze boomeranged to her once more as he wondered if she realized her slipup. She looked back at him, unaware. It was enough to break his black mood.

"Except when you bake, I guess. Did you use it all up when you made the cinnamon rolls?"

Bailey's face turned three shades of crimson, and

warmth snaked through him. Belatedly, he realized
just how much he'd enjoyed teasing her, watching
her squirm. He'd been alone for a long time. His
self-imposed banishment from social scenes, no re-
lationships with women, had been bearable up to
this point. It was a way of punishing himself, although for what he couldn't quite decide. Because
he couldn't save Sarah? Because he hadn't been
strong enough to take care of her and still manage
to hold his marriage together?

Whatever the reasons, he hadn't dwelled on them.
All he knew was he wanted to be alone, and he'd
been fine doing that, until Bailey came along. He
wasn't sure what it was about her that brought out
this side of him, one that had lain buried for so long.
Guilt threatened to take hold of him. He didn't deserve to be happy or have fun. Sarah was gone.
What right did that leave him to go on living, loving
and laughing? None, as far as he could see. But
something about Bailey swayed his reservations and
demanded he let loose and enjoy a little friendly
bantering with her.

Maybe he'd give in. Just this once.

He knew damn well she hadn't made those cinnamon rolls. She might have heated them in the
oven, but he'd recognize Camille Kendall's recipe
anywhere. Nobody baked like Camille. The town's
café owner constantly asked her to supply him with
baked goods.

Besides, Trent had seen the burned bottoms of the cinnamon rolls in Bailey's trash can and the bread knife in the sink, which she must have used to cut them. He'd gotten a kick out of the lengths she'd gone to to keep him from knowing she couldn't cook.

"They take quite a bit of sugar," Bailey said, lifting her arms in a casual gesture. "I hope the tea is all right with just lemon."

"It's fine," he said, letting her off the hook. She was damn good at sidestepping the truth without telling an out-and-out lie.

"I'm going to the feed store to pick up the chain link," Bailey said. "Would you like a sandwich before I go?"

Trent shook his head. "Maybe later, thanks." He wiped the sweat from his eyes with the back of his forearm and looked up at the sun. It must be about noon. The time had slipped away from him while he worked, as it always did, one hour fading into the next, one day into another.

He focused on the here and now. "How do you plan to haul the wire?" He glanced pointedly at her Mustang convertible parked in the driveway.

"I have a pickup truck," Bailey said. "If you change your mind about the sandwich, help yourself." She started to leave.

"Bailey, wait." The words were out before he could stop them, though he knew he should leave well enough alone. It was best to keep his distance from her. He'd made a choice to spend the rest of his life alone, and he aimed to stick with it.

Bailey paused, and Trent ran his hand through his hair, unable to leave things the way they were between them. No matter what his innermost feelings were. "Look, I'm sorry about how I acted earlier. I know you didn't mean anything by what you said."

"Forget it." She smiled softly. "I'd better go before the feed store closes. Apparently, they roll up the sidewalks shortly after lunch on Saturdays here in Mayberry." She headed for the garage.

Trent leaned on the posthole digger and watched her walk away, still liking what he saw far too much. A moment later a familiar pickup truck shot away from the building, with Bailey behind the wheel.

"I'll be damned." Trent shook his head and chuckled dryly. The '53 Chevy Bailey drove was one he'd often seen parked outside the Texaco station where local mechanic Lester Godfrey worked. Coated with primer-gray paint, the truck bore the loving touch of countless hours of work getting body and engine back to near-new condition. The tires probably hadn't seen fifty miles, and the 389 Pontiac V–8 engine, with three 2-barrel carburetors, purred like a cream-fed cat. That truck was one of the few things Lester gave a damn about, outside of his kids and his fondness for Budweiser.

How the hell had Bailey gotten possession of Lester's pride and joy?

Trent wasn't sure he wanted to know.

By the time Bailey returned from the feed store, he had the holes dug and had stopped to take a break. He sat under the shade tree and tried to coax the dog to come to him. As the morning had worn on, he'd noticed the heeler-mix had relaxed somewhat, at least to the point where he was no longer choking himself. But now, as Trent held out his hand and spoke, the dog tensed once more and retreated.

"I hope I'll be able to win his trust sooner or later," Bailey said, coming up behind Trent.

He rose to his feet, causing the heeler to move away as far as the rope would allow. "Good luck. Do you want to back your truck over here so I can unload the posts and wire?"

"You don't have to do that," Bailey said. "You've already done enough."

"I might as well set the posts for you," he said. "That way the cement will have a chance to harden and you can finish the rest tomorrow."

"We'll do it together, then," Bailey said.

The simple meaning of the word sent a shiver creeping up his back. *Together.* It was something he really couldn't relate to anymore. But he had to admit, working with Bailey turned out not to be such a bad way to spend the afternoon. She helped him mix the cement and they did half the job, stopped to eat a sandwich, then finished the rest. By late afternoon, the steel posts jutted from the ground around the entire perimeter of the yard like so many elongated teeth.

Bailey stood back to admire their handiwork. A satisfied smile curved her lips. "Looking good."

Trent thought the same thing, though it wasn't the fence he admired. Bailey's long legs had grown all the more brown from being in the sun all afternoon, and moisture flecked the cleavage between her breasts. Swallowing, Trent put his shirt back on. "We might as well call it a day. You want to go see the horses? Ride a couple of them?"

He told himself he'd extended the invitation because he wanted to get it over with. He'd string the wire on his fence that evening by himself and be done with it. Done with the day's work and with Bailey. There was no point in drawing things out. The sooner he showed her the horses, the sooner she could choose one and the quicker he could get her out of his hair. Fun was fun, but he had to come back to reality. After today, he'd be wise to remember Bailey Chancellor was off-limits.

"I'd love to." Bailey nodded toward the dog. "Let me feed him and change my clothes first."

A short while later she stood dressed in Levi's, a sleeveless blouse and, to Trent's surprise, cowboy boots. He raised his eyebrows. "You actually own a pair of boots?'' Somehow, he'd expected her to ride in tennis shoes, which was dangerous and exactly the type of fool thing he'd thought a woman like her would do.

Bailey eyed the toes of her black boots. "Sure I do. I told you I've been taking riding lessons."

Trent grunted and led the way across her pasture, toward the gap in the fence. The route was quickly becoming familiar and comfortable. It was a good thing the fence would be back up soon, putting an end to that.

In the barn, Trent gathered the tack and grooming tools they would need, then set them outside near the hitching post. Halters in hand, he and Bailey headed for the pasture. They brought back the horses she was interested in and worked them in the arena. Somehow, he wasn't surprised when, after riding all of them, Bailey chose Star.

"Are you sure?" Trent asked.

"Yes, I'm sure."

"He'll need special handling and lots of understanding."

"I'm fully aware of that." Bailey stroked the gelding's nose and held on to the lead rope possessively. "I'll give him everything he needs."

Trent didn't doubt that for a minute. He only hoped he wasn't making a mistake. If Bailey got hurt because Star shied and threw her... Well, he couldn't dwell on that. Her mind was made up, and

while he could have refused the sale of the horse to
her, somehow he couldn't bring himself to do it. The
two of them looked as though they belonged together, Star's head hanging over Bailey's shoulder,
the gelding's blind eye closed as he sighed and wal-
lowed in the attention Bailey lavished on him.

"Okay," Trent said. "You've got yourself a
horse."

Bailey grinned at him like a kid with a new bi-
cycle.

She had a horse, and he had an incurable ache for
something he had no business wanting.

IT TOOK BAILEY two days to put up the fence once
the cement dried around the posts. She'd planned to
rent a fence stretcher, but Trent had insisted she bor-
row his. She frowned, recalling the way he'd tried
to restring the wire between their properties without
her Saturday afternoon after she brought Star home.

He'd acted as though he was calling it a day and
told her to lock Star in the corral next to the barn
until they could string the wire. She had done just
that, and had been brushing and petting Star when
she'd spotted Trent putting the fence back up. Annoyed, Bailey had marched straight over and con-
fronted him. After all, he'd worked hard helping her
set fence posts, and the cinnamon rolls hardly qualified as sufficient payment. His generosity had gone

beyond neighborly duty, so why had he tried to side-step her offer of help?

Her question had remained unanswered. Trent simply acted as though it was no big deal. He came up with a string of excuses—he hadn't wanted to bother her, had thought she was tired; he'd decided at the last minute to put the wire up and be done with it... Though she bought none of it, Bailey let the subject drop.

Trent had reluctantly let her help, and he'd taught her how to pull the wire tight with the fence stretcher, which looked like a pulley with two big metal hooks on each end. But he'd hardly said two words to her the whole time.

She certainly couldn't figure the man out. It was probably best not even to try.

Today was Tuesday, and Bailey had gotten home from the bank at four, then gone straight to work on the fence, stopping only for a quick bite to eat. The poor dog had finally accepted the rope, but she knew he was still afraid of it. The sooner she could untie him, the better.

Bailey finished just before dark. She'd spent the better part of the day on Sunday gathering rocks to line the bottom of the fence so the heeler couldn't dig his way under it. She would turn on the yard lights now and complete her job by laying the rocks. She'd already unloaded them from her pickup Sunday night before the fence was up, piling them in the yard where she could easily get to them.

She spoke to the dog. "I guess I might as well let you loose." After all, he couldn't dig his way out with her watching him. If he tried, she'd catch him and put him back on the rope. "I bet you'll be glad to get off that rope, won't you, boy?" Bailey walked slowly toward him with the back of her hand outstretched. He'd grown to trust her a little over the past few days, in spite of the fact that she'd initially cornered him in the barn in order to catch him and tie him up. She petted him each night when she fed him, though he tolerated her touch grudgingly and quickly moved away when he'd had enough.

"You need a name, fella," Bailey said, gently grasping the rope near his neck. "And a collar, and shots..." She stroked his head, soothing him. The heeler pinned his ears, but slowly relaxed beneath her touch. Bailey untied the rope and slipped it off his neck. "There you go." She smiled and stood watching him. It took him a moment to realize he was free, but once he did, he trotted around the yard with obvious relief.

Bailey moved toward the rock pile, still watching the dog. Her heart swelled. It felt so good to help the animal. To give him a real home. Every living creature needed a place to call his own. She eyed the fence. She hadn't done a professional job but the fence looked all right and seemed sturdy enough. She was confident it would hold the heeler.

Her elation turned to dismay a heartbeat later. The dog loped faster along the length of the fence. Then in one quick motion he shoved his head and shoulders under the bottom of the diamond-mesh wire.

"Oh, no!" Bailey inched forward, afraid to scare him, yet not wanting him to escape. "Hey, boy!" With not much time to weigh her choices, she hesitated a split second, then grabbed hold of the dog.

Startled, he let out a yelp that tore at her heart, and ducked back into the yard. "I'm sorry, fella. I'm not trying to frighten you." She attempted to calm him, but he wriggled out of her grasp and raced across the yard. Bailey watched, helpless, as the heeler gathered his haunches and sailed into the air. He hooked the top of the six-foot fence with his forepaws, scrambling to find purchase with his back legs. Up and over he went, to drop cleanly onto the other side.

Knowing it would do no good to call him, Bailey fought the urge to do so anyway as he took off at a full run. "Damn." She blew out a breath and unclenched her hand. *After all that.* She stared at the pile of rocks and shook her head. The fading light of day had all but surrendered to night. There was no sense looking for him now. She'd get up early tomorrow morning and hunt for him before she went to work.

Feeling more tired than she had in weeks, Bailey put her tools away and headed for the house.

AT FIVE-THIRTY, Bailey awoke, took a quick shower and dressed in jeans and a cotton blouse. The pleasantly cool morning required a light jacket, unzipped. In spite of the fact that she worried about the dog, she couldn't help feeling elated as she walked toward the barn. Dew sprinkled the grass, and the air smelled unbelievably crisp and clean. Birds sang from the trees, and Star whinnied to her from the pasture.

Bailey felt as if she'd entered a fantasy world where all was perfect. This place was everything she'd ever dreamed of. She caught Star and saddled him with the used tack she'd bought from the feed store yesterday. The gelding seemed eager to go as Bailey swung into the saddle and headed down the driveway. She would ride along the county road to a bridle trail she'd noticed that wound through the trees. She had no idea where the heeler might have gone, but surely he wouldn't have strayed far.

Star pricked his ears and stepped out at a brisk walk. Bailey kept him on the shoulder of the road, off the pavement, since the gelding had no shoes to protect his feet from the harsh surface. She'd have to remedy that situation before she did much more riding.

She was almost to the break in the trees where

the bridle path began when Star let out a welcoming whinny. Engrossed in the surrounding scenery and the way the early-morning sun played on the dew-damp grass, Bailey hadn't been paying attention to much else. Now she spotted a rider coming down the road. A spark of warmth ignited within her. Trent. He rode toward her on the horse he called Bronnz.

"I didn't expect to see you this morning," Trent said as he pulled the chestnut mare to a halt.

Hating to admit she was looking for the dog, Bailey started to pretend she was simply out for a ride before work. But there was no point in lying, and if she told Trent, maybe he could help her search for the heeler and get him home.

"The dog got away from me last night," she said. "It was too dark to look for him."

Trent gathered his reins as Bronnz moved impatiently in place. "How?"

"He jumped the fence."

"You're kidding." He shook his head, then surprised her with a grin. "Ornery critter, isn't he?"

"Just scared," Bailey said. She let Star move down the bridle path, and Trent fell into place beside her. "I don't know how much luck I'll have finding him, but I thought I'd better give it a try."

"What are you going to do with the dog…if you can even catch him again?"

Bailey sighed. "I hadn't really thought that far

ahead. I guess I'll worry about that later.'' She focused on guiding Star along the trail and tried not to notice how close her knee was to Trent's as they rode side by side. He wore a straw cowboy hat today, and a denim jacket over a black shirt. His profile made a heart-stopping contrast against the morning sky. Easy on the eyes. She wasn't so sure he'd be easy on her heart. Bailey forced herself not to stare.

''How's Star working out for you?'' Trent asked.

''Fine. This is the first chance I've had to take him out for a real ride. I've been too busy putting the fence up for that crazy dog.''

''Now, Bailey, you know all that dog needs is a little love and understanding.''

She shot a sidelong glance his way and found Trent watching her with a twinkle in his eye, the corners of his mouth twitching. ''Very funny,'' she said. Then she smiled, too. ''Okay, I admit he can be a pain in the butt. But it's not his fault. I still think I can get him to come around.''

''If you can first get him to stay home,'' Trent said.

They wound their way through the trees in companionable silence. A short distance later, the trail came out on the road again before picking up on the other side where the trees gave way to sagebrush. Bailey heard the sounds before she saw anything:

the muffled call of voices, bleating sheep and the sharp bark of a dog.

Her attention was riveted on the bend in the road as she craned her neck to see, but it wasn't her dog that came into view seconds later. A herd of sheep, with two men on horseback and a pair of Border collies in attendance, swept toward Bailey and Trent, woolly faces a bobbing sea of black and white. Star perked his ears, good eye fixed on the herd, nostrils flared as he sniffed the air.

"Be careful, Bailey," Trent warned. "They're on his blind side."

But it wasn't Star who spooked as the sheep swept in front of them.

Bronnz took one look at the woolly beasts and decided she wanted no part of them. With a snort, she leaped sideways and humped her back. Tensing, Star shied and prepared to bolt. Bailey gasped and pulled up on the reins, barely able to keep the gelding under control. To her horror, Trent bounced in the saddle like a rag doll, then sailed to the ground as Bronnz galloped off down the road. He landed with one arm pinned beneath him as his hat tumbled from his head.

"Oh my gosh!" Bailey swung from the saddle, clutching Star's reins. One of the cowboy sheepherders rode over and halted beside them.

"You all right, Trent?" he asked, looking down from the back of his paint horse.

Bailey kept forgetting that this was a small town where everyone knew everybody. The cowboy shot her a glare of sudden recognition when Bailey approached Trent. She cringed, recognizing him, as well. His wife, Joan Sanderson, was one of the tellers at Colorado Western National. Joan had told Bailey that her husband wanted her to quit her job and stay home with the kids, but now that Bailey planned to institute a day care at the bank, she'd be able to bring her children to work with her.

Apparently, Ben Sanderson wasn't crazy about that idea, if the dark look he cast Bailey was any indication. He scowled at her as though she were personally responsible for Trent's fall.

Bailey glared back, then looked at Trent and echoed Ben's question. "Are you all right?" She had a feeling his pride was more bruised than his backside. But her theory was shot down like a darted water balloon the minute he sat up.

He flinched, cradling his right wrist. "Just peachy," he replied.

"Let me help you." Bailey reached out to take hold of his elbow, but he avoided her touch.

"I'm fine." He pushed himself off the ground, using his left arm for leverage.

Belatedly, Bailey noted that Ben hadn't made a move to help Trent pick himself up out of the dirt. She supposed it was some sort of code of the West.

Never help a man back on his horse, or some such nonsense.

She narrowed her eyes at Ben. He mumbled a "See you later" to Trent and headed after his partner and the departing herd of sheep.

"You can stop your heroics now," Bailey said. "Your macho buddy's out of sight. Let me see what you've done to your arm."

"I said I'm fine. If you'll be so kind as to share your horse with me, we can double up for the ride back to my place. It's not far."

Bailey fought the urge to leave him standing in the dust. Why were men always so stubborn? "What about Bronnz?" she asked, determined not to care one way or the other if Trent's arm was broken or merely sprained.

"She's probably already back to the barn by now." He stepped up beside Star, speaking soothingly to him. "I can't believe she spooked and Star didn't. Go figure." He shook his head.

"I guess you never know what they'll do for sure," Bailey said. She watched Trent swing into the saddle, using his left hand to grip the horn. He clutched the reins gingerly in his right and reached out to her. A shiver snaked down her back as, belatedly, she realized that riding double meant sitting snug and intimate against Trent's backside.

"I can walk," she said. "Like you said, it's not

that far, and I don't want to put a strain on my horse.''

''Now who's being stubborn?'' He stared firmly at her, still holding out his hand.

With a sigh, Bailey took it and vaulted awkwardly up behind him. Riding on the back end of the horse felt strange, and far more precarious than sitting in the saddle. Nearly losing her balance as Star headed out at a fast walk, Bailey clutched involuntarily at Trent's waist, then pulled back as though she'd been scalded. *Silly,* she scolded herself. *This isn't high school.* Determined not to let him affect her, she held on to Trent with both hands as they rode along, and told herself it was no big deal. But, oh, he felt good, and the fact caught her off guard. She'd made up her mind not to be attracted to him, but her body apparently was not in sync with her mind. Her palms wanted to slide beneath the denim of his jacket, and her arms seemed drawn to slip farther around his waist and hang on tight.

Sitting rigid, Bailey shook off the notion and bounced along on Star's butt, grateful when the short ride that seemed endless was finally over. She slid from the gelding's back, freeing Trent to swing from the saddle. He dismounted, stiffly holding his right arm.

Bailey pursed her lips. ''I don't suppose it would do any good to offer to drive you to the emergency room?''

"You're a quick learner, banker woman," Trent said. But his smile softened the words. "Thanks, anyway." he added. "You need to get to work, and I'll be fine. A little Epsom salts will take care of this." He held up the offending wrist.

Bailey shrugged and took Star's reins from him. "Suit yourself. If you see the dog, would you please call me at the bank and let me know?"

"Will do." Trent nodded in farewell as she swung into the saddle and headed down the driveway.

Bailey looked over her shoulder and saw that he'd sat down on the porch steps and removed his jacket in order to examine his wrist. As though feeling her gaze on him, he glanced up, and she quickly faced forward.

She'd better pay attention to where she was riding, or she might end up on the ground, too. Forcing her thoughts away from Trent, she idly wondered where the dog was. She didn't have enough time left to search for him now.

Minutes later, Bailey turned up her driveway, and as she drew near the front yard she did a double take, then chuckled in pleasant surprise.

The heeler lay curled on the welcome mat on the porch as though he belonged there. Pulling Star to a halt, Bailey spoke softly. "Hey, buddy. What are you doing on my doorstep?" And just like that, she thought of his name. Buddy. How appropriate. She could use one.

After all, living in a small town where nearly everyone was against you and your nearest neighbor was a gray-eyed cowboy who gave you goose bumps was enough for anyone to need an ally.

"Buddy!" she called, trying out the name.

The heeler perked his ears and tilted his head sideways, then let it sink back onto his front paws. He appeared perfectly at home behind the white picket fence. He blinked and closed his eyes, as though sending her a message. *You can fence me in only when and if I choose.*

Bailey had a feeling Trent Murdock copped a similar attitude.

Well, no need to worry. Fencing in Trent was about the furthest thing from her mind. Still, it wouldn't hurt to be friendly to him. Maybe then people like Ben Sanderson would begin to think of her as someone other than the wicked witch of Colorado Western National.

She'd make a point to drop by Windsong after work this evening and see if a hardheaded cowboy could use a hand with his chores.

CHAPTER FIVE

BAILEY LEFT the bank at five, a box containing a rabbit tucked under her arm. The day had been hectic. She'd had loans to check up on and a meeting with the contractor overseeing the remodel job on the bank's basement-level offices, which would be used for the day care. And Jenny had come in to talk to Bailey at lunchtime, asking if she would like to have a bunny.

Jenny's elder sister, in the process of a divorce, was looking for homes for her pets, since she'd be moving to an apartment. The bunny was headed for the animal shelter unless Bailey could help. Unable to resist the little black rabbit, she'd agreed to take him. Why not? She had a farm now.

Tired but satisfied that things at the bank were running smoothly, Bailey slipped out the rear exit.

The chalk drawing caught her attention right away. Sketched in lines of pink, blue, orange and yellow, it stretched along the length of the sidewalk beside the parking lot, depicting a girl with skinny pigtails, stick limbs and a big smile. Bailey smiled, too, wondering who her little chalk artist was.

From the corner of her eye, she spotted a child peering at her around the end of the building. The little girl had light blond hair and big blue eyes, and looked to be about eight or nine. She ducked out of sight when Bailey spotted her.

"Hi there!" Bailey called. "I promise I won't bite."

Hesitantly, the girl came around the corner into view and walked toward Bailey. "Hi," she said. "Are you the new banker lady?"

She wore a T-shirt with a barrel racer on the front, blue jeans and lace-up cowboy boots. She had her hair in a ponytail, sticking out from beneath a red ball cap, and held a yellow bucket of jumbo-size chalk in one sun-browned hand.

Bailey's heart danced. *What a cutie.* Just the sort of child she hoped to have one day herself. "I sure am," she said, surprised that even a little girl would have heard of her. *Great.* The kid had probably been told to watch out for the wicked witch of the bank, who undoubtedly made a habit of snatching children to bake into gingerbread in her oven. "My name is Bailey." Balancing the box in the crook of her arm, she extended her hand. "What's yours?"

The girl gave Bailey's hand a tentative shake. "Macy Darland." She looked up from beneath the bill of the cap. "You live by us," she said.

"I do?"

Macy nodded. "Uh-huh. My dad owns the Circle D. We run cows. Mostly Charolais and Hereford."

"I see," Bailey said, not sure what a Sharlay was. "And what's your dad's name?" She hoped to heaven he wasn't any relation to the almighty Ben Sanderson. The ranchers in the community were very close-knit, and everyone in the county was either related to or friends with everyone else.

"Wade. My brother is Jason. Our mom died when we were little."

The child's sudden revelation startled Bailey. "Oh," she said. "I'm sorry to hear that." Something about Macy's open honest expression made her add, "I don't have a mother, either, or a dad."

"You don't?" Macy's blond eyebrows crept upward.

"Nope." Bailey shook her head. "So I guess that means we have something in common."

Macy nodded. "Guess so. Hey, what's in the box?" She stood on tiptoe, and Bailey lowered the box for her to see.

"A rabbit who needed a home."

"Oh, he's so cute!" Macy's voice rose in pitch as she set the bucket of chalk down and cooed to the bunny.

Bailey watched, amused. "You like animals, huh?"

Macy grinned. "Sure do."

Again, Bailey's heart went out to the little girl.

Maybe Macy would like to have the bunny, if that was all right with her father.

She hated to say anything without knowing. "Do you have pets?" she asked, instead.

"Horses and two cow dogs," Macy said. "Red heelers. I'd like to have a kitten, but my dad doesn't like cats."

"Does he like rabbits?" Bailey asked.

"For dinner." Macy grinned, and Bailey laughed at her quick wit.

"Oh. Then I guess we won't ask him if this bunny can go home with you."

"Better not," Macy agreed. "But I'd love to have him. Does he have a name?"

"Licorice."

"That's a good one. Since he's black." Macy tugged at the belt loops of her britches, which sagged slightly on her reed-thin hips. "Do you have a lot of pets?"

"I'm working on it," Bailey said. "I have a horse and a dog."

"No cats?"

"Not really, though there's a stray hanging around my place that stole my sandwich the other day."

Macy grinned. "Do you think I could come see your animals sometime?"

"Sure, if it's all right with your dad."

"Oh, he won't mind," Macy said, waving dismissively. "He keeps so busy with the ranch he doesn't pay much attention to what me and Jason do, as long as our chores get done." She spoke the words casually, not looking for sympathy, simply stating a fact.

Bailey's heart twisted. What kind of father ignored his kids? Reminding herself she didn't even know Wade Darland and she shouldn't be judgmental, Bailey glanced at the street that ran adjacent to the bank's alley. "Where is your dad?" As far as she could tell, Macy was alone.

Macy jerked a thumb over her shoulder. "Down at the feed store with my brother, jawin' with his buddies." She rolled her eyes. "He talks forever."

Bailey chuckled. "So, you were bored and decided to do a little artwork, huh?" She gestured toward the chalk drawing. "I like it. It's adorable." Macy had also drawn a hopscotch pattern at the end of the sidewalk, and a yellow horse with a blue mane and tail.

"I thought you might be mad at me for drawing on your sidewalk," Macy said, quirking one corner of her mouth.

"Heavens, no." Bailey smiled. Already, she liked Macy. "It adds a little ambience to the place."

"What's that?" Macy wrinkled her forehead.

"Mood. Atmosphere." She tapped the bill of Macy's ball cap with one finger. "Don't worry, it's something good."

Macy smiled. "Oh." Then she glanced at the building. "Do you take care of all the money in the bank?"

Bailey hid a smile. "I guess you could say that."

Macy nodded. "Daddy says folks ought to give you a chance before they go and judge you hard-nosed. He says your ideas might make the town a better place."

"I see." Guilt washed over her. And here she'd been thinking ill thoughts of the man. Pushing aside the twinge of hurt that the word *hard-nosed* had caused, Bailey smiled at Macy. "Let's hope everyone else comes to feel that way, too."

Macy retrieved her bucket of chalk. "Well, I guess I'd better get back to the feed store in case Dad's ready to leave now. But I'll ride my horse over and visit you and your dog sometime."

Bailey pulled her keys from her pocket. "You do that."

"'Bye, Licorice," Macy said, giving the bunny a final pat. A smile curved her lips as she looked up at Bailey. "See you later."

She waved as Bailey climbed behind the wheel of her pickup truck. Bailey had bought it from a local mechanic, Lester Godfrey, simply to save the man's pride. He hadn't qualified for a loan, and she'd heard from Jenny that he had four kids to feed and a stack of medical bills to pay as the result of some surgery his wife had undergone. So the next time Lester came to the bank, Bailey approached him and asked about his truck, which had been parked outside.

By the time the conversation was over, she'd convinced him that a '53 Chevy pickup was something she'd always hoped to own and that she'd be beside herself if he wouldn't consider selling the truck. It took less than a day for Lester to make up his mind.

Bailey had the truck, and Lester had enough cash to carry his family through some rough times. Now all she had to do was figure a way to sell the truck back to him later without stepping on his already bruised pride. She drove the truck to the bank now and then so Lester wouldn't suspect her motive in wanting to help him. A man like him wouldn't take lightly to pity or anything remotely resembling charity.

Bailey settled Licorice's box on the passenger side of the Chevy. She knew a lot about pride. And even more about being alone. Growing up, she'd hung on to whatever scrap of dignity she could, no matter what each situation in her foster homes had thrown her way. She'd learned to be strong and to depend on no one but herself. Yet there'd been times she'd felt so alone, even when she shared a room with three other girls, that she'd thought her heart would truly break.

The memory of Macy's little face eased into her mind, and Bailey drove homeward trying not to think about a lonely little girl.

Not the one she'd just met.

Not the one she herself had been.

TRENT SPENT the rest of the morning cussing his own stupidity. He'd been so busy worrying that Star would spook and throw Bailey that his mind hadn't been where it should have: focused on his horse. He couldn't believe Bronnz had dumped him. He'd taken his share of spills over the years, but it had been a while since he'd been bucked off.

Chores were slow going because his right arm was sore. Every time he tried to do something with it, a sharp pain shot through his wrist. Maybe Bailey was right, that he ought to go to the E.R. and have it x-rayed. The thought made him shudder. He hated the hospital. Too many memories of Sarah and the suffering she'd gone through lingered in its hallways. But if his wrist was cracked, he might not have a choice.

His thoughts returned to Bailey. He wanted Star to work out for her. In spite of the fact that getting thrown had punched a big hole in his ego, Trent had been impressed by the way she'd handled the gelding. Not bad for a city woman. Come to think of it, Bailey seemed to do everything well. The more he was around her, the more he found himself wanting to know things about her.

That was not good.

It was safer not to care about anyone. The only

living creatures he had feelings for anymore were his horses, which suited him just fine. No love, no loss, no pain. He was certain he could get through life, one day at a time, living safely by his own rules.

But now Bailey had come along and, for whatever reason, set his feelings on edge.

What had her life in Denver been like? And what had made a high-powered businesswoman like her move to a little town like Ferguson?

He'd lived here for five years. He'd met Amy in college, married her and built their dream home on Colorado's western slope a few years later. But their dream turned into a nightmare when Sarah became ill.

Trent had learned to fit in with the locals, though he now kept his distance for the most part. Still, he'd heard people around town talking, and he'd known things about Bailey even before he'd met her. That the bank's new president was not only a woman but was just thirty-three years old—two years younger than he was. The former bank president, Hal Peterson, had been almost seventy and a longtime local resident. Bailey had her work cut out for her.

The townspeople said she was pretty, but not on the inside. "Hard-core," "all business," were descriptions the rumor mill passed along.

But the more Trent saw of Bailey, the more he wondered if the image was the reality. Again, he recalled the softer side of Bailey—a woman who'd cried over his child's grave, who took in a blind horse and a stray rogue dog.

In spite of what the townspeople said about her, he liked her. But then, what did it matter? He shouldn't be thinking about her that way. He needed to get his mind back to the same safe place it had been in for the past year. One where no one could reach him. Now that Bailey had picked out her horse and had her fence put up, maybe he could get her to leave him alone. He'd call her if he saw her damn dog, but that was it.

Feeling somewhat better now that he'd gotten a grip, Trent finished his chores as best he could. He had work to do with the halter babies, but it would just have to wait. Maybe he should soak his wrist again and then ice and wrap it, and work with the foals this evening. He headed for the house.

It was five-thirty by the time he went back outside, and too hot to think about supper. He'd feed the horses, then maybe drive into town for some ice cream. He frowned down at his wrist. It really didn't feel much better, even though he'd wrapped it. Maybe he would swing by the E.R. while he was in town. He told himself he could do it. After all, it wasn't where Sarah had spent her final days. She'd died at home.

"Hello!"

Trent narrowed his eyes as he spotted Bailey walking across his back pasture. She'd obviously climbed through the fence that adjoined their properties. He mumbled an expletive. Didn't the woman know that trespassing wasn't something people in the country took lightly? She herself had commented on how his acreage gave him privacy.

But the sight of Bailey in her blue jeans and snug-fitting tank top stopped him from telling her she had no business crawling through his fence. It also stopped him from listening to the inner voice that told him he had no business wanting a woman he didn't need and had no intention of pursuing anyway.

"Hi," he said grudgingly.

Bailey halted in front of him. "How's the wrist?"

"Okay," he lied. "I haven't seen your dog, if that's why you're here."

"Actually, I already found my dog. I came to see if you needed some help with your chores."

He didn't want her doing him any favors.

As soon as the thought was out, guilt washed over Trent. Bailey was only trying to be nice. It wasn't her fault he felt the way he did. "I'm fine, thanks," he said. "I can handle things."

"I don't mind," she persisted. "I'm really enjoying Star, and I'm sure it would be fun to help you with your horses."

"How's he doing?"

"Great. I've already got him fed and watered, so

if you could use a hand with your chores, I really don't have anything else to do at the moment.''

Trent felt himself weaken. He hated to admit that her help would be nice, given his injury. Even more, he hated to admit that he enjoyed her company. But if he let her help him, the chores would get done faster, which would allow him to escape to town.

He sighed inwardly. If the people in Ferguson could see this side of her, they'd never think of her as the evil banker woman again.

''All right, if you really want to.'' He headed for the barn. ''So where'd you find your dog?''

Bailey gave a short laugh. ''Would you believe he was waiting for me on the front porch when I got home from your place this morning?''

''You're kidding.''

''Nope. He was lying in front of the door, like he'd been there all along.... I guess I'm going to have to make the fence taller so he can't roam.''

''Let me know if you need a hand.'' The words were out before Trent could consider them. Feeling wishy-washy, he added, ''One good turn deserves another, you know.''

''Works for me,'' Bailey said.

They stepped inside the barn, and she helped him throw a couple of bales of hay onto a wheelbarrow, then protested when he insisted on pushing it himself. He wheeled it out to the paddocks where some of his halter babies and their dams were, and cut the twine on one bale.

"How many pieces do they get?" Bailey asked.

Trent fought a smile. "They're called 'flakes,'" he said. Why was it Bailey always managed to make him grin, no matter how rotten his mood?

"Really?" She pursed her lips. "Makes me think of cereal." She helped him toss hay to the horses, then measure grain into buckets. As they poured each horse its ration, Bailey gestured toward the colts and fillies. "They sure are cute. And full of it, too." One of the colts reared up on his hind legs and nipped at his mother. He then came down on all fours, humped his back and raced away, bucking and kicking.

"They're a handful, all right," Trent said, still wondering how he would work them with his wrist screwed up.

"Have you got them halter broke yet?" Bailey asked as though reading his thoughts.

"I'm working on it."

"Well, if you need help, let me know. I don't know much about it, outside of what I've read in magazine articles, but I'd love to give it a try."

Her offer was tempting. Another excuse to be around her.

One he didn't need.

"I'm glad Star's doing good," he said, using the first thing that came to mind to change the subject.

"Me, too." Bailey leaned against the fence rail and chuckled. "Looks like I'm slowly gathering a farmful of animals. I managed to acquire a homeless rabbit today."

"Oh, yeah?"

She told him about her black rabbit. "I almost gave him to a little girl I met, but then it turned out her father doesn't think of rabbits as pets." She folded her arms. "Do you know Wade Darland? It was his daughter, Macy."

Trent gripped the fence rail. Macy used to play with Sarah. "Sure, I know the Darlands," he said. "How'd you meet them?" Did she make it a habit to get to know all her customers?

"I only met Macy. She was drawing with chalk on the sidewalk outside the bank today when I left. She's a cute kid. Asked me if she could come over and see my animals sometime. Said she'd ride her horse over."

A cold sensation crossed his spine.

Daddy, is it all right if I ride with Macy?

Okay, baby, but only in the arena until you see how Misttique handles.

Nausea churned his stomach as longing pulled at his heart. Longing for times past that would never come again.

He didn't want Macy to visit Bailey. Didn't want to risk seeing her and having memories flood his mind. Sometimes it was less painful simply to forget.

Quickly, he shook off the thought. Hiding from the little girl wasn't reasonable. After all, he'd seen her in town a few times with her dad and brother, though only from a distance. Macy and Sarah had been friends, and that was something he'd have to cope with. It wasn't Macy's fault, and Ferguson, after all, was a small town.

But Macy reminded him of Sarah in another way, too. Though she didn't look exactly like her, the two girls did resemble each other. Both had blue eyes and blond hair, and loved to dress in jeans and boots. *Had* loved to dress, he reminded himself.

Past tense.

Sarah was gone.

Would it ever stop hurting?

The memories flooded him now. Sarah and Macy, two peas in a pod, tagging along with him to horse auctions, to the feed store. Running errands with Amy. People who didn't know them had often asked if they were sisters. The girls loved that. Sarah had looked up to Macy as a big sister, though Macy was only a year older.

"Trent?"

"What?" Snapping back to the present, he met Bailey's gaze.

"Are you all right? You turned a little pale for a minute. Maybe your wrist *is* cracked." She frowned at his injured hand, which still gripped the fence rail as though he'd never let go.

Relaxing his hold, Trent flexed his fingers. "I think it's all right," he said. "But maybe I will have it x-rayed, just in case." He stepped away from the fence and pushed the empty wheelbarrow toward the barn.

Bailey followed, picking up on their previous conversation. "Anyway, I suppose I'd better check with Wade Darland and make sure he doesn't have a problem with Macy coming over."

I do! Trent wanted to shout. *I don't want to run into her, or look over at your place and see her there on a horse she used to ride with Sarah.*

But he clamped his mouth shut, knowing he shouldn't feel that way.

Bailey frowned. "Macy seems a little lonely."

Suddenly, Trent felt selfish. Macy *was* lonely. That was why she'd hung around with Amy and Sarah so much. She missed her mother. And she'd taken Sarah's death mighty hard. Almost as hard as he had.

"She is," he said, shoving the wheelbarrow into the feed room. "Her mother got killed a couple of years ago."

Bailey nodded. "Macy told me she died. What happened to her, if you don't mind my asking?"

He shrugged. "It's no secret. She was coming

home from work one night, and she tried to beat the train at the railroad crossing outside of town.''

''Oh my God,'' Bailey said. ''How awful.''

Trent grunted. He didn't want to talk about death. ''Listen, I was about to head to town when you got here. I thought an ice-cream sundae sounded good, since it's too hot to cook.'' He hoped Bailey would take the hint and leave. He'd slipped far too readily into enjoying her company. She was the first person he'd talked to about anything that had to do with Sarah. Though Bailey didn't realize the connection to Macy, she'd easily drawn him into conversation about her.

''Oh, it does!'' Bailey's eyes lit up. ''I haven't had a hot-fudge sundae in ages. Want me to drive?''

Trent's jaw nearly dropped. He hadn't meant to extend an invitation. He frowned. Apparently that was the way his statement had come out, or at least, that was the way Bailey had taken it. Well, he'd just have to set her straight. He opened his mouth to do so.

But the word *no* wouldn't quite roll off his tongue.

''I'll drive,'' he said.

''Okay. Let me get my wallet and we can be on our way.''

Trent sighed. ''You might as well hop in the truck. I'll take you over to your place.''

"Thanks," Bailey said with a smile that would melt chocolate. "That's mighty neighborly of you."

He grunted.

Neighborly indeed.

Trouble was, he suddenly wasn't thinking of Bailey merely as a neighbor or as the new bank president.

His gaze slid along the length of her legs as she climbed into the truck. He remembered what she looked like in shorts, and his thoughts went exactly where they weren't supposed to go.

Nope.

She wasn't just his neighbor.

She was a woman he wanted very much to take to bed.

CHAPTER SIX

BAILEY WASN'T SURE which was better—hot fudge or hot sex. Considering it had been so long since she'd had the latter that she could barely remember, she'd go with the hot fudge. Wrapping her tongue around a wad of chocolate and ice cream, she nearly groaned out loud. On the other hand, the sight of Trent was almost enough to sway her decision. He sat across from her and watched her devour her sundae with a look of amusement that had his gray eyes sparking and her heart missing a beat or two.

"What?" she asked, gesturing with her spoon. "What are you smiling at?"

"You. The way you're thoroughly enjoying your ice cream."

"I am. It's been a long time since I've had hot…fudge." She grinned and felt her face warm to the roots of her hair.

Trent raised his eyebrows. "It's nothing to be embarrassed about," he teased.

It would be if he knew what she was thinking, Bailey mused. "One of my—" She stopped just short of saying "foster mothers." Dottie hardly qualified for the title. "Someone I used to know growing up once told me that men don't appreciate a woman with a healthy appetite. Not that it's ever stopped me." She smiled and closed her mouth over her spoon once more.

Trent's gaze focused on her lips, and she wondered what he was thinking. "That's not necessarily true," he said, meeting her eyes as she started to squirm. "In college I hated it when I'd take a girl out and she'd pick at her food like a little bird. It was like she was putting on a front, hiding her true self. Made me wonder if, once she married, she would just sit down in the middle of the kitchen and inhale every scrap of food around."

Bailey laughed. "Well, not me. People can take me the way I am or leave me." She shoved her spoon into the sundae dish and reached for her glass of ice water. "So, where'd you go to school?"

"Stanford. My parents own an Arabian ranch outside Sonoma."

"Ah, a California golden boy, huh?" Bailey teased. He didn't really look the part. He wasn't pretty enough. Good-looking yes, pretty no. Trent seemed tough, rugged, the way a cowboy should. But then, most cowboys didn't ride Arabians, so he definitely broke the mold there. He was the type of man who piqued a woman's interest and left her wanting to dig deeper.

Forget it, Chancellor, Bailey reminded herself. *He's not for you.*

"I don't know about that," Trent said in answer to her comment. The way his words matched her thoughts gave her a little start. "I think Colorado's more to my liking, especially the western slope."

"What brought you out here?" For a minute, she thought he wasn't going to answer.

His words came out forced. "Amy, my ex-wife. She was born in Colorado and dreamed of building a home in the mountains." He slowly stirred his spoon through his ice cream, lost in thought.

Bailey wanted badly to ask questions, even though she'd told herself not to get close to Trent. But she didn't want to pressure him about something he obviously had no desire to talk about.

"I can relate to that," she said instead. "This is certainly a beautiful area."

"What made you want to come here?" Trent asked.

Bailey hesitated. Should she open up to a man who didn't want to give her the same courtesy? Maybe doing so would let him know he could talk to her. Everyone needed someone to confide in at some time, even a stubborn cowboy.

"The bank I worked for in Denver is an affiliate of Colorado Western National," Bailey said. "They wanted someone to give this bank a new direction, and I was offered the job."

"But what made you leave the city?" Trent persisted. "Life in Denver has got to be a whole lot more exciting than life in Ferguson."

Bailey shrugged. "I suppose living in the city has its advantages. But it wasn't what I wanted overall."

"Really?" Trent shoved his spoon into his ice cream and leaned on the table. "What *do* you want, Bailey?"

The question startled her, and she gave a short laugh. "That's a little personal, isn't it?" Especially coming from someone who kept his deepest thoughts and feelings locked inside.

Now it was his turn to shrug. "I'm just trying to make conversation."

It was more than that, Bailey decided as she studied the expression on his face. Trent Murdock was curious about her. She'd bet her last dollar on it. Maybe she should open up to him…just a little.

"I also came to Ferguson because I've wanted to live on a farm ever since I was a little girl."

"Is that right." He gave her a crooked smile that sent her heart racing. "A banker turned farmer, huh?"

"Something like that. I've always loved animals."

"Did you have a lot of pets when you were a kid?"

"Not really," Bailey said. When a child was

shuffled from one foster home to the next, there wasn't room for a dog or cat.

"What—your parents didn't like animals?"

In for a penny, in for a pound. "My parents were killed by a drunk driver when I was four."

Trent's expression softened, and he closed his hand over hers. "I'm sorry. I didn't mean to pry."

Heat spread through Bailey. Trent's touch felt warm and strong, and she was surprised by her overwhelming feeling that here was a man she could lean on. But the feeling vanished just as quickly as it had come. Trent didn't want to lean on anyone, and she doubted he had any intention of returning the favor. Besides which, she'd dealt with the pain of her childhood on her own and had managed to find a way to heal. Handling the rest of her life was something she could also do on her own.

Abruptly, Trent drew his hand away. "I know how it feels," he said. "To lose someone."

His comment made her wonder if she'd been wrong. Was he looking for someone to talk to? Maybe he didn't even realize it himself. Should she push him for more? Ask him about Sarah? Bailey felt compelled to comfort him, in spite of her better judgment. At first she'd told herself she didn't want any part of a man with so much emotional baggage. But now that she'd gotten to know Trent, she found herself second-guessing her better judgment. Her heart went out to him.

"Trent, if you ever want to talk about anything, I'm a good listener. It seems we have something in common, and—"

"Thanks. I appreciate the offer, but I'm fine." He turned his attention back to his ice cream. "Tell me more about you." Looking away, he picked up his spoon and dug into the last of his sundae with obvious purpose.

Bailey scowled at him, though he didn't notice. That he should expect her to open up to him when he wouldn't do the same wasn't fair.

"There's not much to tell," she said. "I like my job, I love kids and animals and I plan to spend the rest of my life on my farm."

At the mention of kids, Trent's gaze snapped back to her. He sat silent for a long moment. "You don't have any kids, do you?"

"No," Bailey said. "Not yet."

"Ever been married?"

"No, but I'm not opposed to the idea."

He didn't answer, and she weighed her next words before speaking. She hated to be insensitive, but if Trent really was so devastated by his loss of Sarah that he never wanted kids again, Bailey needed to know. Then she'd be able to tell herself that beyond a shadow of a doubt he wasn't worth wasting her time over.

"How about you, Trent?" she asked softly. "Do you think you'll ever remarry?"

"Nope." He practically bit the word off, as though it would poison him if left in his mouth too long. He let his spoon clatter into his empty dish. "Are you going to finish that sundae before your fudge melts it or not? I need to get moving—get my wrist looked at."

Stung, Bailey glared at him. "Letting it melt is part of enjoying it," she said, unwilling to allow him to see he'd hurt her feelings. "That way the ice cream and chocolate run together." Too bad she couldn't melt him. Too bad they'd never join like vanilla and chocolate.

Purposely, she took her time finishing her sundae, knowing it was childish, not caring.

And when she finally followed Trent out the door, after insisting on paying for her own sundae, Bailey made herself a promise.

She wouldn't let Trent hurt her. No matter what developed between them, she'd keep her good sense and not allow things go any further than she chose them to. Because somewhere out there was a man she could spend the rest of her life with. And if that man wasn't Trent Murdock, then so be it. She wouldn't permit it to get her down.

She wouldn't.

TRENT PAUSED outside the doors of the emergency room, hating the icy, pins-and-needles sensation that crawled across his skin. Bailey stood beside him, unaware of his reaction to the place. That was fine. He had no intention of letting her know how he felt. Though he'd called himself a jackass for treating her the way he had at the ice-cream parlor, he'd had no choice. Something about Bailey made it easy for him to talk to her, but opening up to her wasn't smart. That he felt attracted to her was bad enough. To give her any other part of himself was something he simply could not do.

Taking a deep breath, Trent stepped through the automatic doors to the E.R. He scanned the surrounding hallway…and his eyes fell on the waiting room. How many hours had he spent there, and in one just like it in the third-floor pediatrics wing? More than he cared to count. Forcing his gaze away, he headed to the receptionist's window.

"May I help you?" She was a cute little redhead, who did absolutely nothing for his libido. Trent held up his right arm. "I might've cracked my wrist," he said.

"Oh." The redhead frowned sympathetically. "How did you do that?"

He explained, while she sat in front of her keyboard and tapped the information into the computer. His name, address, what time the accident took place.

From the corner of his eye, he saw Bailey waiting in a chair. It was as though she belonged here with him. The thought comforted him in spite of his resolve to push her away, and in spite of the fact that his injury was a minor one. He wouldn't even be at the hospital if not for his injury interfering with his work. He simply wanted to get it taken care of so he could go back to his routine and stay busy; back to his everyday, normal life. A life, he reminded himself, that didn't include Bailey.

Somehow, *that* thought did not comfort him.

He didn't care to dwell on the why of the matter. He pushed away from the chair he'd been seated in and followed the receptionist's instructions to sit in the waiting room until a nurse came for him. Bailey walked silently beside him. He supposed he'd hurt her feelings at the ice-cream place. He hadn't meant to; it was just that he didn't want her prying.

Nor did he want to open up and share his fears and sorrow with her. He was afraid if he ever did, it wouldn't stop there. He might be tempted to go a step further and share more with her than information. And that was something he'd promised himself not to do with any woman.

But Bailey wasn't just any woman. Like it or not, he felt closer to her than he had to anyone in a long time. There was something special about her, though he knew he shouldn't think about that. She wasn't his and she never would be.

Trent sat in a chair next to her in the waiting room. "I hope we're not here long," he grumbled. "I hate this place."

Sudden realization passed across Bailey's face. Her beautiful, violet-blue eyes filled with concern, making him wish he'd kept his mouth shut.

"Trent, I'm sorry," she said, laying her hand on his arm. "I'm sure being here isn't easy."

To say the least. How could he describe what he felt each time he drove past Our Lady of Mercy Hospital? He hadn't stepped inside its doors since he'd taken Sarah home to die, and even just driving past gave him a sick feeling in the pit of his stomach. "Yeah, well, I guess it can't be helped," he said, not wanting to talk about Sarah's last days here.

Daddy, are the angels going to come for me? What if they can't find me here? I don't want to be here. I want to be in my room when they come.

Trent closed his eyes, fighting for control as sweat began to drip down the back of his shirt collar.

"Trent?" Bailey squeezed his arm. "Are you all right?"

Take me home, Daddy. Please take me home.

It was all he'd needed to hear. All he'd needed to make him go against his own wife's wishes and do, instead, what Sarah had wanted most. He'd taken her home. Home to die.

The walls closed around him. He couldn't breathe.

The room swam.

His vision blurred.

He stood. "I have to get out of here."

"Mr. Murdock?" A nurse stepped into the room. Concern lined her face as she peered at him. "Are you all right? Why don't you come with me."

He wanted to bolt. He could barely focus on what the woman was saying, or on Bailey as she held his arm in a steady grip. "Trent? Oh, God," Bailey said. "Here—lean on me."

He didn't want to. Didn't want to lean on anyone ever again. Amy had abandoned him. Sarah had been snatched away from him coldly and cruelly.

Trent swayed, clapping a hand to his forehead. His skin felt clammy to his own touch, beaded with cold sweat.

Bailey slipped her arm around his waist, and he leaned against her. She guided him to an exam room and helped him onto the padded gurney. He felt like a fool. The nurse took his blood pressure, his temperature, his pulse. Bailey fussed over him. It was too much.

"Damn it, I'm fine!" he snapped. Then, seeing the startlement on both women's faces, he forced himself to use a softer tone. "Really. Thanks, but I'm fine. I just stood up too fast."

Bailey graced him with a look that said she knew better, but she said nothing. It seemed to take forever for the doctor to come in, send Trent down the hall to X ray and finally come back with a diagnosis. Trent's wrist was sprained, though that could often be worse than a break, according to Dr. Bevins. Trent barely listened as Bevins gave him instructions to soak the wrist in Epsom salts, use ibuprofen to relieve the inflammation and take things easy for a few days.

He wanted only to get out of there, drop Bailey off at her house and go home to Windsong, where he felt safe from prying eyes. Away from Bailey.

They'd just stepped into the hallway that led to the exit, when a man came out of one of the other exam rooms, his left index finger encased in a huge wad of gauze and adhesive tape. Trent recognized him even before Bailey smiled and spoke to the guy. Mr. Tool Belt, her buddy from the bank. The man he'd wondered if she was involved with.

Trent bristled.

"Bernie," Bailey said. "What on earth happened to you?"

Bernie flashed her a sheepish grin, displaying those even, white, toothpaste-commercial teeth of his. "I had a little run-in with a table saw," he said. "Twelve stitches." His grin widened. "But don't worry, I'll still manage to get the rooms for your day care remodeled on schedule."

Just as Trent wondered if Bailey was going to introduce them, she faced him. "Trent, this is my contractor, Bernie Tuttle. He's remodeling the lower level of the bank to make room for our day care."

Tuttle? Trent felt a grin creep across his face. Not

exactly the macho name he would have imagined for Mr. Tool Belt. Actually, neither was "Bernie." *As in Bernard?* Bernard Tuttle. Suddenly, Trent liked the guy.

He stuck out his hand and gave Bernie's good one a firm shake, even though it pained his wrist to do so. "How're you doing? Nice to meet you."

"Likewise," Tool Belt–Tuttle said affably. "Well, I'd better get home and prop this thing up on a pillow." He lifted his good hand in a wave. "Take care." His comment included Trent.

"You, too," Bailey said.

"Watch out for those saw blades," Trent couldn't resist adding.

Bailey elbowed him in the ribs, her lips curved in a mischievous smile. A smile that made him forget the way he'd been feeling a short time ago.

"You're just plain ornery, you know that?" she said.

He shrugged. "That's what my mom always told me." He stepped up to the E.R. doors. "Come on. Let's get out of here."

THE WHOLE WAY HOME, Bailey fought the emotions that swirled inside her. Trent's reaction to being at the hospital had all but knocked her flat. She hadn't expected to care so much about him or the fact that being at Our Lady of Mercy was obviously a tough thing for him. She kicked herself for not making the connection sooner. Here she'd bugged him about going to the hospital, never once thinking it might bring back horrible memories of Sarah's illness.

She should have known. Our Lady of Mercy was newly remodeled and boasted one of the best pediatric wings in the county, from what she'd heard. Sarah must have spent her last days there. *How sad.* No child should have to suffer that; no parent should have to feel such a cruel, senseless loss.

Trent pulled the truck to a halt in Bailey's driveway, and she hesitated, her hand on the door handle. "Would you like to come in for a few minutes?" she asked, hating to let him go home to be alone with his memories. "I've got cold lemonade and root beer. We could sit on the porch and enjoy the night air." The sun had lowered in the sky, and an evening breeze stirred the tops of the trees.

"No." Trent shook his head. "Thanks."

Still Bailey hesitated. For a minute, back at the hospital, Bernie Tuttle had provided a distraction. She'd seen Trent grin widely when he shook Bernie's hand, though she wasn't really sure why. She'd just felt relieved that his face no longer looked pinched and white. But her relief had been shortlived once they'd gotten out to the parking lot.

Trent had immediately fallen into a brooding silence, one she didn't have the foggiest idea how to penetrate. Small talk hadn't worked, and though she'd longed to tell him to let everything out and

get it all off his chest, she had a feeling now wasn't
the time or place. He didn't know her that well.

"Come on. Just one glass. If I have to spend one
more evening out here alone, talking to my animals,
I'll go crazy."

He smiled crookedly at her, and her heart jumped.

"What's the matter, city girl? The isolation of the
country getting to you already?"

Bailey laughed, suddenly realizing what she'd
said. Though she'd meant it mostly as an excuse to
get him to stay, she had to admit her comment held
a grain of truth. "Well, maybe just a little. I'm not
used to being so alone, although I wouldn't trade
living here for anything." She gestured to encom-
pass the surrounding area. "I love these mountains,
this land. I'll get used to it, I'm sure."

Trent stared at her, his gray eyes lit with some
emotion that had her nerves jangling like warning
bells. *God, the man was good-looking.* Too much so
for his own good, or for hers.

"I'm sure you will," he said. He turned off the
ignition and left his keys dangling in it. "All right,
one root beer, and then I'm history."

Warmth snaked through her and her pulse picked
up tempo as though the high-school quarterback had
just asked her to the prom. *Silly,* she chided herself.
But she didn't care. Being with Trent felt good, and
what was wrong with enjoying his company? As
long as she kept things in perspective. She already

knew there was nothing serious to be had with the man. Entertaining thoughts of a future with him bordered on the ridiculous. So, if she kept these things in mind, she'd be fine.

Really.

Bailey swallowed hard and tried to look away from the pockets of Trent's Wrangler jeans as he made his way up her porch steps. Buddy came around the corner, halted when he saw Trent, then eyed Bailey and actually wagged his tail.

"Will you look at that," she said, her jaw dropping. "He wagged his tail at me."

"I don't blame him," Trent said, shooting her a teasing smile. "You offered me something cold to drink and here I am. He's not stupid."

She graced Trent with a mock glare. "In other words, he's not liable to bite the hand that feeds him."

"Exactly."

"Hmmph," Bailey said. "Goes to show how much you know. I think he's starting to like me." She wondered if she could say the same for Trent.

As soon as the thought was out, she pushed it back where it had come from. Silly! He liked her well enough, in a friendship sort of way, but that was as far as it would go. She knew that, and it was fine by her.

"Come here, Buddy!" she called, snapping her fingers, determined to prove her point.

The heeler took one glance at her, trotted toward the fence and leaped over it as though it wasn't even there.

A chuckle rumbled up from Trent's chest. "So much for your theory and your fence," he teased.

Bailey shot him a glare for real. "Very funny."

"Guess I'm going to have to get better in a hurry," Trent said, holding up his sprained wrist, "so I can help you raise that fence higher."

A retort that she didn't need his help was on the tip of her tongue, but the warmth in his eyes was enough to stop her. "I guess so," she said. "Now, do you want that root beer or not?"

"Sure do." He followed her into the kitchen, and Bailey took two cans of Barq's from the fridge.

"Would you like a glass?" she asked.

"No. The can's fine." As he took it, their fingers brushed, making the pulse in her throat leap. What was wrong with her? She was acting as silly as a filly on locoweed.

Outside, Bailey sank onto the porch steps, thinking Trent would find a place away from her. No such luck. Instead, he sat on the step above her, his knees grazing the side of her arm. She turned toward him, searching for something to say. Something that sounded as though it came from a woman who had good sense and knew her own mind.

"You smell good." *That definitely was not it.*

Bailey looked at her root beer and wondered half-heartedly if it had somehow been tampered with at the factory—spiked with truth serum.

Trent's eyebrows shot up like two caterpillars on a twig. "Thanks," he said. "Though I don't see how I could, after an evening doing chores." His mouth quirked in a half grin.

"That's just it," Bailey said, trying for a save. "You smell like hay and—and wood shavings..." *And musky cologne that obviously lasts all day.* "And you remind me of—of a warm summer afternoon."

"I do?"

"Oh, yeah." She groped for something to add, something that would kick her brain back into gear and make her stop thinking how nice it would be to wrap her arms around Trent and inhale that musky cologne at close range. "I love the scent of hay and wood shavings."

"So do I," Trent said. "I've always loved the smell of horses and barns, especially a show barn where all the horses are shampooed and groomed to the nines, smelling of baby oil and pine shavings."

"I got to go to a horse show once," Bailey said. "The stock show, as a matter of fact." It was one of the best memories of her childhood, one of the few that were truly good. "I was ten years old. I think that's where my longing for a horse began." She smiled as she recalled her twelfth set of foster parents taking her to the Denver National Western Stock Show.

Suddenly, she felt Trent's hand on her shoulder, gently massaging. Startled, Bailey met his gaze. "Who took you there?" he asked softly.

She could read the unspoken words in his eyes. *Not your parents.* She'd told him they'd died when she was four. Bailey froze beneath his touch, afraid to move. Afraid that he'd take his hand away, yet at the same time wishing he would.

Again, the feeling she'd had at the ice-cream parlor overcame her—a reluctance to open up to Trent. She wasn't quite ready for that. "My foster parents," Bailey said. There was no need to tell him that she'd been moved from one home to another, for one reason or another, for the better part of her life.

Trent's gaze softened, and he continued to stroke her shoulder. "You should've been able to share things like that with your own parents," he said, his voice husky. "But instead, it was all taken from you. Just like that." He snapped the fingers of his other hand, and sadness filled his eyes, tearing at Bailey's heart. The look of deep understanding she saw there was enough to undo her. Completely.

Here she'd thought to relate to Trent, when indeed it was the other way around. That he might feel sympathy for her had never occurred to Bailey, and the knowledge swept through her like a shock wave, leaving her feeling vulnerable.

"Yes." She nodded, unable to wrench her gaze from his. Her throat tightened with emotion, and she reached up to lay her hand on his, watching him over her shoulder. "I have only a few vague memories of my parents, yet I've always felt a part of me died with them, a part I could never get back." The words came out barely above a whisper, as if she had something stuck in her windpipe.

Bailey told herself to look away from him, that what she saw in Trent's eyes couldn't possibly lead to anything. A hunger, a longing, lingered there, as though he too suffered from wanting something he couldn't have. His gaze darkened.

Bailey held her breath.

And then she turned toward him. He lowered his face to hers and raised his hand to cup her jaw. She shut her eyes and ignored the warning in her mind that screamed at her to move away before it was too late.

But it was already too late. Trent's mouth closed over hers in a kiss that was neither gentle nor harsh. Instead, it was needy, possessive, both giving and taking. He wound the fingers of his left hand through her hair and she placed her hands at his nape, drawing him near. Their mouths sought frantically with a hunger neither Trent nor Bailey could deny or contain.

He kissed her over and over again, until she was breathless, until her heart cried out for him to stop and to never stop, both at the same time.

When at last he pulled away, his eyes were the color of a stormy sky, his features taut with longing. "Bailey," he whispered. His strong fingers massaged her neck, still caught in the curtain of her hair. He trailed the back of his free hand over her cheek, his sprained wrist forgotten.

And that one word, just her name, held so much...spoke volumes.

Like her, he felt a loss and a need to compensate for it. And like her, he was scared. Afraid to give love to the wrong person, afraid to lose again.

For the first time, it hit home. What scared the hell out of her was knowing that they really had something in common, something that could lead to a strong bond between them. She was afraid to be vulnerable, afraid to offer her love openly, only to have it crushed into nothing. That was what frightened her most about him. That was what had kept her pulling away from him, telling herself she didn't need to be burdened by the emotional baggage he carried.

Trent rose from the step and retrieved his pop can. "Thanks," he said simply. For the kiss? The root beer? For sharing ice cream and an evening full of emotion?

Bailey couldn't speak.

She just watched him stride to his pickup truck and leave without a backward glance.

And one thought stayed with her.

They had something in common, all right, she and Trent. And oddly enough, it wasn't bringing them together—it was tearing them apart.

CHAPTER SEVEN

TRENT TOSSED and turned in his bed that night, then finally got up and went outside to sit on the porch. He could not stop thinking of Bailey.

He couldn't believe he'd kissed her! Yet he'd been powerless to stop it from happening. And if that wasn't bad enough, he'd thoroughly enjoyed it. Bailey was a beautiful woman, inside and out, and knowing that she understood what it was like to suffer a tragic loss served only to draw him closer to her. But he didn't want to be closer to her. He'd made a promise and he meant to keep it. Falling for Bailey could only spell trouble with a capital T, in more ways than he could even begin to count.

She was all wrong for him, for crying out loud. Clearly, she was a woman who knew exactly what she wanted—a family. She'd come right out and said so, and then she'd asked him if he ever planned to marry again. Her statement had seemed innocent enough at the time, but now he wondered if it really had been. Not that she was trying to corner him or anything. It was just that Bailey obviously felt as attracted to him as he did to her, and therefore needed to find out if he wanted to settle down again.

She might as well get that idea out of her head right now, and he might as well forget about what had happened between them.

If only he could.

Good God, he'd known the woman mere days! What was he doing kissing her, much less thinking the thoughts he was thinking about her? Disgusted with himself, Trent stared into the darkness. The yard light over at Bailey's place cast a silver glow, illuminating enough of the pasture for Trent to make out Star's silhouette against the backdrop of night.

This was doing him no good.

How the hell was he ever going to get past what he was feeling for Bailey with her living right next door? Trent stood and shoved his hands through his hair, his wrist throbbing. This was crazy. He was a grown man, and there was absolutely no reason he couldn't forget about that kiss and move on.

So why couldn't he sleep?

Trent stalked back into the house, letting the screen door slam behind him. He glanced at the kitchen clock. Twelve-thirty; eleven-thirty in California. His dad had always been a night owl, unlike most horsemen. But he was also usually up by six or seven at the latest. Vigorous and youthful beyond his sixty-eight years, Zachary Murdock was a man who loved his horses and his children almost equally, and who'd reacted with nothing short of joy the day he'd found out he was to become a father for the fifth time.

Trent smiled at the knowledge that he'd been the only one of the kids who'd arrived unplanned. With ten years between him and his youngest sister, he'd been coddled by all four of his sisters, who'd never felt one ounce of jealousy or resentment because he was the only son. Maybe that was because his parents had never shown favoritism for one child over another.

His dad had missed out on college by becoming a father at seventeen, but he'd made up for it by working hard, building his Arabian ranch into one envied by most people in the Sonoma Valley, where Zach eventually went to live. People from all over the world paid good money to own a Zadel Arabian—the ranch name a combination of Trent's father's and that of his mother, Della.

Trent came from a family so filled with love, he'd had no doubt he would find the same in his own marriage to Amy. But all his dreams had shattered, and he had no desire to go that route again. He needed to stay away from Bailey.

Maybe talking to his dad would help.

He reached for the phone and dialed.

Zach's voice stretched across the miles, sounding so close. "Hello, Trent."

Trent grinned. "How'd you know it was me, and

don't say caller ID, because you haven't bothered to subscribe.''

His dad chuckled, his voice deep and friendly. ''Who else would be phoning me at this hour?'' Then he sobered. ''Is everything all right, son?''

No, everything isn't.

He had a horrible case of lust for Bailey, and he'd kissed her and wanted to do so again.

''Everything's fine, Dad. I just wanted to hear your voice.''

''Well, I'm glad about that,'' Zach said. ''Your mother's sound asleep. I was just sitting here watching the *Late Show* and thinking of you, believe it or not.''

''You were?''

''Indeed. Guess what I got today.''

''No!'' Trent didn't even have to guess. He could tell by the little-boy quality in his dad's voice exactly what it was. A new horse, and if that was the case, it would be none other than the one his father had passionately longed for, a seven-year-old stallion owned by Zach's neighbor and friendly rival on the show circuit. Zach had coveted the animal for years, and ever since his neighbor had fallen into poor health and debated putting the stallion up for sale three months ago, Zach had talked of little else. Ibn Ra Jahim, a half brother to his own mare Bronnz, was a chestnut with flaxen mane and tail, his coat a brilliant red-gold.

"I did!" Zach laughed. "Fifty thousand dollars' worth of horseflesh, son, and I feel like a boy again!"

Trent chuckled. "You always feel like a boy, Dad."

"Well, horses will do that to you, I'm telling you. They keep you young. So, do you want me to ship some semen to you come February?" It was the usual start of the breeding season, which ran into late spring.

The eleven-month gestation period of a mare was a long time to wait for a foal. But the reward a breeder felt when that foal finally arrived, simply could not be described. "Sure, Dad, that would be great," Trent said dryly. "I doubt I can afford your stud fee, though."

"Stud fee schmud fee," Zach said, and Trent could picture him characteristically waving dismissively. "Consider it an early birthday present. Just remember who your friends are if you ever want to sell his sister."

Trent laughed. With Zach's collection of stallions, he no doubt had the perfect mate already lined up for Bronnz. "That I can do, Dad, but I still wouldn't feel right not paying you for the semen."

"Well, then, I guess you'll have to talk to your banker about a loan," Zach joked. "How is Hal Peterson, anyway?"

"Hal retired," Trent said.

"The hell you say! I didn't think that old codger would ever give up banking. He loved that job more than his wife, maybe even more than his horses." The comment was good-natured. His dad had met Hal Peterson on more than one occasion, when Zach came to visit. The two horsemen got along like peanut butter and honey.

"Yeah, well, a lot of folks aren't too happy about it, but I guess that's the way it goes," Trent said.

"So who took his place?"

"A woman, name of Bailey Chancellor."

"A lady bank president, huh?" Zach's voice piqued with interest. "Is she good at her job?"

She's a good kisser.

Trent curled his fist around the phone cord. "I think she probably is. She's making changes in the bank's policy that have a lot of folks up in arms, but her intentions are good." The Bailey he'd seen was a woman full of compassion and idealism. Surely she didn't turn down farmers' loans for the pleasure of imitating Ebenezer Scrooge.

"Well, hopefully she'll work out. Some folks just don't like change. It might take time for them to come around."

"I would imagine."

Zach paused. "Is something wrong?" His ability to pick up on the mood of his children had never ceased to amaze Trent.

"No, Dad, not really."

"You're sure?"

"Bailey's my neighbor."

"And that's a problem?"

"I kissed her."

"I see. Well, that might not be especially good for business relations, but it's not exactly a crime, you know. Not unless she threatens you with sexual harassment, that is. But that's not what's going on, is it?"

Trent sighed and sank onto a chair at the kitchen table. "Nothing's going on. I kissed her—that's that. I won't let it happen again."

Zach's tone softened. "Son, it's perfectly normal for you to want a woman. Why are you beating yourself up over it?"

"I'm not beating myself up." The denial came out a little too sharply even to his own ears. "Look, Dad, we've been over this before. I just don't have any desire to be with somebody right now. I'm happy by myself, and I don't expect that to change."

"Trent, I know you're still hurting. Your mother and I are, too. You'll always grieve for your daughter, but time will ease your pain."

"Dad—"

"Hear me out. What you went through was horrible, something no parent should ever have to suffer. Life isn't always fair, but just because you lost your wife and your child doesn't mean you don't have a right to happiness." The rattle of cellophane

on the other end of the line told Trent his father was
doing what he always did when he was about to
settle into a deep, serious discussion—opening a bag
of pretzels and pouring them into his favorite
wooden bowl. That and a ginger ale were his dad's
version of a good cigar and a glass of brandy.

Trent didn't want to get into a serious discussion,
but Zach was already off and running.

"I know you miss Sarah like there's no tomorrow. But you can't crawl into the grave after your
daughter, man! You've got to snap out of this lone-
wolf thing and get out and enjoy your life. You're
young, son, and I hate seeing you this way. You say
you're happy, but you're not. You've wrapped yourself in a cocoon where nobody can reach you and
you don't have to be afraid to love again. And that
bothers me more than you can know."

Trent stared at the wall without seeing it. "I'm
sorry you feel that way, Dad. I'm not trying to make
you feel bad. I just want to be left alone. It doesn't
bother me. I'm doing fine, and I don't want you to
worry over me. Now, tell me more about your new
stallion."

Zach sighed, and pretzels rattled against the
wooden bowl as he fished around for one and
popped it into his mouth.

They talked horses for almost an hour. Before
they hung up, Zach tried one last time. "Promise
me one thing before you go."

"What?"

"That you'll give your new lady banker a chance."

"I'm sure she's quite competent, and that her new loan policies won't keep me from borrowing money if the need arises," Trent said, being deliberately obtuse.

"That's not what I meant, and you know it. Give it a little time. See where things go. What you and Amy went through would strain any marriage. Maybe she just wasn't the right gal for you. After all, a woman like your mother comes around only once in a lifetime."

Trent chuckled in spite of himself. His parents shared a love as sweet and strong as the day they'd first met. "That's true enough."

"Just think about it. I love you, son."

"I know. I love you, too, Dad."

Trent sat in the chair for a long while after the line disconnected, mulling over his father's words.

The problem wasn't that he didn't want to give Bailey a chance.

It was exactly the opposite.

And that was what scared the hell out of him.

BAILEY DREAMED of a sheikh, riding toward her on a horse the color of the sun. As horse and rider drew near, she saw that the sheikh was Trent, and he wore cowboy boots beneath his robe. He reached out to her, and, smiling, she moved to take his hand. But at the last minute he pulled back, his face full of sadness. "I can't be with you, Bailey," he said. He glanced over his shoulder at another rider on a white horse, a little girl. She looked like Macy, but somehow Bailey knew she was Sarah.

Bailey opened her mouth to speak, but the words wouldn't come out. It was as though they were frozen in her throat. As the child galloped away, Trent spun his chestnut horse around and set out after her. *Wait!* Bailey tried to shout. *Come back—*

She awoke with a start, shaken by the dream. Sitting up in bed, Bailey tossed the covers aside and reached for the lamp on her bedside table. The digital reading on her clock glowed red—2:00 a.m. Bailey rose and headed for the bathroom, wisps of the dream still clinging to the back of her mind.

After washing her hands, she went to the kitchen and poured a glass of water from the pitcher in the fridge. She supposed thinking of Trent and his Arabians yesterday had caused her to envision him as a sheikh. And his riding away in pursuit of Sarah probably meant that because of the loss of his little girl, he refused to be with Bailey or have another family. But what had made her dream that? She wasn't after Trent as husband material.

True, she'd questioned him about his getting married again, but only to prove to herself that he wasn't the man for her. And she'd been right. Both his answer and her dream told her so. Why had the little girl in the dream had Macy's face? Was it simply that Macy had been on her mind lately?

Realization struck home. Macy was barely older than Sarah would've been had she still been alive, and since the Darlands lived a short distance away, it stood to reason that Macy and Sarah had known each other and had probably even been friends. Bailey felt stupid for not making the connection sooner. But why hadn't Trent said anything to her when she'd mentioned meeting Macy? He'd told her he knew the Darlands, but that was all.

She supposed Jenny was right. He didn't like to talk about Sarah at all. She couldn't help wondering how healthy that was. Wouldn't it be better to share memories of her with others? Surely, letting his emotions out, rather than bottling them up would help Trent cope with his grief. But then, men often had a problem with that. Every man Bailey had ever known kept things inside, and Trent was no exception.

And this locked-up pain festered. Or did it? Maybe she was wrong. Different people coped with grief in different ways. Maybe Trent had already made peace with his loss and was perfectly comfortable living his life alone. Well, that was fine with her.

Bailey stood at the sink, gazing out across the darkened pasture at Trent's house. She could just discern the outline of it beneath the glow of the moon and stars. Her mind drifted to the memory of the kiss they'd shared.

Why had he kissed her? Clearly, he didn't want to get involved, so what was it all about? She supposed that, like her, he was lonely. Maybe he'd simply reached out to her because she'd been handy. Yet she hadn't felt used; she'd felt...

Bailey hated to admit what she'd felt. Trent's arms around her had been more than wonderful, his touch beyond nice. She could easily have lost herself in his embrace, in his kiss, and most likely would have, had he not pulled away and left. How far would things have gone if he hadn't driven off? She liked to think they wouldn't have gone far, that she would have come to her senses before that happened. But she wasn't so sure.

Maybe it would be best if she stayed away from Trent for a while. Her feelings for him frightened her, and could surely come to no good for either of them. Keeping her distance was the smartest thing she could do, and Bailey was determined to stay smart.

She'd moved to Ferguson to start a new life, and she was determined to have everything she'd worked hard for and longed for, including a family. If that wasn't in Trent's plans, then he wasn't in hers. It was time to accept that and move on. The only trouble was, her heart disagreed with her head.

Well, too bad, Bailey silently reprimanded herself. *Get over it! He's not for you.*

For the hundredth time, he's not for you.

BAILEY SPENT the next week avoiding Trent, which wasn't hard since apparently he was avoiding her. Fine. She focused on work and on figuring out how to add an extension to her fence that would keep Buddy in the yard. By Wednesday, she'd purchased the materials she would need to get the job done, and planned to start on the fence once she got home from the bank.

At lunchtime, Bailey headed over to Audrey's Café. She'd no sooner taken a seat in a corner booth than the bell above the door tinkled and Camille walked in. Bailey smiled and waved her over. "Well, hi there, stranger. Long time no see."

"How's it going?" Camille asked, sliding into the booth, across from her. "I haven't seen you in days. What's keeping you so busy?"

Bailey shrugged. "This and that." She pushed thoughts of Trent to the back of her mind. "Mostly the remodeling for the day care."

The waitress brought menus, and Camille opened hers, came to a quick decision, then put it down, propped her elbows on it and locked her gaze on Bailey. "So, how are things between you and Mr. Tall, Blond and Handsome? Did he like your home-made cinnamon rolls?"

Bailey tucked her tongue in her cheek. "Oh, he loved them, all right. But I don't think he believed for a minute that I baked them."

Camille chuckled. "Well, you can't blame a girl for trying." She leaned forward and lowered her voice. "I heard he took you out for ice cream the other night."

Bailey stopped short of letting her mouth fall open. "Who told you that?"

"A little bird," Camille said, then grinned. "Named Jenny."

Rolling her eyes, Bailey smiled. "Figures. Well, it was no big deal. He'd sprained his wrist. I helped him with his chores, and then we went for ice cream and to the emergency room."

"The E.R.?" Camille drew back. "Girlfriend, what kind of date is that?"

Bailey smothered a grin. "I told you, it wasn't a date. We'd taken his truck to town, so I had to go with him." She kept her tone light, as though the outing had been no big deal. But the kiss she and Trent had shared lay heavy on her mind, filling her with longing.

She felt her face redden beneath Camille's scrutiny. "What?"

"*Had* to?" Camille humphed. "I doubt there's a man on this earth who can make you do anything." She narrowed her eyes. "Is there more to this than you're letting me in on?"

Bailey sighed. Should she tell her about the kiss?

"There *is*," Camille said, pushing her menu aside. "Come on, Bailey, tell me. What's going on?"

"He kissed me," Bailey said.

Camille's eyes widened. "Really?" Her pretty lips spread in a slow smile. "Was it good?"

Bailey smiled back in spite of herself. "Yes, it was good. Too good."

"What's that supposed to mean?"

Bailey met her friend's steady gaze. "I don't know, Camille. I really like him. It's just that he's so hung up on the loss he suffered I don't know if he's ready to move on. I've got dreams and plans, and if he doesn't want to be with anyone, then why waste my time?"

Camille shrugged. "Maybe it's not such a waste. Maybe the man just needs a chance."

"Could be," Bailey said. "It's just that he's so annoying sometimes, running hot, then cold. I'm not sure I want to risk falling for someone who's going to end up breaking my heart."

"Yeah." Camille sighed wistfully. "I can sure relate to that." She sobered. "You know, it isn't easy losing someone you loved."

Sorrow washed over Bailey at the knowledge of how much Camille had suffered from her husband's death. She put her hand on Camille's arm. "I know, hon, and I'm really sorry you lost Caleb. But you'll find somebody to love again one of these days.''

Camille quirked her mouth. ''Well, if I do, it sure won't be a rodeo cowboy. My point, however, is—healing takes time. Give Trent a little. I'll bet he comes around.''

''Maybe,'' Bailey said, though she wasn't so sure. Even if Trent did get past his pain, was she willing to risk loving him?

''Hey, speaking of Trent...'' Camille said. ''I dropped one of my cats off at the vet clinic just before I came over here, and I heard Doc Baker had to go on a call to Windsong.''

Concern for Trent's horses instantly filled Bailey. ''What for?'' she asked.

''Colic.''

Bailey's heart jumped. Colic was not a good thing, she knew that much. The term was used to refer to any number of gastrointestinal disturbances in horses, and could be caused by a number of factors. Bottom line—a horse did not have the ability to vomit; therefore, gut impaction or severe abdominal pain might lead a horse to roll in an effort to relieve the discomfort, twisting its intestines in the process, which would likely prove fatal. ''Oh my gosh. I wonder which horse it is?''

Camille lifted a shoulder. ''Dunno. Maybe you ought to go over there after you get off work and see.'' Her tone suggested it was a good excuse to check up on Trent as well as the horse.

Bailey graced her with a mock look of reprimand.

''What?'' Camille put on an expression of innocence. ''That's only being considerate. I mean, you do care about animals, right?''

''Of course,'' Bailey said, closing her menu. She'd barely even looked at it. She fought the voice inside her head that told her she cared about Trent as well. ''Whichever horse it is, I hope it'll be all right.''

''Only one way to find out.'' Camille winked, then turned to give the approaching waitress her order.

BAILEY STOOD next to Star, debating. Should she go over to Trent's and see how everything had turned out with the colicky horse? Or should she mind her own business? Leaning against Star's shoulder, she breathed in the warm, comforting scent of the gelding's satin-smooth coat. If she was smart, she'd do exactly that—mind her own business.

But she could see Trent in the pasture above, leading a horse back and forth along the fence line. That horse looked like Bronnz, and with a sigh, Bailey walked to the dividing fence and ducked through the wire. She could hardly turn her back on the man when one of his best mares was in danger of losing her life.

Cutting across the pasture, Bailey focused on the horse and tried not to think about facing Trent for the first time since they'd shared cold root beer and hot kisses on her porch. Spotting her, Trent waved but kept walking. Bailey fell into step beside him, and immediately, warmth spread through her, causing her temperature to rise and her pulse to pick up. She'd forgotten how good he looked, how tempting he smelled.

As usual, his woodsy cologne overrode the pleasant scents of horse and leather that were Trent. He wore a black T-shirt with the name of an Arabian-horse association on the front, and his dark gold hair brushed the neckline of his shirt beneath the back of his ball cap.

"I heard you had a colicky horse," Bailey said in an attempt to shrug off the feelings of desire and longing he stirred in her. She eyed Bronnz, and worry tugged at her heart. The mare was beautiful, and obviously Trent's pride and joy. She hoped the animal was okay.

Surprise registered briefly on Trent's face as he glanced at Bailey, then kept walking, concentrating on the task at hand. "I wouldn't think the condition of my horses is a bank topic," he said.

"It's not. Camille was at the vet office today when Dr. Baker got called out here." Bailey touched Bronnz's sweaty coat. "She feels warm. Is she all right?"

Despair twisted Trent's features. "I sure as hell hope so." He glanced at the mare. "Doc Baker gave her a dose of mineral oil and a shot of Banamine to help relax her gut, and it seemed to help for a while. But she lay down again a few minutes ago and acted like she wanted to roll."

"Is there anything I can do to help?" Bailey asked.

He shook his head. "Thanks. I've already called Doc Baker again."

"Here." Bailey reached for the lead rope. "Why don't you let me walk her for a while. I'm sure you're getting tired."

Trent looked down as their hands brushed when Bailey reached for the rope. He licked his lips, and Bailey's heart hammered. Just touching him set her on fire. Obviously, the stern and macho Trent Murdock was not immune to a similar reaction, if the expression on his face was any indication.

Now Bailey's pulse thundered. Good Lord, she should be thinking about the fate of poor Bronnz, rather than entertaining fantasies of Trent caressing her hand, her arm…and any other part of her body he cared to put his hands on. What was wrong with her?

She took hold of the lead rope, and Trent made a token protest. "Really, I'm fine," he said. "There's no need for you to concern yourself." He tightened his grip, their hands still touching.

She should be the one to get a grip, Bailey thought. On the rope *and* on her emotions. "I don't mind," she said. "Bronnz is a magnificent animal. I'd hate to see anything happen to her."

Reluctantly, Trent relinquished the rope but kept right on walking beside Bailey. "Me, too," he said. "She's the best mare I've got. Not to mention my favorite."

"I thought so." Bailey smiled. He didn't smile back, and she let her expression fade to a scowl. Trent had no reason to be so darned standoffish. She was only trying to help.

But his next words made her realize the reason he looked so serious. "Bailey, about the other day—on your porch."

Oh, Lord, here it came. He was going to say the kisses were all a mistake and that he'd never meant for them to happen. She didn't want to hear those words. She already knew she'd been a fool to let him kiss her—a fool to begin to fall for a man who could never love again.

She cut him off. "You don't have to explain. I already know."

"Know what?" His deep voice vibrated with something akin to intimacy. Bailey had to force herself to look away from those cool gray eyes that set her soul on fire every time she saw them.

"That kissing me was a mistake." She swallowed over the words that seemed to stick in her throat.

She hated that he thought of it that way. Heaven help her, she longed to feel warm and wanted in Trent's arms, and to kiss him again.

"That wasn't exactly what I was going to say." Trent spoke the words gently, shoving his hands in his pockets as though to keep from touching her.

"No?" Bailey ignored the shiver that danced along her spine as her shoulder brushed his while they walked.

He made no move to step away. "No." He stopped and put his hand over hers, causing her to pull Bronnz to a halt. "Let her rest a minute," he said.

"Won't she roll?" Bailey grasped at straws. She needed to keep walking, needed to move away from the proximity of Trent's maleness. From his hard, tanned body standing so close to her in that damnable T-shirt that showed off every muscle he had.

"We won't let her. Besides, she needs a little breather." He reached over and brushed a lock of Bailey's hair from where it had escaped the braid she'd put it in once she'd gotten home from the bank. "And so do I."

She glanced sharply at him. His touch froze her in place.

He looked back, and his eyes spoke volumes. He wanted her, just as much as she wanted him. "Kissing you wasn't a mistake, Bailey. It just wasn't something that should've happened."

She raised her eyebrows. "And the difference is?"

He lowered his hand and shoved it in his pocket once more. "A mistake is something you wish you'd never made. I don't wish I hadn't kissed you, Bailey. I just wish things could somehow be different. And because they can't, then I'd say it shouldn't have happened. It wasn't right for me to kiss you like that. I'll make sure I don't do it again."

Bailey's blood went hot, then cold. An unreasonable mixture of hurt and anger churned inside her, and her face grew warm. She knew he was right. Wasn't that the very reason she'd been avoiding him? So why did his words fill her with anguish?

"No problem," she said, focusing on Bronnz. She ran her hand along the mare's sweaty neck. "How long should we let her stand?"

"Bailey." Trent spoke her name softly yet firmly.

She fumed, angry with herself, annoyed with him for making her feel this way. She hadn't asked to be attracted to him; hadn't asked to care one way or the other. But she did. More than she'd realized.

She faced him.

"I don't want to hurt you."

"You're not," she lied. "How could you? Don't you know we bankers don't have any hearts?" She forced a smile. "Really, Trent, it's all right. That's why I haven't come over lately. I was a little embarrassed by what happened. Oh, don't get me wrong," she held up her hand, palm out. "The kisses were nice. But that's all." The lie rolled off her tongue so easily Bailey was stunned at how believable, how rational, it sounded. "I don't expect anything else from you."

"I didn't think you did," Trent emphasized. "I just wanted to clear things up, that's all." He shifted uncomfortably. "I was worried I'd offended you."

"Well, worry no more," Bailey said. "You didn't. So let's forget about it." With relief, she noticed what must be Doc Baker's mobile veterinary truck pulling into the driveway beyond the barn. "Looks like your vet is here."

"Yeah." Trent took the lead rope from her hand. Then his mouth curved in a slight smile. "You wanna come up to the barn and get a firsthand lesson on treating colic?"

"Why not." Bailey brushed her deepest feelings aside. After all, Trent wasn't saying he never wanted to see her again. He'd only let her know what she was already fully aware of. He had no interest in falling in love again.

She was glad for his honesty.

Glad for knowing that her initial reaction to him was right on target.

But sorrier than she could say that things had to be this way between them.

CHAPTER EIGHT

TRENT FOLLOWED the path now clearly visible in the grass of his lower pasture and climbed through Bailey's fence. Though he had to admit this route was handier than taking the road, he ought to stop using it. Every time he noticed the worn path, it reminded him that he and Bailey had a connection. He was having a hard enough time trying to work her out of his system. He didn't need a constant reminder that the two of them had grown closer than he'd planned.

He probably shouldn't even go over to her place right now, but he'd told himself that helping Bailey finish the extension on her fence, as he'd said he would, was the right thing to do. After all, she'd stayed with him for hours last night after Doc Baker left, walking Bronnz, making sure the mare didn't roll.

The night had been exhausting, but the colic had abated, then disappeared altogether, and this morning when he'd checked on Bronnz, she'd been quietly munching grass hay in her stall. Relief and happiness had flooded him. He hadn't wanted to lose her, too.

Bailey's genuine concern for the horse's well-being had touched him more than he cared to admit. He liked the woman, and the more he saw of her, the more he wanted to see. A part of him wondered if maybe his father was right and he should give her a chance, yet another part of him warned it would be foolish to do so.

If he started dating Bailey, what might come of it? While he didn't want to ever get seriously involved with anyone again, neither did he want to have a fling. It just wasn't his style. Being alone might seem a harsh alternative, but that was the way things had to be.

Besides, there were too many uncertainties in becoming attached to Bailey. Putting aside the fact that she wanted a family, would she even stay here as planned? Ferguson was a nice little town, if small towns were your thing. But who was to say Bailey wouldn't become bored once the novelty of small-town life wore off, and decide to return to the city? Trent had lived in a big city once. He didn't plan to do so again.

Like his father, he wanted to be the best Arabian-horse breeder he could be. He loved his horses, his ranch and his way of life. No one was going to take that from him. No one was going to take anything from him again, which was why he had to get a handle on his feelings for Bailey.

Last night she'd accepted his offer to help her finish the fence, since he'd told her it was a way to return the favor of walking Bronnz. They'd been doing a lot of that lately—one good turn for another—and he knew that once the fence was up, he'd have to make a greater effort to distance himself from her.

He crossed the pasture, pausing to give Star a pat, then walked toward the gate that led into the driveway by the yard. As he swung the gate open, he halted, squinting against the late-afternoon sun.

Belatedly, he noticed the palomino horse penned near the barn. Macy was there with Bailey, tagging along as Bailey carted a roll of wire across the yard in a wheelbarrow.

Macy, with her cowboy boots and blond pigtails...so much like Sarah.

Trent took a deep breath and headed for the yard.

Bailey glanced up and smiled. ''Hi there.''

''Hi.'' Even to his own ears, his voice sounded gruff. He cleared his throat and tried again. ''Looks like you're all set to string some wire.''

She nodded toward the roll of V-mesh and let the wheelbarrow come to rest on the ground. ''Buddy's roaming days will soon be over.''

''Hi, Trent,'' Macy said, walking over to stand in

Do You Have the Lucky Key?

PLAY THE
Lucky Key Game
and get

HOW TO PLAY:

1. With a coin, carefully scratch off gold area at the right. Then check the claim chart to see what we have for you — **2 FREE BOOKS** and a **FREE GIFT** — **ALL YOURS FREE!**

2. Send back the card and you'll receive two brand-new Harlequin Superromance® books. These books have a cover price of $4.99 each in the U.S. and $5.99 each in Canada, but they are yours to keep absolutely free.

3. There's no catch. You're under no obligation to buy anything. We charge nothing —ZERO — for your first shipment. And you don't have to make any minimum number of purchases — not even one!

4. The fact is, thousands of readers enjoy receiving books by mail from the Harlequin Reader Service®. They enjoy the convenience of home delivery...they like getting the best new novels at discount prices, BEFORE they're available in stores...and they love their *Heart to Heart* subscriber newsletter featuring author news, horoscopes, recipes, book reviews and much more!

5. We hope that after receiving your free books you'll want to remain a subscriber. But the choice is yours — to continue or cancel, any time at all! So why not take us up on our invitation, with no risk of any kind. You'll be glad you did!

YOURS FREE!
A SURPRISE GIFT

We can't tell you what it is...but we're sure you'll like it! A
FREE GIFT—
just for playing the LUCKY KEY game!

Visit us online at
www.eHarlequin.com

FREE GIFTS!

NO COST! NO OBLIGATION TO BUY!
NO PURCHASE NECESSARY!

PLAY THE
Lucky Key Game

Scratch gold area with a coin.
Then check below to see the books and gift you get!

336 HDL DH2S
135 HDL DH2J

YES! I have scratched off the gold area. Please send me the 2 Free books and gift for which I qualify. I understand I am under no obligation to purchase any books, as explained on the back and on the opposite page.

NAME   (PLEASE PRINT CLEARLY)

ADDRESS

APT.#   CITY

STATE/PROV.   ZIP/POSTAL CODE

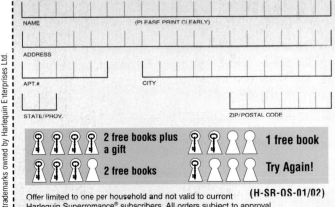

2 free books plus a gift

1 free book

2 free books

Try Again!

Offer limited to one per household and not valid to current Harlequin Superromance® subscribers. All orders subject to approval.

(H-SR-OS-01/02)

The Harlequin Reader Service® — Here's how it works:

Accepting your 2 free books and gift places you under no obligation to buy anything. You may keep the books and gift and return the shipping statement marked "cancel." If you do not cancel, about a month later we'll send you 6 additional books and bill you just $4.05 each in the U.S., or $4.46 each in Canada, plus 25¢ shipping & handling per book and applicable taxes if any.* That's the complete price and — compared to cover prices of $4.99 each in the U.S. and $5.99 each in Canada — it's quite a bargain! You may cancel at any time, but if you choose to continue, every month we'll send you 6 more books, which you may either purchase at the discount price or return to us and cancel your subscription.

*Terms and prices subject to change without notice. Sales tax applicable in N.Y. Canadian residents will be charged applicable provincial taxes and GST.

BUSINESS REPLY MAIL
FIRST-CLASS MAIL   PERMIT NO. 717-003   BUFFALO, NY

POSTAGE WILL BE PAID BY ADDRESSEE

HARLEQUIN READER SERVICE
3010 WALDEN AVE
PO BOX 1867
BUFFALO NY 14240-9952

NO POSTAGE
NECESSARY
IF MAILED
IN THE
UNITED STATES

If offer card is missing write to: Harlequin Reader Service, 3010 Walden Ave., P.O. Box 1867, Buffalo NY 14240-1867 front of him. "How are you? I haven't seen you in a while."

Trent forced himself to smile at her. "I'm okay. How's your dad and Jason?"

"They're fine. Are you going to help us put up the fence?"

He sighed inwardly, ignoring the tight knot in his stomach because of Macy's presence. She'd grown since he'd last seen her. Sarah would've grown, too.

He picked up the roll of wire. "Looks like it. Guess we'd best get started."

They worked side by side, the three of them, for the rest of the evening. When they were done, the fence was two feet taller, and Trent had managed to work most of his anxiety out of his muscles. But his head ached from the emotional Ping-Pong he'd played with himself as he'd bounced back and forth between keeping silent, walling his thoughts and emotions, and unconsciously becoming caught up in trivial chitchat with Bailey and Macy. He tried not to focus on the feelings that welled up inside him. Tried to pretend that every time Macy said something to him, he did not recall Sarah's sweet little voice, in his mind, in his heart.

Let me swing the hammer, Daddy. I can pound fence staples.

I'm your best helper, huh—

"Not bad." Bailey's voice broke through his reverie. He brought his mind back to the present, looking first at the fence, then at her. She stood with one hand on her hip as she scanned the length of the fence. He thought she'd never looked better, the setting sun playing through the gold streaks in her hair, her skin damp from her hard work.

He wanted to pull her close and use what he felt for her to block out all other thoughts, all other emotions, all the memories of what he'd lost.

Instead, he laid down the hammer and looked at the fence again. "I'd say we did a passable job, though I'm not sure if Buddy's all that happy with it." Trent glanced at the dog, who lay resignedly on the porch with his head resting on his speckle-tipped paws. Soulful brown eyes gazed back at him as Buddy gave a long, humanlike sigh.

"What's wrong, boy?" Macy asked.

The heeler perked his ears, his eyes following Macy as she moved across the yard. Oddly enough, the dog had taken an instant liking to her, and had spent a great deal of the evening tagging along at her heels as she helped with the fence.

"Look here, Buddy," Macy went on, bending to retrieve something from the grass.

Buddy raised his head from his paws and cocked it sideways, following her every move. His eyes came to rest on the red rubber ball she gripped in her small fist.

Bailey smiled and shook her head. "He won't play with it. I've already tried."

"He might," Macy said. "Some dogs just don't know what to do with a ball at first." She crouched down and tapped the toy on the ground. "Come on, Buddy! Come on, boy." She dragged the ball across the grass as the heeler watched. Every muscle on the alert, he rose to a sitting position, and his tail began to wag.

"You want it?" Macy asked. "Huh, you want it?" With a flick of her wrist, she pitched the rubber ball across the yard. "Then go get it!"

Buddy sprinted after it, and as the ball arced across the sky, the sun behind it seemed to burn a hole in Trent's vision.

Pain flashed in his head as a memory pushed through to consciousness.

Sarah's voice.

Get the ball, Jax! Get it, boy! That's it.

And Macy's— "Good dog. Good boy."

Their voices blended, here and now, then and there…

Bring it to me.

"Good dog."

Come on.

"Trent, are you all right?" Bailey's words cut through his mental fog. She edged toward him. "Did you get a little too much sun?"

But he barely heard her. An odd feeling roiled through his stomach as he watched Buddy grip the ball in his teeth and race back toward Macy.

The image of Jax and Sarah grew in his memory, churning, fading, blending anew as Macy stooped to ruffle Buddy's fur.

And the awful, sinking blackness that had plagued him for the past year, the sorrow that had gripped him, seemed to shift—just an inch. Making way for something so unfamiliar that for a moment he almost didn't recognize it for what it was.

Warmth.

Pleasure.

The kind that came when a father witnessed his daughter at play. The deep-down, good feeling of savoring a simple moment in time.

But this wasn't his little girl; it wasn't her dog.

It was Buddy and Macy, and he felt like a traitor for enjoying their company.

"Damned if you don't look like him," he muttered.

The smile that had begun to tug at his mouth gave way to a scowl, and he tucked the warm, pleasant sensation deep down inside where it belonged, along with the grief he'd nurtured and fed for so long now. So long that he didn't know how to do anything else.

"Look like who?" Bailey's question pulled him into the present.

He'd hardly been aware he'd spoken out loud.

"Nothing. Nobody." Trent began to gather scraps of wire from the ground, ignoring Bailey's puzzled frown. He tossed the scraps into the wheelbarrow.

"Trent, what's wrong?" Exasperation laced her words.

"Nothing," he replied gruffly. "I need to clean up this mess and get back to Windsong. I have chores of my own to finish before dark."

"Do you want some help with them?"

"No. Thanks." He pushed the wheelbarrow around behind the barn and disposed of the wire pieces in the trash barrel, trying to ignore Bailey's presence. Trying to fight the urge to stay and talk to her, to Macy, just a little while longer. It was time to go.

"Thanks for your help," Bailey said.

Her tone had turned from exasperated to chilly. He could hardly blame her. He knew he was being abrupt, but it was necessary. If he was to keep his distance from her emotionally, then he had to focus on doing just that. He couldn't have fun with her or with Macy. It just wasn't right.

Facing her, he found that the look in her eyes nearly undid his every resolve. He wanted to reach out to her just once more, and simply brush his hand across her cheek. He remembered how silky her skin had felt beneath his touch when he'd kissed her on the porch.

Instead, he shoved his hands into his back pockets. "No problem. Hopefully the fence will hold Buddy now."

They stood, silent, for the span of a heartbeat.

Macy's laughter carried through the air as she continued to play with the dog.

"So, I'll see you later," Trent said.

Bailey gazed solemnly at him. "Yeah, okay."

BAILEY HAD NO IDEA what had caused Trent's abrupt mood swing. One minute he'd been fine and the next he'd pulled back inside his shell like some damn turtle, cranky and unwilling to poke its head out. What was wrong with him? She replayed everything that had happened.

She'd been having a good time, working with him and Macy, enjoying the way Macy coaxed Buddy into a game of fetch with the red rubber ball. She couldn't believe Macy had actually gotten the dog to do it. Bailey had tried and tried to get him to play fetch, to no avail. Maybe he'd just been waiting for the right person to come along. Maybe he had a little girl in his past who'd played with him.

Again, realization dawned with the sudden impact of a ball cracking against a bat.

A little girl in Buddy's past.

A little girl in Trent's.

Had Macy triggered some specific memory of Sarah? *Damn.* She should've thought of the possibility. If she'd been a little more careful, she might have avoided putting him in a situation that made him uncomfortable. But darn it, tiptoeing around

Trent's feelings all the time was hard, and frankly, she was getting tired of it.

Feeling guilty for thinking that way, Bailey caught Star and saddled him, half listening to Macy's chatter while Macy saddled her horse, Amber, the little palomino she'd ridden over earlier in the day. With evening settling into dusk, Bailey wasn't about to let Macy go home unsupervised, and besides, a ride sounded pretty good right now. Maybe it would help clear her head.

She understood Trent's grief and felt the depth of his loss, so why should she feel guilty for trying to make him smile? She wondered what he'd meant when he mumbled something about "looking like *him.*" The only "him" present besides Trent was the dog. He had to have been referring to Buddy.

"Macy," Bailey said as they swung onto their horses and headed down the driveway. "Did Sarah have a dog?"

"Mmm-hmm." Macy's little face grew serious as she glanced over at Bailey. "She had a Border collie mix—I think he was part blue heeler—named Jax. Why?"

"I just wondered," Bailey said. She had to know. "What did he look like?"

Macy shrugged. "He was black and white with some speckles on his nose and paws. He looked a little bit like Buddy. Except his ears sort of flopped over on the tips."

Bingo. "Ah." Bailey rode along, her thoughts on the child Trent had lost, and suddenly it dawned on her that she had no idea what Trent's little girl had looked like, either. "And Sarah?"

Macy grinned. "Like me. People thought we were sisters." Her smile faded and sadness filled her blue eyes. "We used to ride together. I sure miss her."

"I'll bet you do," Bailey said softly.

Minutes later, they halted at the bottom of the Darlands' driveway. Waving, Bailey watched Macy trot Amber toward the barn. Then she turned Star and headed down the road. She'd already decided exactly where she was going. Over to Windsong.

She'd obviously upset Trent, albeit unintentionally, by having a little girl around who reminded him of his daughter, and a dog who looked like Sarah's Jax. But maybe that wasn't such a bad thing. Could be it was time Trent started to face what had happened and begin to work his way through it.

And maybe it's none of your business, her inner voice reprimanded.

Perhaps not, but she did care about Trent—more than she liked to admit—and it was possible he simply needed to find a way to deal with his grief. Some way other than crawling inside himself. It was also possible he needed a little help to do so.

He'd said his parents lived in California, and Jenny had told her Trent had locked himself away from everyone, both emotionally and physically, since Sarah's death. Could it be he really had no one to turn to, or at least, no one he wanted to turn to? Apparently, his wife had pushed him away, or turned away from him. Something had to have happened to make them go their separate ways. Bailey had often heard that the death of a child could break a marriage.

Sympathy and sadness warred with determination as Bailey headed for Windsong. Reminding herself that Trent required not sympathy but support, she took a deep breath and urged Star into a lope.

Trent was feeding the broodmares and foals. He looked up, and his eyes held hers for a moment before he resumed his task. Bailey steeled herself for what she could already see was going to be a chilly reception. If nothing else, she'd learned that Trent was stubborn.

Well, she could be stubborn, too.

"Hi," she said, pulling Star to a halt as the gelding whinnied a greeting to his former stablemates.

"Didn't we just say goodbye?" Trent looked at her but kept right on tossing hay.

Bailey gritted her teeth. Caring about someone so hardheaded damn sure wasn't easy. "We did, but I rode home with Macy to make certain she got there safe. And since there's a full moon out, I thought it might be fun to take a moonlight ride. I've never done that before."

He merely grunted, and Bailey held her patience by a thread.

"Would you like to go with me?"

"No, thanks."

The thread snapped. "Why not? Are you scared?"

"What's that supposed to mean?"

"Well, it doesn't mean I'm asking if you're scared to ride in the dark." Bailey glared at him. "You're afraid you might enjoy it, aren't you?"

He scowled darkly at her. "Don't be ridiculous." And he went back to tossing hay.

"I'm not. It's true. You're afraid you might have fun. That's why you came home a little while ago. It frightened you that you were having fun with me and Macy." Her heart pounded. She knew she'd crossed the line, but it was too late to back down now. Maybe it wasn't her place to say to him what she was saying. But she didn't see anyone else around to do it.

Trent froze, his hands on a flake of hay, his back to her. His shoulder muscles tensed beneath his shirt, and when at last he moved, he threw the hay to one of his mares just a little too hard.

"Is that so?" He faced her again.

Bailey leveled her chin at him. "Yes, it is."

"Humph. Shows how much you know." But the flicker of pain in his eyes told her she'd hit home.

She bit back an apology. She didn't want to be

mean, yet maybe he'd been coddled too long. From what Jenny had said, the entire town had given him a wide berth since Sarah's death. Could be it was time someone intruded on his space, if only a little.

"So, are we going riding?" Bailey asked again.

Trent heaved another flake of hay over the fence. For a moment, she didn'ty think he was going to answer. But then he faced her. His cool gray eyes hid whatever emotion stirred within. "Yeah, I'll go riding with you, Bailey. Somebody ought to, or you'll probably get lost in the dark." He reached for the last of the hay bale, but Bailey could've sworn the tension melted from his posture a little.

She breathed a quiet sigh of relief. Calling Trent's bluff had apparently been the thing to do. "Need any help finishing your chores?" she asked, trying to hide the note of triumph that lightened her tone.

"I can handle it," Trent said.

Okay, so she hadn't completely softened him up.

He flicked a glance her way. "I'm about done, anyway," he said grudgingly. "But if you want, you can pour some grain to the weanlings."

"All right," Bailey said, matching his cool tone of voice. "I can do that." She tethered Star to a nearby hitching post and hauled sweet feed to the foals.

"I'll get saddled," Trent said, edging past her.

Bailey nodded, ignoring the way her stomach did a little flip when his shoulder brushed against hers as they passed each other in the barn doorway. He got a halter and lead rope, and she fed the weanlings, then put the feed buckets back in the grain room. She watched Trent lead Dokina to the barn.

Minutes later, they rode down the driveway to the road and headed off along the gravel shoulder.

Trent frowned down at Star's hooves. "He's got a loose shoe. Who put those on him?" His tone sounded accusatory.

Bailey frowned back. She'd seen a farrier's ad in the local paper and phoned about it. The young man who'd responded had told her he was fresh out of horseshoeing school and was just getting started in the business. She'd figured someone new would be eager for customers and would therefore give her horse the utmost attention. "Owen Preston," Bailey said. "Do you know him?"

"Yeah, I've heard of him," Trent said, looking disgusted. "He's barely out of high school." He glowered at her. "I wouldn't trust him with my horses. Why'd you call him?"

Bailey almost let her jaw drop. "Why do you think? You told me Star needed shoes, so I looked in the newspaper and found Owen's number." Defensiveness rose in her. "He seemed competent."

"Well, he's too young to know what he's doing yet," Trent said. "You should've asked me for a name."

"Fine," Bailey said sweetly. "Who do you use?"

"I do all my own farrier work, but I can give you the names of a couple of good shoers. Meanwhile, you can't ride Star with his shoe like that." He'd slowed Dokina and now pulled her to a halt. Bailey tried not to notice the way his eyes appeared even more gray in the surrounding dusk. "Let's head back to the barn," he said. "I'll fix the shoe."

He'd done enough favors for her already. "I don't want to put you to any trouble," Bailey protested.

"You're not. I offered, didn't I?"

She bristled, wondering if it was his gruff manner that irritated her, or simply her own reaction to him. There was something about Trent she found appealing, something that tempted her to dig beneath the armor he'd covered himself with and get to the man beneath. What was he really like? What had he been like before Sarah's death?

Bailey told herself she didn't really want to know. She could enjoy his company without delving too deeply. Just because she was curious about him and attracted to him didn't mean she had to think beyond that. Yet, getting Trent to open up to her, even a little, gave her a sense of satisfaction. It made her feel she at least meant something to him, friend-shipwise. After all, he didn't seem to hang around with or talk to anyone else.

"All right, then," she said, turning Star around.

They headed back to the barn, and now Bailey did notice the clank and rattle of the gelding's loose shoe, which she'd previously missed. Leaving Dokina tied to the hitching post outside the barn, Trent haltered Star and led him inside, where he put him in cross-ties—a lead rope attached to each side of his halter—in the aisle.

"I'll get my tools," he said. "There's a fridge in the office if you'd like a can of pop." He gestured toward a room near the stalls.

"Thanks," Bailey said. She wasn't all that thirsty, but it would give her something to do. Something to take her mind off the confusion she experienced every time she was around Trent. She entered the office, groped for the light switch and froze when brightness flooded the area.

Her gaze riveted on the twelve-by-fourteen photograph of Sarah that hung on the wall over Trent's desk. Her quest for a can of pop forgotten, Bailey stepped around behind the desk, her hand reaching out automatically to touch the oak frame.

Oh, God. Her heart fluttered, then squeezed painfully.

Sarah had been a beautiful child, even more so than Macy. As a matter of fact, she really didn't look all that much like Macy beyond the way she was dressed and the way she wore her pale blond hair. Twin braids lay over the shoulders of her sequined purple western shirt, her big blue eyes shadowed by the brim of a cream-colored cowboy hat. Dimples creased her cheeks as she smiled for the camera.

The photo had obviously been taken at a horse show, and Sarah's little hands gripped the end of a fancy leather lead attached to a pale gray Arabian that Bailey didn't remember seeing on the ranch among Trent's other horses. It had never occurred to her to wonder if he still had Sarah's horse.

The photo was a head shot of Sarah and her gray, and she wore a banner of some sort across her shoulder, like the ones donned by rodeo queens. Her smile was enough to have won the heart of any horse show judge—or anyone who so much as looked at her. It was the happiest, most genuine smile Bailey had ever seen on a kid. Not a fake, posed for the photo.

Bailey's heart twisted. Trent's loss of his daughter had saddened her before, but now that she had a face to put with the name, she felt even more deeply for him than ever. Such a horrible tragic waste of a short vivid life.

She blinked back the burning sensation behind her eyes and turned her attention to the huge blue ribbon fastened to the outside corner of the picture frame. Slowly, she reached up and ran her fingertips over it. *First Place—Halter Class—Peewee Division.*

Happier times.

That he was able to leave Sarah's photo hanging above his desk, a daily reminder of the little girl who'd been taken from him, told Bailey just how strong he really was. Put in his position, she wasn't sure she'd be able to do the same.

"She was the princess."

Trent's voice startled her, and Bailey swallowed a gasp as she swung around to face him. Sadness filled his eyes, and the guarded look he usually wore was gone.

Bailey felt much the same way she had that day he'd caught her at Sarah's grave—like an intruder. "She was beautiful," she said, meaning it. "Inside and out, I'd bet." She looked once more at the photograph.

"That was her favorite picture of her and Misttique." Trent's eyes took on a faraway look, but a smile underlay his words. "It was taken two years ago, at her first horse show."

Impulsively, Bailey moved around the desk and reached for his hand. "I know how you must miss her," she said.

He swallowed, blinked, then squeezed her hand. "Yeah," he said, his voice husky. "Yeah, I do."

"I'm sorry," Bailey said, lowering her voice to a near whisper. "Really, truly sorry." She choked back the tears brought on by seeing the moisture in Trent's eyes.

He said nothing but continued to grip her hand.

She sensed this wasn't the time to push him. It was simply a time to let him know she was here if he needed her. And she felt she'd done that with this small gesture.

She gave their clasped hands a little shake. "So, did you think I'd gotten lost?" She forced a smile, willing her voice not to tremble. "Figured I couldn't find the refrigerator?" She'd obviously been in his office longer than she'd thought, longer than it would take simply to get a can of pop.

For a moment, he seemed surprised by her light comment, as though he'd expected her to probe, instead, about his little girl. He squeezed her hand once more, then released it.

"The thought had crossed my mind, banker woman." He gave her a sad little half grin, then left the office.

Bailey moved to the mini fridge in the corner and extracted a can of pop without even noting the flavor. Her thoughts were elsewhere.

Something had happened between them just now. Something had passed from her to Trent, a form of understanding. It wasn't much, but it was a start.

Bailey popped the top on the soda can, not entirely sure what to make of that feeling of closeness.

CHAPTER NINE

WITH STAR'S SHOE INTACT, Trent rode beside Bailey through the trees, toward a trail that led to the river. He wasn't sure why he hadn't just fixed the horseshoe and called it a night. It would have been easy to tell Bailey he'd changed his mind, that the ride would have to wait until another time.

But the damn fool woman had no business going out on the trail in the moonlight, much less on Star, with his one eye, when she barely knew how to handle a horse. While it wasn't Trent's responsibility to take care of her, he somehow felt the need to look after Bailey and make sure she didn't end up getting herself in trouble. Besides, he'd actually begun to enjoy her company, though he knew he shouldn't. That she hadn't pressured him into talking about Sarah tonight meant a lot.

They rode in silence, and Bailey seemed content simply to enjoy the scenery. Dusk had all but given way to darkness. "There's a nice trail through here," Trent said. "It leads to the banks of the Colorado." The river wound alongside the frontage road, past Ferguson and its surrounding towns, cutting through private property here and there.

"I love the way the river looks in the moonlight," Bailey said. "When I drive alongside it, I often find myself pulling over for a closer look."

Trent nodded agreement. Like an oil painting, the Colorado spread out before them as they broke from the trees. Moonlight spilled across the water, turning everything around it surreal, glowing with a brightness akin to early-morning light. He watched as Bailey sucked in her breath and pulled Star to a halt, taking it all in.

"What's wrong?" he teased, turning in the saddle to see the expression on her face. She looked like a kid viewing Disneyland for the first time.

"God, but I love this part of the country!" Bailey said, shaking her head in awe. "How many people are blessed with a sight like this in their own backyard?" She gestured to include the expanse of land and river. Then she spoke as though thinking out loud more than talking to him, her gaze still on the river. "How many of life's simple pleasures have I missed by living in the city all these years?"

He smiled. "I don't know, city girl. You tell me." He kept his voice soft and even. But his heart pounded and he couldn't help wondering what he himself had missed out on before he'd met her. He tried to shake off the thought, but it wouldn't go.

He swung down from the saddle and offered her his hand. "Want to see it close-up?"

She hesitated but a moment, then took his hand and eased from the saddle. Heat snaked up his wrist from where their palms linked, and the urge to take Bailey into his arms and kiss her washed over him like the river that flowed below. Instead, he held the reins of his horse in his free hand and walked with Bailey toward the water's edge.

They let the horses drink while they stood on the banks and stared across the river. "Look." Trent pointed. Two mule deer had come down from the mountain to drink, and they lifted their heads and gazed with a mixture of curiosity and apprehension at him and Bailey and the horses.

"Oh," Bailey whispered, gripping Trent's arm with excitement. "They're gorgeous! I've never been this close to a deer before." She smiled. "Except in a zoo."

"Not quite the same, huh?" He grinned back at her and, from the corner of his eye, saw the deer bound up the riverbank and disappear into the trees and brush.

"Not even close," Bailey said. "That was incredible." She smiled and squeezed his hand. "I'm glad you brought me here."

So was he, and he could no longer resist the urge to kiss her. He pulled her against him so fast it made her gasp. The impulsive action took him by surprise, as well. But before Trent could give it a second thought, Bailey was in his arms, her lips soft and warm beneath his. She groaned as he slipped his tongue into her mouth, and the sound brought heat rushing to his groin. From the moment he'd seen her, he'd wanted to make love to her, and that had not changed. No matter what his better judgment told him, he wanted Bailey in the worst way.

He needed to get himself under control.

"We'd better go back," he murmured. Unable to resist, he traced kisses along her earlobe, her jaw, then found her mouth again. Her hands laced behind his neck, her mouth eagerly responding. Her tongue wrapped around his, warming his blood, making it hard to stop.

He did so with effort.

Bailey's eyes sparkled in the moonlight, eager, alive. She made him feel alive for the first time in over a year, and he tamped down the guilt that feeling brought him.

She licked her lips, sending his pulse into a frenzy, and nodded. "Yes, I suppose we'd better."

They rode back toward Windsong, and Trent could barely focus on keeping his horse on the trail in the moonlight. He wanted to relish this moment with Bailey, and try as he might, the longing to make love to her would not abate, though it scared him. He'd been with no one since his breakup with Amy, and even then it had been a long time since they'd had an intimate relationship. Sarah's illness had put such stress and strain on their marriage that Amy had moved out of his bed weeks before she'd moved out of his life.

Blocking the thought, Trent focused only on the moment. He'd had every intention of pushing Bailey from his life, and certainly had never thought—not seriously, anyway—to take her to bed. But maybe he should. Maybe it would be the one way to get over what he felt for her. He told himself it was purely a sexual thing. Hell, he'd gone so long without sex that he'd probably just reached the end of his rope. He was only human. He'd met a beautiful woman he liked and was attracted to, and now he wanted to have her. It was nothing more than that.

Right.

He knew that was a lie. Deep down, he also knew that Bailey turned him inside out and upside down, and that if he'd just allow himself a little slack, he could fall in love with her. But that wasn't going to happen. He couldn't let it. Making love was one thing; falling in love was another.

Lost in thought, Trent let his horse move along the trail automatically, barely aware that Dokina veered onto a fork in the path that they usually took as a route home. Bailey's sharp intake of breath caused him to look up, and only then did he fully realize where they were. The narrow trail branched away from the main path, flanked by tall mountain grass, wildflowers and Russian olive and cotton-wood trees. Just above it, on the overlooking hill, was the cemetery.

The expression in Bailey's eyes as she met his gaze was enough to shock him into shame. Here he'd been letting wanton thoughts of her fill his head, not even realizing that he now rode on the trail he usually took when he wanted to think about his daughter. He'd made weekly visits to the cemetery without fail ever since Sarah's death. He often chose this trail, too, on his way back from a ride to the river, so that he could look up and see Roth Hill and know that Sarah had been laid to rest in the shelter of these mountains. She suffered no more and was now in a far better place than this earth had to offer, though he missed her so much he thought his heart would surely shrivel up into nothing.

"I didn't realize you could see the cemetery from here," Bailey said. Sadness filled her pretty eyes. "It's so peaceful."

Trent pulled Dokina to a halt, and Star automatically stopped, bumping Bailey forward in the saddle. She quickly regained her balance, loosened her reins a little and let the gelding stand. Though he couldn't see Sarah's grave, Trent focused his gaze on top of the hillside. A few of the headstones and marble crosses stood in view, shadows in the moonlight.

"It's close to home," he said, "where I can visit

often.'' He sighed and leaned forward, resting his crossed wrists on the saddle horn.

He'd never talked to anyone except his parents about Sarah's death, and even then he'd held back. Because sharing his pain meant exposing his heart, and that he could not bring himself to do. He still wasn't sure he would ever be able to talk about Sarah's death at length, but something about Bailey let him feel comfortable in talking a little.

''Amy's only visited Sarah's grave once since the funeral. I guess she just can't handle it. She didn't want to help me plant the blue spruce or decorate it.''

''Why did you?'' Bailey asked, her voice a near whisper.

He noticed she was holding her breath, as though afraid that if he realized he was telling her these things, he might stop. Normally, he would have. Only three people besides him knew the reason behind Sarah's tree: Amy, his mother and his father. But somehow he didn't mind including Bailey.

''Sarah loved Christmastime,'' he said. ''We had a routine we'd followed since she was real small. On Christmas Eve day, I always took her sledding. And that night, weather permitting, we'd go for a short horseback ride.'' He smiled softly in remembrance. ''I used to carry her on the front of my saddle when she was real little, then behind it as she grew bigger, until finally, she could ride her own horse.''

''That sounds like fun,'' Bailey said.

''Yeah.'' The memories folded around him, taking him back to a snowy day with his little girl. ''After our ride, we'd have hot chocolate, then we'd each choose one present to open.'' He let out a small laugh. ''Sarah never could decide which one until the last minute. She'd pick one, then change her mind and pick another.'' He looked at Bailey and found she was smiling, though her eyes had misted over.

Trent swallowed to ease the constriction of his throat. ''She'd be up at the crack of dawn on Christmas Day, and we'd have a huge dinner with my family. By bedtime, Sarah was so worn-out she could hardly hold her eyes open. But she always made me read her the story from the Bible of how baby Jesus was born in the stable. And just before she dropped off to sleep, she'd say, 'You know what I wish, Daddy?''' His voice thickened, and he fought the tears that burned his eyes. ''I wish every day could be Christmas, because it's just like magic.'''

He looked at Bailey. Tears streaked her cheeks, and she swiped at them with the back of her hand. ''I'm so sorry,'' she said. ''You shouldn't have had to lose her the way you did.'' Nudging Star closer, she reached out and touched his arm. "I wish I could do or say something to ease your pain."

He nodded. "It's not something parents ever think they'll have to go through. You just don't expect to outlive your child."

"No." She sniffed and wiped her eyes once more. "She had stomach cancer?"

He nodded. "Yeah. The cancer spread to her liver." He took a deep breath. "She died six months after being diagnosed."

"Dear God." Bailey tilted her head back to look up at the sky, then let her gaze come to rest on the cemetery atop the hill. "I'd like to visit her grave again sometime," she said, "if you wouldn't mind, and take her some flowers."

"Sure." Dokina shifted beneath him, then pinned her ears at Star. "Hey." Trent spoke to the horse. "Be nice." He tightened his reins, forcing Dokina back a step. "I guess we'd better head for home. Someone's tired of standing still."

Bailey managed a small smile. "Okay." They rode along single file at first, until the trail widened. Then Bailey rode up beside him. "What happened to Sarah's horse?" she asked. "The one in the photo I saw tonight?"

Another source of pain on the long list of decisions he'd had to make.

"I couldn't bear to see Misttique every day. Sarah loved that horse more than anything. But I couldn't bear to sell him, either. So I shipped him to my parents' ranch in California.''

"They still have him, then?''

He nodded. ''Mom finds comfort in taking care of Misttique and riding him. She says it makes her feel close to Sarah.''

Bailey's mouth twisted in a sad little smile. ''Sarah probably would've liked that.'' She hesitated. ''What about her dog?''

He frowned. ''How did you know she had a dog?''

''Macy told me.'' She eased Star along the trail, and in the moonlight, he could see the soulful expression in her eyes. ''He looked like Buddy, didn't he?''

Trent sighed. How had this conversation gotten started? He really didn't want to rehash all this. ''Yeah, pretty much. He was a Border collie–blue heeler mix. His name was Jax, and I bought him for Sarah just before we found out she was sick. He stayed by her side constantly. And he moped when she went to the hospital.'' He didn't tell her that Jax had howled outside Sarah's bedroom window the night she died, until Trent could stand it no longer.

That mournful, near-human sound would haunt him for the rest of his life. Even the better part of a bottle of whiskey hadn't been enough to drown out the plaintive wail. He'd brought the dog into his room and let Jax sleep on the rug beside the bed.

Trent had lain awake all night, staring up at the ceiling, his eyes dry and achy. He'd cried so many tears there were none left inside him. Dangling his hand over the edge of the bed, he'd rested it on Jax's head, finding comfort in the animal's presence.

Amy had left hours before, unable to sit by and watch her daughter die. She'd been staying with a friend since their marriage had officially ended, when he'd brought Sarah home from the hospital. The next day, Amy came back to get the remainder of her things while Trent was at the funeral home, and she took Jax with her.

"My wife and I had separated shortly before Sarah died. She moved back to California right after that, dog and all, and filed for divorce." He steered Dokina over a fallen log. "Careful. Don't let Star trip over that."

Bailey guided the gray horse over the log. The look she gave Trent told him she knew he was trying to shift the conversation elsewhere. She grew silent, then asked, "How long have your parents raised Arabians?"

Relieved and grateful that she understood his need for a change of subject, Trent let out a breath he'd barely been aware of holding. He'd already told Bailey more than he'd intended. "Since before I was born," he answered.

They spent the remainder of the ride talking about Zadel Arabians and his mother and father. "Your parents sound wonderful,'' Bailey said as they halted at the foot of her driveway. "Do they visit often?''

He stiffened. Was she hoping to meet them? A part of him would love to introduce Bailey to his mom and dad. Another part ran scared at the thought of what that implied. "Usually once or twice a year. I'm not sure when they'll be out again.''

"Well, thanks for riding with me.'' Bailey grinned crookedly. "It wasn't so bad, was it?''

He chuckled. "No, it wasn't. Do you want me to help you unsaddle Star?'' He was making up an excuse to prolong the evening, but he couldn't stop himself. He'd enjoyed their ride together far more than he wanted to admit, and now that it was over, he hated to leave Bailey.

"No, thanks,'' she said. "I can handle it.''

"All right.'' He turned his horse around, then looked back over his shoulder. "Hey, Bailey. Let's do this again soon.''

She appeared startled by the invitation, but she quickly recovered. "Sure.'' Her lips curved, making him remember the kisses they'd shared by the river. "That way I won't get lost in the dark.'' She winked and lifted her hand in a little wave, then headed up the driveway.

Trent rode away, heart pounding, not sure why he'd tacked on the last-minute invitation. Maybe the night air had gone to his head.

Then again, maybe Bailey had.

He glanced over his shoulder, unable to resist just one more look at her, and saw her do likewise as she rode Star toward the barn.

Quickly, he faced forward in the saddle. The sight of Bailey riding in the moonlight on a horse the color of a phantom was enough to make him believe she was merely a figment of his imagination. He'd hardly be surprised if he woke up in the morning to find he'd dreamed all the things that had occurred in his life since he'd met her. Since a woman with big-city ways and a small-town heart had stirred feelings long dormant in him.

The memory of her parting smile followed him home.

He couldn't remember the last time he'd enjoyed a ride as much as he had tonight. And though he hated to admit it, it had sort of felt good talking to Bailey about Sarah.

Trent continued to dwell on Bailey as he unsaddled Dokina and brushed her down. Surely he was losing his mind. He seemed to sway between wanting to steer clear of Bailey and wanting to take her to bed. He couldn't help thinking it would be interesting to see which of the two ended up happening. But for now, he was satisfied to take things one day at a time. A day with Bailey in his life often felt like ten. Still, he had a sinking feeling that one without her might feel like a thousand years.

He turned Dokina out into the pasture and stood near the gate, looking across at Bailey's house. A light was on in the barn. After a while, it went out, and a short time later, so did the one in an upstairs room that was probably her bedroom.

He pictured Bailey climbing between a set of crisp cool sheets, possibly wearing a scrap of lacy panties and a teddy. Or a sheer silky nightgown, or maybe nothing at all.

A heated mixture of longing and apprehension filled him.

If only he could switch off his feelings for her as easily as she'd turned off the light in her room. He turned his face toward the heavens. "Sarah, honey, what on earth is your daddy going to do?"

A shooting star streaked across the night sky. Trent followed its path, then stared at the place in the star-studded blackness where it had disappeared.

Closing his eyes, he made a wish. He wished for guidance, and hoped that whatever was meant to happen would happen soon, so that he might either forget Bailey and get on with his life, or have the courage to pursue a relationship with her and see where it led.

Then he went inside and climbed into bed. And as sleep curled around him, he drifted away on a dream in which he held a phantom lover, and lost himself in her gentle touch and her mesmerizing violet eyes.

CHAPTER TEN

BAILEY NEVER THOUGHT she'd consider a branch audit a blessing in disguise, but that was exactly how she felt as she prepared for her first one as president of Colorado Western National. Her job depended on all bank records being in order, which turned out to be a good thing. It left her no time to dwell on the kisses she and Trent had shared by the river last week.

. They hadn't talked since their moonlight ride. True, Bailey had worked late every night this week. Still, she'd thought Trent would call. He'd said he wanted to go riding again sometime soon. Normally, Bailey would have assumed he, too, was busy. But she'd caught sight of him across the pasture several times while she did her chores, and all he'd done was wave. He'd made no effort to come to the fence and talk to her.

In all fairness, she had to admit that she hadn't made an effort to walk over and talk to him, either. She felt stressed and exhausted from working late every night. Preparation for the branch audit meant poring over everything from safe-deposit sign-in cards to night-drop logs. The bank would be scored on a scale of one to a hundred. If it didn't receive at least an eighty-five, Colorado Western National would go on written warning, and Bailey could lose her job.

The thought terrified her. She had every confidence she'd kept things running properly, but what if she'd overlooked some important detail? Without her job, she could hardly afford the payments on her farm, and without the farm, her dreams would all go down the tubes. She'd be forced to move back to the city.

And she'd probably never see Trent again.

Bailey shuddered at the thought of giving up her farm. She'd come to care a lot about Trent, but the farm meant everything to her. She'd promised herself that nothing would stand in her way of obtaining the solid, permanent home she'd always longed for—a place to put down the roots she so desperately needed for her and her future children. She'd also vowed she would accomplish her goals with or without Trent Murdock.

She intended to keep those vows.

Obviously, her relationship with Trent must mean something to him, or he wouldn't have trusted her enough to talk about Sarah. But exactly how far he was willing to take things, she didn't know. Bailey was actually surprised he'd talked about Sarah at all, and wondered if he would have, had they not ridden

past the cemetery. It didn't matter. At least he'd
opened up to her a little. She only hoped she wasn't
a complete fool for thinking things might continue
to develop between the two of them.

She'd already made it clear to Trent that she cared
about him. If he wanted to be with her, he was going
to have to meet her halfway.

Determined to push Trent out of her mind for
now, Bailey headed for the bank. As she entered the
lobby, she spotted Lester Godfrey in the waiting
area.

Jenny approached her. "Bailey, Lester's here to
see you." She frowned. "He said he needed to talk
to you about something, but he wouldn't say what."

Bailey glanced at the clock and sighed. She still
had some last-minute things she wanted to go over
before the auditors arrived. "I can give him a few
minutes," she said reluctantly. "Send him into my
office."

Bailey sat down behind her desk, and Jenny
showed Lester inside. He removed his ball cap and
clutched it in his work-worn hands, twisting the bill
into the shape of a taco shell.

"Hello, Lester." Bailey smiled and indicated one
of two chairs facing her desk. "What can I do for
you?"

Lester sat on the edge of the chair and cleared his
throat. "I was wondering if there was any way

you'd reconsider giving me that loan, Ms. Chancellor. I really need the money.''

Bailey frowned. ''I don't understand. I thought the money I paid you for your truck was enough to carry you through for a while.''

''It did help.'' Lester shrugged one shoulder and avoided making eye contact. ''But it didn't go as far as I'd hoped. My wife, Jolene—she had some female surgery recently, as you know. And the bills just keep pourin' in.'' His gaze returned to hers. ''Besides that, Jolene's madder'n a wet hen at me for selling you that truck.''

''Oh?''

He puffed out his cheeks, then sighed. ''We had our first date in the Chevy, at the old drive-in theater that used to be out east of town. And I've spent a lot of time and money fixing the truck up.'' He grinned crookedly. ''We brought each of our four kids home from the hospital in that pickup, and Jolene wants it back. So I was thinking if you could see your way to giving me the loan, then I could buy the truck back and maybe have some money left over to pay the doctor bills.''

Sympathy for Lester's plight flooded Bailey, but there was nothing she could do. ''I'm sorry, Lester. I'd like to help you, but as I told you before, you don't qualify for a loan.''

He nodded. ''I know when you ran everything through your computer it didn't come up lookin'

real good. I ain't got much in the way of credit."
He gestured dismissively. "But can't you just skip
all that and do things the old-fashioned, small-town
way? Maybe pull a few strings and get me the loan?
I'm good for the money, I swear."

Bailey held on to her patience. "I'm truly sorry,
Lester, but it just doesn't work that way." She offered him a sympathetic smile. "Times have
changed. Unfortunately, we no longer give loans
based on a man's word and a handshake."

The earnest smile left Lester's face, and with it
his friendly attitude. "I see. Guess I'm beginning to
understand why folks in this town have a problem
with you running the bank." He jammed his cap
down on his head and pushed away from the chair.
"Thanks a lot for your time." With that, he stormed
from her office.

Startled by his abrupt change in attitude, Bailey
rose from her desk and walked out to the lobby
where Jenny's desk stood. Jenny had turned in her
chair to look out the window, craning her neck to
watch Lester stride down the street. "Uh-oh," she
said, her face clouding over.

"What?" Bailey stepped up beside her and
peered through the tinted glass that lined the top half
of the wall. Across the street, Lester disappeared
through the doors of the Silver Saddle Saloon, lo-
cated just down the block.

"He's drinking again." Jenny faced her, exasperation in her eyes. "Poor Jolene. She's had trouble keeping that man sober ever since they got married. But he'd been doing so well lately. I thought he might've stopped for good this time. He hasn't touched a drop since New Year's Eve." She shook her head. "Lord, what will Jolene say? Maybe I should call her."

"It might be best if you didn't," Bailey said. "It's usually not a good idea to interfere in someone's marital problems." For the life of her, she couldn't understand why any woman would stay with a man who had a drinking problem, much less continue to have children with him. But it was none of her business.

Bailey headed back to her office. By the time the lunch hour approached, her palms were sweaty. The auditors were due to arrive at one o'clock. Everything was in order. She couldn't wait to get the whole thing over with. She was too nervous to eat anything substantial. Maybe a cup of yogurt would settle her stomach.

As she walked to the break room, she spotted Lester, standing next to Jenny's desk once more. Jenny had risen from her chair and was trying to calm him down. He gestured vehemently and shook his head, shrugging away from the hand she laid on his arm.

Spotting Bailey, Jenny strode her way. "Lester wants to see you again." Irritation flushed her face. "I tried to tell him you were tied up in a meeting, but he got very belligerent.'' She shot a disgusted look in Lester's direction. ''He's drunker than twelve skunks. He must've spent the last three hours slamming down longnecks.''

''Never mind, Jenny. I'll handle it.'' Her patience rapidly thinning, Bailey headed purposefully toward Lester. Lord, she didn't need this right now.

He gave her a lopsided grin. ''Just the woman I want to see.'' He held out his arms as though the two of them were bosom buddies. As he tried to sling one arm around her shoulder, Bailey side-stepped him and took him by the elbow.

''Lester, why don't you come into my office for a minute.''

''Good idea,'' he slurred, glaring at Jenny. ''*She* said you were in a meeting and didn't have time for me.'' He drew back and frowned. ''Whatsa matter, Ms. Chancellor? Are you too busy to talk to a workin' stiff like me?'' He staggered sideways, drawing the attention of the customers in the lobby.

''I'm making time for you now, aren't I?'' Fully irritated, Bailey marched him into her office. ''Have a seat.'' She closed the door behind them.

Lester sat down. Bailey took her chair and folded her hands on top of the desk blotter. ''Now, what seems to be the problem?''

''I already told you what the problem is.'' He enunciated each word slowly, as though his tongue were too thick and tied in knots. "I'm out of money."

Holding on to the last of her patience by a thread, Bailey spoke calmly. "Yes, and I already explained to you that you don't qualify for a loan. There's nothing I can do about that."

He waved her statement aside. "Aw, c'mon. You and me both know that's all just red tape. You can get around it." He leaned forward, sending alcohol-laden fumes her way.

Bailey leaned away from him. "What happened to the money I gave you for your truck?"

Lester's face reddened. "I told you, it's gone. Spent." He waved his hand in the air in a gesture that said farewell to the money.

She couldn't help wondering if he hadn't drunk away a good deal of it, rather than spend it on the bills he needed to pay.

"And you know what else?" Lester pressed his forefinger against the top of the desk for emphasis. "If I don't get that truck back now, Jolene is not going to be a happy camper, let me tell you. She's hell on wheels when she's mad."

Bailey folded her arms in front of her. "I'd be happy to sell the truck back to you whenever you can come up with the money to buy it. But there's no way I can give you a loan, Lester. Now, if you'll excuse me..."

"Then how the hell am I supposed to get the Chevy back?" he all but shouted.

"Please lower your voice," Bailey said. "Shouting at me is not going to help your situation."

"Is that right?" Lester rose from his chair and leaned against the desk with both hands. "Look. Just loan me the money and I'll pay you back in installments. Hell, this bank's got plenty of it." He gestured at the surrounding furniture and office equipment. "All this fancy-schmancy stuff you've got, and your fine clothes." He raked her with a gaze from head to toe. "It won't hurt you a bit to help me out. I already told you I'm good for the money. I've got a job." He tapped his chest proudly. "I just need'ta get on my feet a little, that's all."

Not willing to waste another minute trying to get through to him when he obviously wasn't coherent enough to listen, Bailey rose and walked around the desk. "I have to ask you to leave, Lester."

"Nope." He shook his head and crossed his arms in front of his chest. "I'm not budging until you say yes."

"I'm not going to stand here and argue with you." She moved toward the door. "I don't have time for this."

Lester grabbed her roughly by the arm, his fingers biting into her skin, and yanked her backward. Startled, Bailey gaped at him.

"Why won't you help me?" he demanded. His face scrunched with drunken fury.

"Let go of me." Furious, Bailey jerked her arm from his grasp, and Lester responded by shoving her. Staggering backward, she fell against the filing cabinet and banged her elbow on the corner of it.

Fear mingled with anger. In his drunken state, Lester could be far more dangerous than she'd bargained for.

"You don't hear too good, do you?" Lester's eyes darkened, and he took a threatening step toward her, his hand clenched at his side.

Bailey stood her ground, determined not to let him see she was frightened. "I'd say you're the one who doesn't hear very well."

The door swung open at that moment, and two police officers stepped over the threshold, Jenny right behind them. "Is there a problem?" One of the officers, tall and slim, fixed Lester with a stare. The second one, shorter and stocky, kept his hand on his hip near his pistol.

Jenny glared at Lester. "I heard him shouting, Bailey. He's violent when he's drunk."

Lester's eyes shot daggers at Jenny. "This is none of your business," he grumbled.

"Sir, step outside with me," the first officer said, beckoning Lester to come forward.

Instantly, the fight went out of him. Lester held

up his hands, palms out. "I don't want any trouble, Officer."

"Neither do we. Now, just step outside."

The policemen escorted him to their waiting patrol car.

Shaking, Bailey stepped into the lobby to address the half-dozen customers who stared at her. "I apologize for the commotion. There's nothing to worry about, just a bit of a misunderstanding." She lowered her voice and spoke to Jenny. "I'll be in the break room if the police need to talk to me." She had to calm down before the auditors arrived.

Jenny nodded, her face pale. "I'm so sorry I didn't tell you about Lester's drinking problem before, Bailey. I truly thought he had it under control."

"It's all right. Don't worry about it."

"Did he hurt you?" Jenny spotted the mark on Bailey's arm. Her eyes widened. "Oh my gosh."

"It's nothing," Bailey said. "Lester grabbed me and shoved me, that's all. But it's probably a good thing you called the police, Jenny. Thank you."

"No problem."

Bailey went to the break room and closed the door. After pouring a cup of coffee, she sat at the table and rubbed her bruised elbow. She'd had some experience with violence as a foster child, under the care of a woman whose brother-in-law often got drunk and caused a ruckus. Still, he'd never raised a hand to her or anyone in the family. Then there'd been Ruth, the foster mother she lived with when she was eleven. Ruth had never hit her, but she'd had a habit of grabbing Bailey by the arm and shaking her whenever she wanted to get a point across.

Bailey ran her hand over the place where Lester's grip had pinched into her flesh. Angry, red-hued fingerprints stood out against her skin. She felt violated, and hated that what he'd done brought unhappy childhood memories rushing back to her.

Minutes later, one of the police officers came in and questioned Bailey about what had happened. Though furious with Lester, she declined to press charges, not wanting to make more of the incident. Lester would be hauled to detox for an overnight stay. Hopefully, the experience would shake him up enough to make a difference. Maybe he would seek professional help.

Once the policeman left, Bailey returned to her office and waited for the auditors to arrive. But the incident with Lester had upset her more than she cared to admit. Her elbow smarted where he'd slammed her into the filing cabinet, and the red fingerprints on her arm promised to turn into a bruise.

What a jerk. And here she'd tried to help him out. Well, no more. Let people in town think of her as the hard-core banker woman if they wanted to. This would be the last time she'd bend over backward to help anyone.

The auditors arrived promptly at one o'clock and

spent the rest of the day poring over the bank's records. It took Bailey's mind off her problems. By the time the audit was over, she was tired but elated. Everything had gone smoothly, and the bank had received a score of ninety-five.

Bailey headed for home. She fed the animals, prepared a light supper and thought about calling Trent. But she was simply too exhausted to do anything more than eat and fall into bed. It was just as well. She'd resolved to leave him alone for a while, and she meant to stick to that resolution.

So why was it she couldn't keep thoughts of the kisses they'd shared by the river from running through her mind? Flopping onto her side, Bailey punched her pillow into submission and closed her eyes.

The next morning, she woke up feeling sick to her stomach. Not sure if it was due to the excitement with Lester the day before, combined with the stress of preparing for the audit, or if she had a flu bug, she telephoned Jenny.

"I'm not feeling well. I think I'll stay home today and rest. But if anything urgent comes up, call me."

"Never mind that," Jenny reassured her. "You just get some sleep. After what Lester did to you yesterday, it's no wonder you don't feel well. I'm telling you, he shook me up, and I wasn't even the one he attacked. Lord, he's a mean drunk!"

Bailey thanked her, then crawled back under the

covers. Maybe a little extra sleep wouldn't be such a bad thing, provided she could get her mind to shut down long enough to cooperate.

But thoughts of Trent whirled through her head anew, and only with effort was Bailey at last able to fall back asleep.

TRENT HAD SPENT the past week contemplating just exactly where things were headed with him and Bailey. He'd foolishly wished upon a falling star, as though that would solve all his problems. If only it were so easy.

He hadn't called Bailey or gone to her house because he wasn't sure he should. The more he was around her, the more he found himself wanting to be with her. No matter how much he'd enjoyed their moonlight ride a week ago, or how tempted he was to get to know her on a much deeper level, it wasn't what he'd planned.

Still, he missed her more than he'd ever thought he would, and he wanted to see her. It wasn't her fault that his emotions were a mass of confusion. He had no idea what he would ultimately do about the situation, but he knew for certain that he didn't want to burn any bridges right now. Maybe he could keep seeing Bailey, provided he took things slowly.

He had to stop thinking about taking her to bed. Hell, he'd even purchased a box of condoms on impulse the last time he was at the grocery store. When he'd gotten home, he'd held the box in his hand, sure he'd lost his mind. He'd started to heave it into the trash. Instead, he'd shoved it into the drawer of his nightstand. Just in case.

Disgusted with his actions—those of a silly, love-sick fool—Trent climbed into his truck and headed for town. He'd heard the bank was offering high-interest-rate certificates of deposit, and logically, it made sense for him to transfer some of his money into one. But more important, it would give him a good excuse to see Bailey on neutral ground. Maybe talking to her at the bank would be better right now than seeing her alone at his house or hers.

He searched the lobby as he entered Colorado Western National but didn't see Bailey anywhere. She was probably in her office. Spotting Jenny, he walked over to her desk.

She beamed a smile at him. "Hello, Trent. What can I do for you?"

"Is Bailey in?" he asked, shifting uncomfortably beneath Jenny's knowing gaze. He couldn't help wondering how much Bailey had confided in her. Did she know he'd kissed Bailey on more than one occasion?

Jenny's eyes widened. "Didn't you hear about our excitement yesterday?"

Apprehension twisted his stomach as he glanced toward Bailey's closed office door. "What excitement?"

"Lester Godfrey came in drunk off his butt," Jenny said. "It was awful." She clutched her hand to her chest. "He jumped all over Bailey for not giving him a loan, and then he grabbed her and shoved her. Bruised her up a bit. I had to call the police, and they hauled Lester off to detox. Poor Bailey woke up not feeling so good this morning. And who can blame her, after all that. She didn't come to work today."

Trent clenched his hands. Deep black fury filled him. "Lester hurt her?"

"Well, not badly, but still..." Jenny let the words trail away.

Trent barely heard her. He was already on his way out, torn between the desire to find Lester Godfrey and beat the hell out of him and the need to go to Bailey and make sure she was all right.

After slamming the door of his pickup, Trent headed out of town to Bailey's house. Why the hell hadn't she phoned him?

Both her car and truck were parked in the driveway. Buddy lay on the porch, and he thumped his tail at Trent before trotting out of reach. Trent knocked on the door. It was a minute or so before Bailey answered. She wore a tank top and shorts, and her hair was mussed, as if she'd just woken up. A large bruise in the shape of a man's fingers marred the golden-brown skin of her left arm above the elbow.

Concern mingled with the anger that pooled in his stomach.

Bailey appeared surprised to see him. "Trent. Come in." She held the door wide, and he stepped into the kitchen.

Already, the day was warm. Bailey left the door open and moved toward the kitchen counter. "I was just fixing some tea. Would you like a cup?"

"Why didn't you call me?"

She faced him, not even bothering to pretend she didn't know what he was talking about. "You heard what happened."

"Yeah," he said, his voice tight. "I heard. And I damn near drove straight to the gas station to knock some sense into Lester. What the hell got into him?" Unable to hide the feelings that had gripped him the moment Bailey opened the door—fear that she could've been hurt far worse than she was, and anger that he hadn't been there to protect her—Trent reached out to her. He wanted to hold her, but instead, he simply ran his hands gently up and down Bailey's arms. "Are you all right?"

"I'm fine," she said, shivering beneath his touch. "If you'll sit down, I'll tell you exactly what happened."

He sat, and Bailey pulled out the chair next to him, leaving her empty teacup on the kitchen counter. Her violet-blue eyes hid her emotions, but not so much that he couldn't tell something was bothering her. "I started to call you, but I wasn't sure I should."

"Why not? Bailey, I'd hope by now you know I care enough about you that you can call me anytime you need to." The admission was out before he was scarcely aware of what he'd said.

She gazed apprehensively at him. "I'd like to believe that. But frankly, I'm not sure how to read you sometimes, Trent. One minute you're kissing me and the next you're pushing me away." Hurt clouded her gaze for the span of a heartbeat, followed by a flash of irritation.

Guilt stabbed him. She was right. But how could he make her understand how he felt? Short of opening up the floodgates to his emotions and letting them all out, he simply couldn't make her see where he was coming from.

He wasn't ready for that.

He folded his hand over hers on the table. "Bailey, I'm sorry. I'm not playing mind games with you. It's just that ever since Sarah died and Amy left me, things have been hard. Can you understand that?"

"I'm trying."

He set his jaw. "It's been a long time since I've felt anything but emptiness inside me." Gently, he squeezed her hand, not wanting to admit that she'd stirred that emptiness into something he couldn't define. "I'd like to know I can see you, Bailey, and

spend some time with you.'' No matter how confused he felt, there was no way he could simply
walk away from her. Though his better judgment
told him he should, his heart simply wouldn't let
him.

He wondered which inner voice he should listen
to. He was far from ready to make a commitment,
to her or to anyone, but he also wasn't willing to
stay completely away. Maybe he'd feel differently
in time, but right now he couldn't bring himself to
turn his back on Bailey.

She held his gaze for a long moment. His gut
twisted as he waited for her answer, and a part of
him wanted to run.

''I don't know if I can give you what you want,
Trent,'' she said. ''But while we're busy trying to
figure each other out, I'm not opposed to seeing
you.'' The hard-core businesswoman was back,
ready to negotiate, and he sensed she used her tough
facade as a shield. Hell, he knew she did, just as he
used his seclusion on the ranch as one.

Bailey graced him with a firm stare that said she
wasn't about to let any man walk all over her. He
had no doubt about that. It was one of the things he
liked and admired about her. Still, a part of him
longed to take care of her. But that was impossible,
for more reasons than one.

Tamping down his emotions, Trent slowly let go

of her hand. "I'm glad to hear that. Now, tell me exactly what happened with Lester."

She took a deep breath and explained. When she told him about buying Lester's truck simply to save the man's pride, it was all Trent could do to keep control of his temper. Now he really wanted to tear Lester in two. Bailey had been kind enough to help him out, and the creep had repaid her with violence.

"I'd wondered how in hell you'd talked him out of that pickup." He shook his head, and his anger faded as he looked at Bailey. On the outside, she was steely. But on the inside, she was a cream puff. A sucker for a hard-luck story, a caregiver to needy animals. A chuckle rose in his throat.

Bailey's eyebrows arched. "May I ask what you find so amusing?"

The situation was far from funny, but Bailey always made him see through the darkest moment to the lighter side. "You're something else," he said. "Looks like the coldhearted banker woman really has a heart of gold." He leaned toward her. "What would the townspeople think if they knew you were just a big ol' marshmallow inside?"

Her eyes sparked as she rose to the challenge. "I am not."

He fought the urge to kiss her senseless. Every aspect of Bailey made him lose his mind. "Yes, you are. And I have a feeling it's a side of your personality you don't often let people see."

She pursed her lips and held his gaze. "Maybe. Could be I'm a lot like a hardheaded cowboy I know, who doesn't let anyone into his heart or his life very often, either."

"Touché," he said. He leaned back in his chair and folded his hands behind his head to keep from pulling Bailey into his arms. "So, should I go find Lester and pound him senseless? Or did you have him thrown in jail?"

She shook her head. "No on both counts. A— he's not worth it, and B—I didn't press charges because even though he made me mad, I can't help but feel sorry for him."

"Sorry?" It wasn't what he'd expected her to say.

She nodded. "Mmm-hmm. The man's been down on his luck, and apparently he has a drinking problem. That's an illness. He shouldn't be condemned for it."

"He tried to hurt you."

"If he'd really wanted to, he would have. Lester's not my favorite person at the moment, and he's a bit of a bully. But he needs help, not a jail sentence."

Trent chewed his bottom lip. "I swear, I don't know what to make of you. Just hearing what he did to you made me want to have a piece of his hide."

"Why?"

The simple question struck him speechless. "What do you mean, 'Why?'"

She folded her arms and stared back at him. "Normally, that's the type of reaction a woman might get from a lover or a big brother, or even a very close friend. You're sure not my brother, so which of the other two choices does that leave us with?"

Trent's pulse thundered.

If she wanted a choice, he'd give her one.

His resolve forgotten, he leaned forward and drew her toward him until their lips were all but touching. "I'd say we've gone a step beyond friendship. Shall we see where it leads?"

Without waiting for an answer, he kissed her hungrily. She groaned and kissed him back, bracing her hands against the table as though to refrain from touching him. Then, slowly, she ran her palms across his shoulders until her arms circled his neck. He lost himself in her kiss, knowing he shouldn't but unable to stop.

When he pulled back, he saw fire in her eyes. "I'll wager it leads to trouble," she said.

He held her gaze for a long moment, then rose from his chair. "You may be right. But then, I've never been one to shy away from trouble. Why start now?" He headed for the door, then faced her as he held the screen open. "Don't ever hesitate to call me if you need anything, Bailey. I can't figure out what it is you do to me, but I'm damn well afraid I like it. I'll see you later."

He let the screen door close behind him, but not before he noticed the startled look in Bailey's eyes.

Well, at least she couldn't accuse him of being dishonest.

Walking toward Windsong, he licked his lips, still tasting her, warm and sweet on his tongue.

CHAPTER ELEVEN

BAILEY BIT into a slice of pepperoni pizza and tried to forget what Trent had said to her that morning. Which wasn't easy, considering he was the topic of discussion at the moment.

Macy sat beside her on the porch steps. "Do you think he'd say yes?" she asked hopefully. She twirled a dangling string of cheese around her finger before plopping it on top of her pizza slice.

"I guess there's only one way to find out," Bailey said. "We'll just ask him." Why not? Trent had told her not to hesitate if she ever needed him for anything, and Macy's request for Trent to be a guest speaker at her 4–H club meeting tomorrow seemed a reasonable one. A woman who owned cutting horses was supposed to come talk to the group and give a demonstration, but she'd fallen ill and had to cancel. Disappointed, the group's 4–H leader was frantically searching for a last-minute replacement. Asking Trent was a safe, not-too-personal way to see him again.

Bailey knew she must be out of her mind even to consider him anything more than a friend. What on earth had come over her last night? He'd given her the perfect opportunity to tell him she thought it best that the two of them stop seeing each other. Instead, she'd opened a Pandora's box. Her sensible side reminded her that exposing her emotions to Trent would lead to nothing but trouble, just as she'd told him. Yet she was so drawn to him she simply couldn't resist giving a relationship with him a try.

He'd told her he'd never been one to run from trouble.

She'd never been one to back down from a challenge.

In fact, facing one always gave her a natural high, and meeting the challenge successfully never failed to fill her with a sense of accomplishment and power. Not to mention that she liked Trent and was deeply attracted to him. He'd practically dared her to give him a chance. She wondered how much of his attitude was pure bluff. She'd wager that he was just as apprehensive about what might happen between them as she was, but if he thought she'd back down first, he'd better think again.

"I hope he will," Macy said. "Otherwise we'll have to work on our record books." She made it sound like torture.

"What are those?" Bailey asked.

"They're notebooks where we record every single detail about our 4–H project. It's like doing homework."

Bailey chuckled. "Well, I guess we can't have that."

Macy plucked a slice of pepperoni from her pizza, held it aloft between thumb and forefinger, then curled her tongue around it. "So," she said, chewing carefully, "can we go over and ask him after we finish our pizza?"

Bailey's heart raced at the thought of seeing Trent. "Sure, honey, we can do that."

A short time later, she and Macy headed across the pasture and ducked through the fence. Trent was in the round pen, halter-breaking a bay-colored foal. He looked up as they approached, and Bailey shivered at the expression in his eyes. He seemed glad to see her for once. Then his gaze fell on Macy, and like a shadow, his expression shifted.

A deep sadness filled his eyes, and Bailey perceived a wall rising between them, blocking from view what Trent must feel when he looked at the little girl who had once been his daughter's best friend.

"Hi, Trent," Macy called out.

"Hello." His greeting was neither unfriendly nor warm. He kept his focus on the filly he led, then glanced at Bailey. "What's up?"

She walked over and leaned against the fence, bracing one foot on the bottom rail. "I've come to take you up on that favor you offered."

"What favor is that?" He continued to lead the filly around the corral.

Bailey frowned. "My, is your memory that short, cowboy? Wasn't it only yesterday you told me if there was anything I ever needed, just to let you know?"

He grunted. "I suppose. So what is it you need?" His expression remained neutral.

She could have throttled him. *Here we go again,* she thought. Mr. Hot-Then-Cold. "Actually, it's more of a favor for Macy."

Trent halted in his tracks, gripping the foal's lead rope. He faced Bailey, his eyes shadowed beneath the straw cowboy hat he wore, but there was no mistaking the look in them.

"What would that be?"

"The guest speaker who was supposed to talk at her 4–H Club meeting tomorrow canceled at the last minute. Macy would like you to address her group, instead, on the finer points of raising Arabian horses."

He sighed visibly. "I can't do that."

"Why not?" Bailey glared at him, determined not to back down. Whether he realized it or not, Trent needed to get out and socialize more. He'd had fun with her and Macy when they'd worked on the fence together. He would probably enjoy himself at the 4–H meeting. All he needed was a shove in the right direction.

"Please, Trent," Macy begged. "If you don't come, we'll get stuck working on our record books." Her blue eyes pleaded, and Bailey couldn't see how Trent could refuse her.

"I'm sorry, Macy. I'm just not up to it."

"Why?" Bailey repeated. "You look perfectly fine to me." She gestured toward the filly and the rope he held. "Your wrist seems to have healed quite well, and addressing a group of eight-to-ten-year-olds is hardly strenuous."

He clenched his jaw. "That's not the issue. You know why I can't do it."

And he obviously knew she didn't really believe his refusal had anything to do with a sprained wrist. But before Bailey could speak, Macy clambered up on the fence rail and hung there, her little face pinched with sorrow.

"I know why, too," she said quietly. "It's because of Sarah." Her eyes clouded over. "You don't have to explain, Trent." She sighed in a very adult-like way. "If you could only know how bad I miss her. Sometimes my heart just feels like it's going to crumble and blow away on the wind." She swallowed. "Sarah was my best friend ever. Practically my sister. I don't know why she had to go to heaven, and I hate it that she's not here anymore. But I know she watches over me. And I know she wants me to ride my horse and have fun like the two of us used to."

Macy clung to the fence and glanced down at the ground. "Though some days it's just so hard not having her around to talk to, especially at the 4–H shows." She looked up at Trent once more. "So if you don't feel up to coming to the meeting tomorrow, I'll understand. Really."

Bailey nearly burst into tears. *Jesus.* She put her arm around Macy and gave her a hug. "I'm sorry, honey. It's so awful to lose someone you love." She brushed Macy's bangs off her forehead. "Maybe I can help your group think of someone else."

"No."

The word came out so abruptly, for a moment Bailey thought she'd imagined Trent said it. She glanced at him and saw that his features had softened. Gone was the stoniness she'd seen moments before. In its place were genuine sorrow and empathy.

"I'll do it," he said. He led the bay over to the fence and reached hesitantly through the rails to pat Macy's arm. "What time do you need me there?"

Bailey heaved a mental sigh and gave Trent a smile of encouragement. He didn't smile back, and for an instant, guilt gripped her. Had she simply used Macy to manipulate Trent and interfere in his life? But the guilt quickly faded. Her intentions had been honorable, and she knew she'd done the right thing. After all, getting Trent to address the 4–H group would help Macy out, and it might do Trent some good, as well. What possible harm could come of it? Wasn't it high time he got out and did something useful with his life? Shouldn't he be glad that she cared enough about him to try to help?

But the look he gave her said he was anything but appreciative.

"We're meeting at the arena at nine in the morning," Macy said. "Is that okay?"

"That's fine," Trent said quietly. "I'll be there. Should I bring a horse?"

"Oh, yes." Macy's face lit with enthusiasm.

It was enough to clinch Bailey's feeling that she'd done the right thing, Trent's look notwithstanding. Macy needed some happiness to override the loneliness she often seemed to experience. Again, Bailey could relate to that.

"All right, then. I'll bring a good one." Trent stared pointedly at Bailey. "Now, if there's nothing else... I need to get back to working the foals. Maybe we can talk more about this a little later."

"Fine by me," Bailey said, leveling her chin. "Come on, Macy. What say we go for a little ride."

"Okay. 'Bye, Trent. See you tomorrow."

Trent waved, the end of the lead rope threaded between his fingers. His eyes remained locked on Bailey.

She could practically feel his gaze burning a hole through her shoulder blades as she walked away.

THE NEXT MORNING, Bailey showered, dressed in jeans and a lavender tank top and plaited her hair in a French braid. Following the directions Camille had given her, she drove to the arena.

She'd spent the evening at Camille's house last night, watching movies, eating popcorn and talking. Bailey brought Camille up-to-date on all that had happened between her and Trent and asked for her friend's advice. Was she wasting her time with Trent? Would he ever decide that he could move on with his life? Or should she simply get out from being involved with him now, before it was too late and he broke her heart?

Camille had looked at her wisely. "Seems to me it's already too late, girlfriend. You've fallen for the man, haven't you?"

Bailey was afraid she was right. "God, is it that obvious?" She sighed. "I don't know, Camille. Trent leaves me so confused. One minute I'm hopeful we could actually share a relationship and the next minute I'm frustrated that Trent seems to want nothing more than to be left alone. And maybe he really does want that." She gave a short laugh. "I've been trying to tell myself my intentions were honorable in getting him to address Macy's 4–H group, but now I'm not so sure."

"What do you mean?"

Bailey dug into the bowl of popcorn. "Could it

be I want him at the fairgrounds for selfish reasons?"

"Like...?"

"So he'll begin to heal?" She pitched several kernels into her mouth.

"What's wrong with that?" Camille frowned.

"Well, nothing, if I was thinking only of Trent. But I have to admit that a part of me is hoping he'll find some way to recover from the loss of his little girl and be the kind of man I want him to be. The kind who wants a family."

Camille shook her head. "I don't think so, hon. You don't seem like the 'I'm gonna catch myself a husband' type to me at all." She chuckled, then squeezed Bailey's hand. "What I do think is that you're a kindhearted person who'd like for Trent to work through his grief, simply because you care about him. If you can help him do that, go for it. Afterward—well, just take it as it happens." She shrugged. "Who knows? Maybe he's Mr. Right and maybe he's not. But you won't find out if you don't give it a shot."

Though she'd felt somewhat better after talking to Camille, Bailey still wasn't certain she was doing the right thing. She'd already suffered enough rejection in her life. Opening herself up to more wasn't exactly the smartest thing she could do.

Still, she'd come this far with Trent, and Camille was right. Bailey had fallen for him, her feelings growing the more they were together. Unless she was willing to cut things off with him right now, then she might as well hang in and give him a chance. After all, they really hadn't known each other that long. Maybe she was simply trying to push things along too quickly. Could be she needed Trent every bit as much as he did her.

Bailey shivered. The thought of needing anyone scared her. While she wanted a family, she never again wanted to feel the hungry yearning she'd experienced as a child.

Her thoughts still racing a mile a minute, Bailey pulled her pickup into the fairgrounds and parked near Trent's big black Ford.

His horse trailer sat behind it, and when she reached the bleachers facing the arena, she saw that he'd brought Shafana with him. With her dappled gray coat and silver-black mane and tail, the mare was one of Trent's prettiest, in Bailey's opinion. Taking a seat, she watched Trent demonstrate some of the unique qualities of the Arabian horse as he talked to the group of fifteen kids. He put Shafana through her paces, and again, Bailey was reminded of a cowboy-turned-sheikh.

Warmth crept through her. Trent was a very attractive, sexy man, and not only that, he seemed to be having a good time with the kids. She suddenly got a picture of what a wonderful father he must have been. Could he ever be one again?

When he'd first begun to address the group he'd been a bit reserved, but now, as he rode Shafana in a circle, then answered questions the kids threw his way, he looked relaxed and in his element. She hoped he was. She wanted him to learn to live again, for his sake as well as hers.

"Excuse me, Ms. Chancellor?"

Bailey faced the man who'd spoken her name. Lanky but handsome, he wore a short-sleeved western shirt and faded jeans, and a pair of boots and cowboy hat that looked as if they'd seen better days. His blue eyes stood out against tanned skin.

He sat down beside her on the bleachers and held out his hand. "I'm Wade Darland, Macy's dad."

"Oh." Surprised, Bailey accepted the man's handshake. "Nice to meet you." Somehow, she'd never thought Wade Darland would bring Macy to her 4–H meeting. She'd figured Macy would probably ride with a friend, given that her dad didn't spend a lot of time with her or her brother.

"I wanted to thank you for having Macy over to your place so often," Wade said. "I hope she's not making too much of a pest of herself."

"No, not at all," Bailey assured him.

He thumbed back the brim of his sweat-stained hat, revealing short-cropped brown hair. "I'm afraid I don't get a lot of time to do fun things with the kids. Keeping up the ranch is a lot of work. But I do try to participate in their 4–H events whenever I

can.'' He nodded toward a tall, sandy-haired kid
who stood near Trent's horse in the arena. ''That's
my boy, Jason, in the dark blue shirt. He's just a
year older than Macy, but he's a lot of help on the
ranch. Macy is, too. Still, with her being a girl, I
don't work her quite as hard as I do Jason.''

Bailey couldn't help but bristle at his male chau-
vinism. She felt her eyes narrow involuntarily.

''Whoa, no offense toward the fairer gender intended,'' Wade quickly added, smiling broadly as
he held his hands up in surrender. ''My hat's definitely off to any woman who can come into a town
like Ferguson and run the bank in the face of so
much opposition.''

Bailey raised her eyebrows, startled by his unexpected compliment. ''Thank you.''

''I know folks have had a tough time accepting
some of your ideas,'' Wade said. ''But hang in
there. They'll come around eventually.'' He glanced
toward the arena once more. ''Anyway, my kids
miss their mom, especially Macy, and I'm much
obliged to the attention you've shown her. She
thinks a lot of you.''

''I'm glad to hear that,'' Bailey said. ''I can assure you, the feeling is mutual.''

Wade nodded. ''She's a good girl, my Macy.''
He smiled proudly, dispersing the last of Bailey's
impression of a negligent father. ''Looks like they're

about to wrap this meeting up.'' He tipped his hat. "Nice to meet you, Ms. Chancellor."

"Likewise," Bailey repeated.

She watched him walk across the bleachers, then turned her attention to Trent. He'd finished his demonstration, and a few of the kids stuck around to ask him further questions. Macy beamed proudly, obviously taking credit for having invited him to be their guest speaker.

Bailey smiled to herself. Trent made quite a picture, standing in the arena surrounded by kids. She knew how hard it had to have been for him today, how it surely had brought back memories of his little girl and the things they'd shared.

Bailey chewed on her bottom lip and hoped she hadn't made a mistake in coercing him here. That she might have caused him pain was too awful to contemplate. But if she'd been responsible for getting him to enjoy himself for a while with these kids, then the effort had been worth it.

She caught Trent's gaze as he led Shafana onto the racetrack that circled the arena. Trying to read his expression was impossible. There was only one way to find out how he felt about today. Bailey headed down the steps of the bleachers and was about to walk across the racetrack when she spotted Lester Godfrey in the parking lot. He glared at her, then opened the car door to admit a boy who'd attended the 4–H meeting. Bailey hadn't known that one of Lester's kids was in Macy's group. With a final dark look at her, Lester climbed behind the wheel of the car, slammed the door and drove away, his tires spitting gravel.

"If I'd known he'd be here, I might have invited him to stick around for a private talk."

Bailey whirled around to face Trent, who stood behind her, clutching Shafana's reins. His gray eyes smoldered with anger.

"There's no sense in that," Bailey said. "What happened is over and done with."

"Maybe," Trent said.

"What do you mean?" Her pulse picked up a beat, and she wasn't sure if it was because of the words he spoke or because of the way he looked in his snug Wrangler's and black western shirt. The leather-and-sage scent of his cologne drifted her way, and the longing to slide into his arms and kiss him rocked through her.

"Lester's not the sort of man to let the matter go that easy," Trent said. "And I'm betting it didn't sit too well with him that you drove his truck here today."

Bailey glanced at the '53 Chevy, which had seemed so much more practical to drive to the fairgrounds than her Mustang convertible. "I never gave it a thought," she said. Then she scowled. "Besides, it's *my* truck now, not his."

"Maybe in your eyes," Trent said. "But not in Lester's."

"Well, I'm certainly not going to let him intimidate me," Bailey said.

Trent quirked one eyebrow. "Now, why doesn't that surprise me?" he teased.

Bailey reached out to stroke Shafana. "Do you need some help getting her unsaddled?"

"No, thanks. I can handle it." He smiled crookedly, and she realized he was echoing the words she'd spoken to him the night of their moonlight ride, when he'd offered to help her with Star.

Bailey punched him lightly on the arm. "You're ornery, you know that?"

"Look who's talking," he said as they walked toward the horse trailer.

"What's that supposed to mean?" She flipped her braid over her shoulder.

Trent gave a dry laugh. "As if you didn't know. Using a little girl to get me to socialize." He shook his head. "I'd say that's pretty ornery, not to mention sneaky."

Bailey leaned against the horse trailer and folded her arms in front of her as Trent haltered Shafana. "Are you saying you didn't enjoy giving the demonstration to the kids?" She graced him with an inquiring smile.

"No, I'm not saying that." He tied Shafana to the trailer, then loosened the cinch on the mare's saddle.

"I'm just saying you could've went about asking me a little differently."

Bailey thought she detected a not-so-teasing note in his voice. Was he truly annoyed at her? "And if I had taken a different approach, would you have said yes?" she challenged.

"Probably not."

The honesty of his answer surprised her. "Well, there you go." Bailey motioned with one hand. "If I hadn't let Macy ask you, then you would've sat at home all by yourself today—as usual—instead of enjoying the sunshine and my good company here."

He faced her, eyebrows raised. "Is that right."

"Yes, it is, Mr. Cool Lone Wolf."

He grunted. "So that's what you think of me, huh?"

Bailey pursed her lips and nodded. "Pretty much."

"Humph."

"Don't tell me you're going to deny it."

He didn't answer right away. Instead, he swung the saddle and blanket from Shafana's sweaty back and laid them in the bed of the pickup. With a brush and currycomb, he went to work on the mare's coat, looking at Bailey over the top of Shafana's back. "I don't deny it, Bailey, and I don't make excuses for it, either. It's simply the way I like my life."

"Really?" Irritation bubbled within her. "You're going to stand there and tell me you prefer being alone and lonely to being here with me and these kids—'' she gestured at the few children who had not yet departed ''—having a good time.''

''That's right,'' he said stubbornly, whisking the brush across Shafana's neck and shoulder.

Bailey gritted her teeth and reminded herself that she'd worried about maybe having caused him pain by getting him here today. Damn it, didn't the man understand that he couldn't crawl in a hole and watch life pass him by?

''You know what?'' She glared at him. ''You're hopeless.''

He shrugged nonchalantly. ''Probably.''

''I ought to just stop wasting my time with you.''

''Maybe so.''

So why didn't she? The voice inside her mocked her, as did the challenging look Trent gave her. Was he hoping she'd rise to his challenge and force him to come out of hiding, both literally and figuratively? Or was this simply her imagination?

Bailey sighed. ''I really don't know why I keep bashing my head against that brick wall you've erected,'' she said. ''Maybe it's because I see more behind that tough exterior of yours than most people do.''

''We've had this conversation before,'' he said. ''Ms. Marshmallow.'' His lips twitched, then curved in a grin.

Bailey shook her head. "What am I going to do with you?"

He ducked beneath Shafana's neck and slipped his arms around Bailey's waist, crossing his wrists as he held the horse brushes behind her. "If there weren't children present, I could show you," he murmured. Then he gave her a chaste kiss before releasing her. Turning his back, he began to brush Shafana once more.

Bailey's lips burned where Trent's had touched them. She placed her fingertips there, loving the way his kiss had felt, yet angry at herself for wanting him so much.

"Is that so?" she said, placing her hands on her hips. "And who says I'd let you?"

His gray eyes sparked as he glanced over his shoulder at her. "You do, sweetheart. I can see it in those violet-blue eyes of yours every time I kiss you."

She wanted to slap him. And she felt like kicking herself because his arrogant words were true, and because she'd love to kiss him again.

Instead, she whispered in his ear. "Yeah? Well, it's obvious how much you want me, as well." Purposely, she made her voice low and husky. "I can see it in the front of those jeans of yours, cowboy— every time you kiss me." She squeezed his hip, letting her eyes drop to the zipper of his jeans. Then she walked away.

He stared after her, agape.

With a smug smile, Bailey waved at him, climbed into her pickup and drove out of the parking lot.

TRENT WATCHED Bailey pull out of sight. Chuckling, he turned his attention back to grooming Shafana. Bailey was the most amazing, most irritating, most interesting woman he'd ever met. He still couldn't believe how she'd manipulated him into speaking to Macy's 4–H group.

There was no way he would have said yes if Macy hadn't looked so damn brokenhearted yesterday. She'd nearly torn his heart in two, talking about Sarah the way she had. Yet that wasn't all there was to it. What had really gotten to him was that he'd never realized just how much pain and grief other people had suffered after Sarah's death.

Sure, he knew Amy had grieved for their little girl, in spite of her inability to face the reality of the situation, as had his mom and dad and dozens of friends and neighbors. But deep down inside, he'd been positive that no one in the world could possibly hurt the way he did. Seeing the depth of Macy's pain was a real wake-up call. He knew Sarah's death had been hard for the girl, but to hear just how hard in Macy's own words staggered him. It was the reason he'd said yes to her request, though at first he'd been angry at Bailey for cornering him that way.

Though coming to the fairgrounds where Sarah

had so often ridden in horse shows had initially been hard, he had to admit he'd enjoyed being around the kids. Again, a wave of guilt rushed over him.

Sarah should be here. She'd be old enough now to be in Macy's 4–H group. Eight was the minimum age for joining. Knowing his daughter hadn't even had a chance to do that sapped all the happiness he'd felt just moments ago.

Would he never get over his futile rage, not to mention the sorrow he experienced every time such a thought crossed his mind?

Once he'd brushed Shafana's coat dry, Trent loaded her into the trailer, put his tack away and climbed behind the wheel of the truck. The fairgrounds were deserted, the last of the kids and their parents gone. Rebecca, the 4–H leader, had thanked him profusely for his time at such short notice. He'd told her it was no problem. But what had it cost him emotionally?

The abandoned fairgrounds only made him realize just how empty his life was, how barren his heart with Sarah gone. He didn't want to feel normal again, because somehow that would betray Sarah's memory. But Bailey's words kept echoing in his mind: *You're going to stand there and tell me you prefer being alone and lonely to being here with me and these kids, having a good time?*

He searched his soul.

And he knew the answer.

He didn't prefer it, but he had no choice. That couldn't change unless he was willing to open his heart to the possibility of pain and sorrow once more. And he couldn't bring himself to do that. Not now. Maybe never. He'd flirted with Bailey, and he'd told her he'd never been afraid to face trouble, but now he wasn't altogether sure that was true.

Putting the truck in gear, he backed out of the parking lot and pulled away from the fairgrounds and its memories that plagued him.

HE'D NO SOONER GOTTEN Shafana unloaded and turned out in the pasture than the phone rang. He started to let the answering machine get it, but it was probably his mom or dad.

He hurried into the house and glanced at the caller ID as he reached for the phone. His parents' number flashed on the screen as his mother's voice filled his ear.

"Trent, honey, it's Mom."

She didn't sound right. "Hi. What's the matter?"

"It's your dad," she said.

Fear gripped him.

"He's had a mild heart attack."

Mild? His mouth went dry. How could any heart attack be described as mild? "Is he okay? When did it happen?" *Dear God, no. Not his father. Not after losing Sarah.*

"This morning," Della said. "He'd just gotten

back from a ride on his new stallion. The damned old fool.'' Tears choked her voice. ''He still thinks he's thirty years old. Trent, I'm so scared. The doctors say he'll be fine, but...'' She let the words trail away.

She didn't have to explain. Trent clenched the phone and momentarily closed his eyes. ''It's going to be all right, Mom. I'll be on the first flight I can get out of here.''

''Call me when you have your flight information,'' Della said. ''I'll pick you up at the airport.''

''Never mind. You just sit with Dad. I'll grab a cab. Which hospital is he at?''

She told him.

''Okay. Hang tight, Mom. I'll be there as soon as possible. Tell Dad I love him.'' He hung up the phone and leaned against the wall. *Shit*. His hands shook. If anything happened to his dad...

He wouldn't think that way. Surely fate could not be so cruel.

He reached for the phone once more and called the airline to make arrangements to fly to California. Luck was with him, and he was able to get a flight out later that day. He'd have to pack quickly, though, and find someone to care for his horses.

Instantly, Bailey came to mind. She didn't know a lot about horses, but surely she could manage to feed his while he was gone. He could ask one of his neighbors, but they were all busy taking care of their own ranches. He started to dial Information to get Bailey's phone number but hung up, instead.

What the hell. He might as well just go over to her place and ask her.

Telling himself it wasn't an excuse to see her again, Trent headed across the pasture to the dividing fence. He'd have to bring her to Windsong and walk her through the horses' daily routine. He wasn't sure how long he'd be gone. It all depended on how well his dad was doing.

Again, fear gripped him, and he pushed it away.

He would take things one at a time. It was the only way he could stay strong for his mother's sake.

As he approached Bailey's house, he couldn't help but think that this was just one more event that had thrown her into his life. Maybe it was an omen.

Then again, maybe going to California would give him the perfect opportunity to think. He prayed his dad was all right. And he prayed that when he returned to Windsong, he'd have an answer to the question that plagued him night and day:

Was he doing the right thing even considering a relationship with Bailey?

CHAPTER TWELVE

BAILEY'S THOUGHTS were wandering like the curves in the road she was taking home from the fairgrounds. Which was just how she'd felt ever since she first became attracted to Trent. How much longer could they keep up this game they played, where they flirted one minute, then retreated the next?

She was just as guilty as he was. She had fun flirting with Trent, but she wanted more than that. Knowing she would likely come out on the short end left a sour taste in her mouth. Unfortunately, Camille was right. It was too late to worry now. She'd gotten in way over her head. All she could do was hang on for the ride.

Bailey parked her truck and headed for the barn. Maybe if she stayed busy, it would occupy her mind and keep her thoughts off Trent for a little while. She was expecting a delivery of two tons of hay this afternoon, and the feed room needed to be cleaned out first to make room for it. She'd been buying hay for Star from the feed store up until now, a few bales at a time, but that was getting expensive, since the cost per bale was higher than buying by the ton.

Bailey set to work clearing out the old boxes and refuse the farm's previous owners had left. A short time later the sound of footsteps in the barn caught her attention. They were too heavy to be Macy's. Surely it wasn't Trent. Heart pounding, Bailey stepped into the barn aisle.

It *was* him. Bailey's breath caught in her throat. She must look a mess. Already she was hot and dusty from working in the feed room, her T-shirt damp against her body. Swiping at stray wisps of hair that had come loose from her braid, she glanced down at her clothes. Good grief. She had a spider-web caught on the belt loop of her jeans.

Brushing it off, Bailey smiled and tried to control her racing pulse. "Hi," she said, wondering what had brought him to her house so soon after she'd just seen him at the fairgrounds. Then she noticed how pale and drawn his face was. "What's wrong?"

"It's my dad," he said without preamble. "He's had a heart attack."

"Oh, no." Dread shot through Bailey. Trent didn't need more tragedy in his life. *Dear God.* "Is it bad?"

"Mom said it was a mild one, but I'm really worried about him. Dad's pushing seventy. I have to fly to California."

"Is there anything I can do to help?" Bailey inquired. "Do you want me to feed your horses while you're gone?"

He nodded. "Would you mind? I'd ask one of the neighbors, but they've all got plenty of work of their own. Not that you don't, with the bank and all," he hastily added.

She held up her hand. "Say no more. I'm happy to do it."

"Can you come up to the house now and let me walk you through my chore routine?" he asked. "I have to leave here shortly."

"Of course."

"You're sure it's no imposition?"

"No, it's fine. I was just cleaning up to make room for some hay I'm having delivered, but it won't arrive for over an hour."

"You should've said something," Trent said as they walked down the barn aisle. "I would've hauled it for you. No sense in you paying extra to have it delivered."

A shiver went up Bailey's spine. What would it be like to have Trent in her life every day, sharing chores with her, there whenever she needed him? Actually, he pretty much did that already. She couldn't help but ask herself why he cared enough to help her out any time whether she asked or not, yet he wasn't willing to trust her with his feelings.

"That's okay," she said. "I didn't have to pay

much extra, since the driver was bringing a load of hay to this area anyway.''

"Well, next time just holler." His gaze fell on hers, soft and compassionate.

Bailey's heart swelled. Whether he admitted it or not, Trent was a kind and generous man. Here he was, thinking of her, even as he worried about his father. Longing pulled at her, and she ached for him. It wasn't fair that bad things kept happening to him. She wished she could take him into her arms and invite him to be a part of her life—forever.

Instead, she followed him across the pasture, along the familiar route between their properties, and ducked through the dividing fence.

Trent walked with her through the barn and showed her where each type of feed and vitamins were kept and which horses got what. "I've written up a feeding chart and schedule," he said, indicating a clipboard on the wall. "It'll help you keep everything straight. Doc Baker's phone number is there, in case of emergency. Don't worry about turning the mares and foals out in the exercise pen if it's too much trouble. They can stay in their paddocks until I get back if need be. And don't mess with Alysana." He glanced toward the bay stallion, in his roomy, pipe-rail paddock.

A frown creased Trent's forehead. "Normally, I stable him in the hottest part of the day to keep his coat from bleaching out, but just leave him be. I don't want you to get hurt."

"Don't give it another thought," Bailey said. "I'll take care of everything."

He hesitated. "Are you sure this won't be too much for you, Bailey? I could probably call Wade Darland and see if Macy and Jason want to help you out. Or maybe—"

"Trent." She gave him a firm look. "I said not to worry. I'll be fine, and as much as Macy likes to come over, I'm sure she and Jason will help me if necessary. You just go and take care of your father."

He sighed, both hands on his hips. Then he moved toward her and slipped his arms around her waist. "I can't thank you enough." He bent and kissed her, softly at first, then more passionately.

Bailey closed her eyes and let his tongue invade her mouth, loving the feel of it, the taste of him. The way his strong arms felt wrapped around her. *Dear God, she loved this man. Why couldn't he love her back?*

With seeming reluctance, Trent ended the kiss, yet kept his arms around her waist. He gazed into her eyes. "Bailey," he whispered, "when I get back, we need to talk. I can't keep going on this way. You're turning me inside out to the point where I can't even think straight. We need to deal with what's happening between us, one way or another."

She pressed her fingertips gently against his lips. "Shh," she said. "Don't think about that now. Just go to your father. I'll be here when you get back."

He nodded, then released her. "Thank you again," he said.

"No problem." She smiled, heart pounding. He wasn't the only one who couldn't think straight. He was right. They needed to sort things out. Her heart couldn't take much more of this.

As she walked home, Bailey made herself a promise. Whatever it took, she would get her feelings for Trent out in the open and ask him to do the same. If her future included him, then she needed to know that. And if it didn't, she needed to move on.

She couldn't afford to do otherwise.

ZACH LOOKED BETTER than Trent had thought he would. Though he lay in bed in the cardiac care unit of the hospital, his color appeared good, and he smiled when Trent walked into the room.

"Hey, son, it's good to see you."

"It's good to see you, too, Dad." Trent leaned over the bed and gingerly gave his father a hug, afraid to hurt him yet craving the physical contact.

"Guess you're going to have to help your mother look after Zadel Arabians for a little while," Zach said, "until I can get back on my feet."

"I'll do that, but you've got to promise me you'll take it easy once you come home. You have to slow down a little, Dad." Trent smiled and squeezed Zach's hand. "You're not twenty-one anymore, you know."

"Well, I felt about a hundred when that heart attack hit me," Zach said, shaking his head.

Della clamped a hand to her own chest. "Lord, I thought I was going to have one right along with him." She gave Zach a stern look. "I swear, Zachary. Wanting to endurance-race at your age! What am I going to do with you?"

"I'm not the only senior-age endurance rider," Zach said, defending himself. He turned to Trent. "Wait till you see Jahim. Best-looking stallion you ever laid eyes on. I had entered the twenty-miler coming up Labor Day weekend. Jahim and I were conditioning when I had my episode."

"Episode, hell!" Della scowled at him. "Let's just call a spade a spade, shall we?"

Trent hid a smile. Keeping Zach in line had always been something Della was proud to call her job. His dad often bit off more than he could chew, and Della was quick to line him out when she thought he needed it. His parents shared not just a strong and binding love but a deep close friendship.

He envied them that.

It felt good to be here with his parents, even if he did wish it were under better circumstances. Yet he wondered how it would be to set foot on the ranch again. Every time he visited Zadel Arabians it was like coming home. He hadn't been there since Sarah died.

Memories of his marriage to Amy and the times they'd taken Sarah to the ranch for a visit when she was a baby flooded his mind. Zach and Della had spoiled her no end, and had been sorry to see him and Amy leave for Colorado. Sometimes he himself wished he hadn't moved there. He felt badly that his parents hadn't been nearby to take part in every day of Sarah's life.

But then, if he hadn't moved to Colorado, he never would've met Bailey.

Trent focused on his mom and dad's conversation. "You just wait," Zach said. "I'll be up and around before you know it, and have Jahim ready to race by next year for sure. I'm no quitter."

"No, but you're crazy," Della said. Then she chuckled. "And I'm crazy about you, you old fool."

Trent laughed, and Della shot him a grin. Her pretty, silver-blond hair, cropped in a practical style, flattered her face and made her blue-gray eyes stand out. Like her husband, Della was youthful beyond her years, her figure still trim, the result of having worked on the ranch for so long.

Trent was proud of his parents. He'd grown up wanting to be just like his dad, and now that he was older, he saw traits of his mother in himself, as well.

To have such close family ties, such deep roots, meant everything. Already, his sisters were on their way to be at Zach's side. They'd always been a tightly knit family.

He could see why Bailey longed for what she'd never had. Yet he still doubted he could ever give it to her.

The nurse came in to check Zach's blood pressure, and reminded Trent to keep his visit short. "Your father needs his rest," she said firmly.

"Yes, you do," Trent agreed over Zach's protest. "How about if I drive out and feed the horses, Dad. I'll come back later."

"Sure, sure. Take Mom's keys." Zach gestured toward Della's purse, and she fished the truck keys out of it.

Trent planted a kiss on his dad's forehead. "Behave yourself while I'm gone, you hear?"

"What fun is that?" Zach asked. But he seemed a bit tired, and his eyes were already fluttering closed.

Trent took hold of his mother's shoulders and kissed her cheek. "See you in a bit, Mom."

He headed down the hall, lost in thought. Maybe it was a good thing he would face the ranch alone for the first time in well over a year. He didn't want to upset his mother if his emotions overwhelmed him. She'd taken Sarah's death hard enough.

Rounding the corner, Trent stopped in his tracks. Amy.

She'd just stepped out of the elevator, and her gaze snagged his and held. She hesitated, then walked toward him, her high heels clicking on the linoleum. He hadn't seen her in months, not since the divorce. She looked good, but different. Dressed in a skirt and suit jacket, her blond hair caught up in a French twist, she appeared every inch the businesswoman. Gone were all signs of the horsewoman who'd lived in blue jeans and once shared his ranch and his life.

"What are you doing here?" He hadn't meant to be blunt, but he couldn't help it. Amy had turned her back on him in the final hours of Sarah's illness, not to mention on their marriage, and he wanted no part of her now.

"Your mother called and told me about your dad's heart attack," she said. "I came to see him."

It shouldn't bother him that his mother still kept in touch with Amy. After all, she'd been Sarah's mother. But his little girl was gone, and Trent couldn't help but wish Amy would vanish from his life. She'd made her choices and she'd hurt him badly. It hadn't taken long for anger to replace the pain of her leaving. That had faded finally. Now he felt nothing toward the woman who'd once been his wife.

Amy stood with her hand fluttering awkwardly at

her throat, while the background noise of the hospital folded around them. "I don't mean to make you feel uncomfortable. If you'd like, I'll leave."

"There's no need," Trent said. "I'm on my way out. Take care of yourself, Amy."

"Trent, wait." She laid her hand on his arm, and a cold chill crept over his skin as though a spider had skittered there.

He tightened his jaw, and she let go of him. For a moment, pain flickered in her eyes, as if it hurt her that he wouldn't want her to touch him. What did she expect?

"I, uh, wanted to tell you something. Before you heard it somewhere else."

"What's that?" He shifted from one foot to the other, impatient to be on his way. To push Amy out of sight, out of mind.

"I'm getting married."

She couldn't have shocked him more if she'd stuck him with an electric cattle prod. Not that he cared what she did with her life. It just felt odd to know she was moving on without him. A voice inside his head whispered that Amy had moved on long ago. Besides, he'd entertained thoughts of what it might be like to share his life with Bailey. Amy, too, had every right to happiness.

"Congratulations," he said. "I hope you're happy with your new life." But even to his own ears, the words did not sound sincere.

"Don't be that way," Amy said.

"What way?" He crossed his arms and glared at her.

"You know exactly what I'm talking about." She rubbed her forehead, as though staving off a headache. "God, here we go again." She laughed without humor. "We haven't seen or spoken to each other for the better part of a year, and we're already sniping." She sighed. "I don't want that, Trent. I still feel a connection to your parents. Can't we at least be civil to each other? Can't you realize that life goes on, with or without us?"

He shrugged indifferently. Amy would never understand how he felt. "Fine."

She shot him a look.

"What?" Irritation flooded him. "Do you want me to kiss the bride? Dance at your wedding? Offer to be your fiancé's best man?"

Anger darkened her eyes as she glared back at him. "You don't have to be sarcastic, Trent."

Suddenly, all the fight drained from him. She was right. He was acting like a jackass. If Amy wanted to remarry, that was her business.

"I'm sorry," he said. "I guess you just caught me by surprise."

She nodded, then smiled. "It took me by surprise, too. I met Eric through a singles' group a friend talked me into attending. He's divorced, with two little boys. And talk about a small world. Eric went to high school in the Denver area.''

But Trent was no longer listening. His train of thought had screeched to a halt at the mention of the two little boys. Hurt and anger flooded him all over again. How could Amy stand there, smiling and talking about her new husband-to-be and his kids, as though this ready-made family was an easy replacement for Sarah?

He worked his jaw muscles back and forth, wondering how he could ever allow himself to fall in love with Bailey and start over. Nothing—no one—could ever take the place of Sarah and the life he'd had with her.

"Look, Amy, I hate to run, but I really need to go take care of Dad's horses." He glanced pointedly down the hall toward the cardiac care unit. "I'll be back in a couple of hours." His tone let her know that his words weren't meant as an invitation for the two of them to meet up again.

She nodded. "Point taken, Trent. I'll be gone by the time you get back." With that, she strode away.

Trent headed for the elevator, where he pushed the down button with more force than was necessary.

Why was he so upset, not just with Amy but with himself? He wasn't the one who'd turned his back on Sarah, the one who'd visited her grave only once. And he'd certainly never seriously considered making a new life for himself, with a substitute family. He could never, ever do that to Sarah's memory.

Yet his relationship with Bailey didn't feel like a betrayal. The feel of her kisses, her touch, the way she smiled, drifted into his mind. What he shared with Bailey seemed more right than he cared to admit.

The elevator doors slid open, and he stepped inside. Just as quickly, they closed.

Life could be like that. One door sliding open, another closing rapidly behind you almost before you knew it.

Did Amy have the right idea after all? Was moving on a natural part of the healing process, one he'd been afraid to face?

He has two little boys...

Trent shivered as Amy's words rang through his mind.

He might fall in love with Bailey, and he might even want to marry her someday. But could he ever really give her what she so desperately wanted?

Children were obviously high on her priority list. But as much as he'd enjoyed the company of Macy and the kids in her 4–H group, and as much as he'd gotten used to being around Macy again, he still didn't think he'd ever want to have more children of his own.

Trent exited the hospital, suddenly glad to be away from its cloying, antiseptic smell—one that would haunt him always. Would the ghosts and the pain of his past never let him go? How in the world was he ever supposed to live and love again, the way he once had when Sarah was alive and well?

And how was he supposed to forget about Bailey, if he ended up unable to make a commitment to her?

Bailey was a lot of fun to be around. He liked her spunk and her positive outlook, even though he didn't really see life the way she did. One of his greatest fears was that her optimism would rub off on him. That had already happened on more than one occasion. Yet how long could it last? That was the problem. There was no guarantee that the two of them could be happy for a lifetime.

So where did that leave them?

Trent headed down the sidewalk, letting the sounds of traffic surround him, feeling frustrated and uncertain. He wanted to love Bailey.

He just wasn't sure how to go about it.

CHAPTER THIRTEEN

TRENT WOULD BE PROUD of her, Bailey was certain. Ten days had passed since he'd left for California, and if she did say so herself, she'd done a more than passable job of taking care of Windsong. Macy had helped out, and even Wade Darland had stopped by to make sure things were running smoothly.

Trent had called three times in the past week, once to let her know his father was doing well and the other two times to see if everything was okay at Windsong.

The first time he'd called, they'd laughed about never having talked to each other on the phone before. It had felt a little strange, but Bailey had loved the way Trent's sexy voice had sounded, low and deep, making her toes curl. He planned to come home tomorrow. She couldn't wait. She'd missed him more than she'd ever thought she would. Yet at the same time, her stomach whirled at her anticipation of the talk he'd promised her they would have upon his return.

Trying not to think about that, Bailey made her way across the pasture and climbed through the fence to Trent's property. The wind picked up, shaking the leaves of the trees in a musical dance, and a chill claimed the air, turning it crisp and sharp. It carried with it the scent of fall, reminding Bailey that summer would officially end in a matter of days. Around her, dark clouds moved across the sky, and as she hurried to get the horses fed, fat drops of rain fell, slowly and intermittently at first, then heavier and more steadily.

In his paddock, Alysana raced in circles, sensing the incoming storm, his black mane and tail flying in the wind. His red coat looked like a streak of fire as he ran, calling to the mares in their nearby enclosures.

Bailey hesitated outside the fence, watching the blood bay stallion. He was used to being in the barn, and she was sure Trent would never leave his prized horse outside in a storm like this. She glanced up at the clouds. The sky looked wicked—dark gray and black—and streaks of lightning split the clouds even as she watched.

Her mind made up, Bailey hurried toward the stable for a halter and lead rope. She knew stallions required firm handling, and she was certainly no expert in the matter. But surely she could manage to catch Alysana and lead him to his stall.

Outside, she opened the paddock gate and stepped through, careful to latch it securely behind her. Quietly, she spoke to the horse. ''Easy, boy. There's nothing to be afraid of. Come on, Alysana, let's get you inside, where it's warm and dry.'' The bay perked his ears, focused on Bailey, then with a shrill whinny, began to race in circles once more.

Bailey spent several futile minutes walking calmly in his wake, unable to draw close to him. He snorted, and continued to circle the enclosure while the rain poured down, soaking her and the horse to the skin.

Frustrated, Bailey stopped and stood still. Alysana halted, as well, gazing curiously at her. He took a step or two in her direction. ''That's it,'' she coaxed. ''Come on, boy.'' The bay stretched his neck to sniff her outstretched hand, then whirled and bolted again. Bailey cursed softly under her breath. This was getting her nowhere.

She headed for the barn, where she scooped some sweet feed into a bucket and pocketed several horse cookies, then made her way back outside. Within minutes, Alysana gave in to the temptation of Bailey's treats. Standing just out of reach, he extended his neck as far as he could and took a cookie from the palm of her hand. Two cookies later, she managed to persuade him to come close enough to stick his nose into the grain bucket. Quickly, Bailey slipped the halter over his head and buckled it in place.

With a feeling of triumph, she abandoned the black rubber bucket, needing both hands free to control the stallion. "See," she crooned, reaching into her pocket for another cookie as she led Alysana toward the gate. "That wasn't so bad, was it? Huh?" She patted his neck, loving the scent of his rain-drenched coat. They stepped through the gate, and as Bailey closed it, a huge streak of lightning split the sky, followed quickly by a resounding clap of thunder.

Startled, Alysana snorted and bolted to the end of his lead rope, nearly jerking it from Bailey's grasp. It was all she could do to hang on to him. She let go of the gate, gripping the rope in both hands as she faced the horse. "Whoa, boy. Easy." The wind caught the gate and slammed it against the pipe-rail fence with a metallic clang, spooking Alysana all over again. He lunged and his shoulder slammed into Bailey. She stumbled backward, lost her footing and plopped down on her butt in the mud.

Fear rushed through her, not so much that the horse would trample her but that she would lose her grip on the lead rope. If Alysana got away, there was no telling where he might run off to. He could get loose on the road and be hit by a car in the downpour. With all her might, Bailey clung to the lead rope as she struggled to regain her footing.

She gained her balance and staggered upright just as she heard the sound of a vehicle pulling into the driveway. With no time to look over and see who it was, Bailey held tightly to the rope, working her way up it hand over hand toward Alysana. If she could get close to the stallion, maybe she could soothe him.

"Easy, boy. Whoa, Alysana. Whoa!" She managed to get up beside his shoulder once more. But he shook his head and fought her, making her arms feel like wet spaghetti as she tugged him toward the barn. She'd just reached the door when Trent's voice sounded in her ear.

"I've got him."

With a start, Bailey looked up, straight into his eyes, as gray as the storm. Her breath caught in her throat. "Trent." Warmth curled through her. "What are you doing home so soon?"

He took the rope from her, and Bailey found it difficult to uncurl her fists after having held on to the lead so tightly. Her fingers burned where the rope had chafed them, and water dripped from her hair into her eyes.

"I took an earlier flight home than I'd originally intended," he said over his shoulder as he led Alysana into the barn. "Good thing, too." He cast her a look of reprimand, and Bailey's heart jumped.

His expression was a mixture of irritation and concern. Again, warmth snaked through her, overpowering the damp chill caused by her rain-soaked clothes. The emotion in his eyes spoke louder than words. It wasn't the horse he was worried about.

God, but it was good to see him. She wanted to

fold herself into his arms and hold him close. Instead, she slid the barn door shut, muting the sounds of the storm outside.

Trent put Alysana in his box stall, then faced her. "What were you doing out there, Bailey?" He gripped her shoulders. "You could've gotten hurt. Didn't I tell you not to mess with Alysana?" He pursed his lips and shook his head. "What am I going to do with you?"

Bailey glared at him. "Well, I could hardly leave him out in the storm, could I?" She squared her shoulders beneath Trent's grasp. "I had the situation under control..."

"Yeah, I can see that." Pointedly, he swiveled her around and stared at her muddy backside.

Bailey felt her cheeks warm. She must look a sight. She turned toward him, tucked her tongue in her cheek, then laughed. "Welcome home, cowboy."

Trent stared at her a moment, then he laughed, too, and the sound filled her with pleasure. "You really know how to roll out the welcome mat for a guy," he said. "I nearly swallowed my teeth when I saw you out there in the middle of the lightning storm, holding on to Alysana for dear life. I wasn't sure which one of you to be most worried about." His eyes sparkled playfully.

"Is that right." Bailey placed her hands on her

hips. "Are you telling me your horse means as much to you as I do?"

With another chuckle, Trent placed his fingers beneath her chin and tilted her face upward. "Maybe more like the other way around," he teased. Then his lips came down upon hers, and Bailey lost herself in the warmth of his arms, her wet clothes and windblown hair forgotten.

Moaning, she wrapped her tongue around his. Trent ran his hands up and down the small of her back, pressing her against him. And as their kiss grew more heated, she could feel his need in the hard length of him, denim against denim. She draped her arms around his neck, feeling the quick beat of his heart as her breasts rubbed his chest.

"Let's go inside," he whispered, his forehead against hers. "We need to get you out of those wet clothes."

Bailey licked her lips. "That's the best offer I've had all day."

Still kissing, touching, they made their way to the barn door. With one hand, Trent slid it open, his other hand still looped around her waist. Already, the storm had blown over, leaving behind a strong breeze and the clean scent of rain-washed earth.

Bailey felt as though the storm now moved inside her. Her heart raced, and her blood heated as Trent continued to kiss and caress her. On the porch steps, they locked in an embrace, Trent's leg thrust be-

tween hers, their lips seeking hungrily, like lovers
sharing a first kiss. She had no doubt where this was
leading.

He pushed the door open and scooped her up in
his arms. Startled, Bailey let out a gasp, then snuggled against him as he pressed his mouth over hers
once more in a kiss that set her soul on fire. He
carried her through his bedroom doorway and set
her down on the floor next to the queen-size bed.

"Bailey," he whispered. "I've waited for this
moment ever since I laid eyes on you." He ran his
hand over her wet hair, looking intently at her. "Are
you sure this is what you want, too?"

Catching her bottom lip between her teeth, Bailey
nodded. She slipped her hands inside his jean jacket,
running her palms across his chest. "More than you
can know," she said.

Trent shrugged out of the jacket and let it fall to
the floor. Bailey took pleasure in the way his muscles rippled as he pulled off his T-shirt and tossed
it aside. His chest was hard and smooth, sprinkled
with a light dusting of hair that veed down and disappeared beneath the waistband of his jeans. The
muted light from the window spilled across his skin,
making him look like a dream lover who'd come to
her, conjured from her wildest fantasies.

He stripped off the rest of his clothes and stood
before her, completely naked. Seeing him without
clothes excited her, making her tremble. Eagerly,

she let him remove her jacket, then her shirt and bra. By the time he'd undressed her, she saw how easy it would be to plunge into an emotional abyss without a second thought. The temptation to give her heart to Trent, even knowing he would likely break it, overwhelmed her.

He laid her down on top of the quilt that covered the bed, as dusk claimed the cloud-studded sky. A half-moon hung high above, breaking up the shadows, just visible through the windowpane.

Trent ran his hand across her bare hip, and his lips curved in a slow, sexy smile. "You wear moonlight even better than the river does," he said. And with that, he lay down beside her and took her into his arms.

Bailey slid her hands across his bare shoulders and let him pull her close, certain she'd lost her last scrap of good sense. She'd questioned the wisdom of this moment, even when it had been a mere fantasy. Yet she'd known, deep down inside, that it was bound to happen sooner or later. She'd been kidding herself, wanting to believe she could control what she felt for Trent.

As a child, she'd divided her feelings into neat little compartments and locked them away so no one could hurt her. As a young woman, trying to find her way once she'd left her last set of foster parents, she'd done exactly the same thing. She'd been so careful to guard her heart from anyone who could cause her pain. And now, here she was, baring her feelings to a man who fell precisely into that category.

Trent had nothing permanent to offer her—no promise of love and commitment, or of the family Bailey so deeply craved. She knew that. But at the same time, she was drawn to him. It was so easy to love this man who reminded her at times of an injured bird, and at other times of a regal hawk…tough, self-sufficient, needing no one. If she was really smart, she'd leave his bed and never look back.

"Bailey," Trent said. "I want to make you feel good. I want to kiss every inch of your skin and know the taste of you on my tongue."

All coherent thought fled as he slid his palm along her thigh. She moaned, loving the way his rough hand possessed such a gentle touch, savoring the way it rubbed across her skin. Common sense told her this was a mistake, yet she didn't care. Her body craved release. She had to know what it was like to lie in his arms and let him love her, if only for a little while.

He paused just long enough to reach into the nightstand and withdraw a box of condoms.

As he tore one open, Bailey raised her eyebrows.

"Planning ahead, cowboy?"

He shot her a smile that made her mouth go dry. "Maybe." He slid the condom over his erection, and the intimate ritual heated her blood as she watched. Then he stretched out alongside her on the bed once more and took her into his arms.

Bailey locked her arms around Trent's neck and slipped her tongue into his mouth. He let out a moan, and heat pooled between her legs. He wanted her. She found power in that, and in the fact that she wanted him, too. They were like two forces of nature, coming together to clash and mesh, until all else was lost.

Trent returned her kisses with hot, fervent ones of his own. One hand caressed the base of her neck, while the other found the small of her back. Pressing her against him, he took advantage of her having wrapped her legs around him, and in one silky motion he slid inside her.

The movement was so unexpected, yet so smooth, Bailey gasped. She'd thought he'd engage in foreplay for a while, and she'd thought she wasn't ready for him yet.

She'd thought wrong.

She was more than ready. She moaned against his mouth, loving the heated way he made her feel, savoring the ache he caused at the center of her core, the throbbing between her legs. Sweet, delicious satisfaction began to pool through her as Trent moved inside her.

Hard, hot, wanting, he stroked her first with his erection, then with his hand, as well. His fingers crept into her nest of curls, and he found the hard nub of her flesh and began to caress it in slow circles, while his hips kept rhythm with hers.

Bailey climaxed so fast her entire body shook. With a cry, she arched against him, her shoulders pressing into the pillows while her hips thrust to meet his. Moments later, he tumbled over the edge with her, then lay with his head nestled on her shoulder, sprinkling kisses against her collarbone, her neck, her throat.

"Bailey," he whispered. "You make me crazy."

"You do a pretty fair job of that yourself," she said, running her hands over his back and shoulders. Bailey's mind and body still thrummed with the passion she'd so quickly spent, passion that was already rising to the surface again, as even now, Trent stirred between her legs.

"I didn't mean to move so fast," he said, rising onto his elbows to look into her eyes. With his thumbs, he rubbed circles at her temple, then stroked her damp hair away from her face. "I'd meant to take my time with you, Bailey, but you're so sweet, so sexy, I couldn't hold back."

"I'm not complaining," she said, letting her lips curve into a smile.

"Does that mean you like what you've seen so far?" he asked, his smile matching hers.

Bailey put on a contemplative frown. "I think so, but I'm not sure."

"Not sure?" His eyebrows arched, and he lowered his voice to a growl. "What do you mean, you're not sure, banker woman?"

"Well, it was all over so quickly," she teased. "I mean, it was great, but I'd really, really hoped to savor you a while longer." She trailed the nail of her index finger along his biceps. "It isn't every day that I crawl into bed with a hot, yummy cowboy."

"I'm glad to hear that." He nipped her earlobe. "So you want to savor me, huh?"

"Mmm-hmm," Bailey moaned as his tongue snaked inside her ear.

"That's good," he murmured, "because I hadn't planned on letting you out of here any time soon."

"Is that right?"

"That's right. It's not every day I get a hot, sexy city woman into my bed."

"I should hope not," Bailey said.

He traced a line of kisses from her ear to her throat, back up to her chin. There he paused, just short of her mouth, his eyes locked on hers. His expression grew serious. "Bailey, I'm not kidding," he said. "It's been a long time since I've wanted to be with a woman. I don't know what it is about you that makes me feel this way, and I can't promise you where things will go from here. But right here, right now, I want you."

Bailey gazed back at him. "Promises often mean nothing," she said. "Honesty does." And his honesty cried out to her soul more than anything else he could've said or done. Shallow words of love and empty promises were not what she wanted to hear. Like Trent, she wanted only to focus on this moment. She would worry about what came afterward later.

"In that case," he said, pressing a kiss against her lips, "I can honestly say that you make me feel something no other woman ever has. I just haven't quite figured out yet what that something is."

With that he covered her mouth with his and rolled to his side with her wrapped in his arms.

Wasting no further time on words, they lost themselves in each other. This time, their lovemaking was leisurely. Trent took his time pleasuring her with his hands and his mouth, and she took equal opportunity to give back what he gave to her. When Bailey was certain she'd never been more fulfilled in her life, she slipped into an easy, dreamless sleep, knowing that no matter what the next moment brought, for this moment, she was happy and content.

Content lying in Trent's arms, and pretending for a little while that he was hers.

TRENT WAS STARTLED from the depths of sleep by a nightmare. For a moment he was surprised to find Bailey nestled with her head against his shoulder, her legs tangled with his among the sheets and blankets. The sweet scent of her hair, her perfume and the aftermath of their lovemaking surrounded him— clung to his skin, his bed. He savored them for a moment, then quietly sat up and disengaged himself from Bailey's warm body.

She sighed and snuggled deeper into the pillows, her features soft, relaxed, as though she hadn't a care in the world.

Dear God, what had he done? He'd led this woman to trust him and to give herself to him, and what could possibly come of it? Like a fool, he'd yielded to the physical desire he felt for Bailey and let all good sense flee his mind. He'd indulged himself in her like some horny teenager, using her body to relieve him of the frustration and wanting he'd known ever since he'd laid eyes on her.

Yet as he watched her sleep, he knew there was more to it than that.

It wasn't simply physical need that had caused him to take Bailey to bed. He hadn't treated her like an object of lust, there simply to fulfill his needs. He was in love with her, and that was why he wanted her in his bed. The thought scared the hell out of him. After losing Sarah and seeing his marriage crumble, one would think he'd be smarter this time around.

Trent pushed back the covers, climbed from the bed and slipped into his jeans. He had to get a grip on himself, had to face reality and decide what he was going to do about the mess he'd just made between him and Bailey. Barefoot, he walked quietly down the hall and stood in front of Sarah's room. His breath lodged in his chest, and he hesitated, wondering if he shouldn't just turn away. He hadn't been in the room for weeks.

Closing his hand over the knob, Trent pushed the door open, and memories rushed over him like a flooded river swelling above its banks.

He could still smell Sarah in this room, despite all the time that had passed. He didn't know if the scent of her was real or imagined, salvaged from his treasury of memories. But as he stepped inside the confines of these walls, it was as though she was here again, alive, real, well. He blocked out the odor of her sickness, and nearly all thoughts of the final days she'd spent curled beneath the canopy of her bed in the corner. Instead, he recalled the lemon-sunshine smell of her blond hair, and the way her clothes always carried the sweet scent of the outdoors, a combination of little girl and horses and wild mountain air.

Crossing to the far corner, Trent sank onto the bed and flicked on the bedside lamp. A soft glow from the Mickey Mouse light flooded the room. The silence gripped Trent as he looked around.

He hadn't left the room as a shrine. Yet he hadn't been able to clear out Sarah's room. It had been another sore spot between him and Amy. She'd thought he should dispose of the haunting memories of those final days of their little girl's life. She'd told him to donate Sarah's toys and clothes to charity, that it would be best if he gave away all the furniture and repainted the room.

He'd flat-out refused.

He'd given Macy one of Sarah's Breyer horses, and some of her things to children in need. He'd even cleaned out the closet, and left only Sarah's favorite T-shirts in the dresser drawers, her boots under the bed. But he hadn't been able to completely empty the room of everything that had been a part of his daughter. He didn't want to. He needed to surround himself with things that kept her memory fresh and clear in his mind, and to have not a shrine but, instead, a place of retreat, where he could come and simply remember.

His gaze traveled the room. A few of Sarah's Barbie dolls still rode on their horses across the topmost shelf of those he'd built for her; below them, her collection of *Goosebumps* and *Saddle Club* books were lined neatly end to end. The two bottom shelves held her stuffed animals, and on her dresser, the trophies she'd won with Misttique in the local saddle club competitions were proudly displayed, ribbons in an array of colors hanging on the wall above them. The closet still held the afghan his mother had crocheted for her one Christmas, and the bed was made up with clean sheets, the ones Sarah loved, with the horses on them.

The pillow was the one where she'd rested her head each night after a long day spent playing, riding or going to school. He'd read her to sleep more times than he could count, sitting on this very bed, and held her hand when she'd had the chicken pox, and brought her soup when she'd fallen out of the tree house and broken her arm.

And he'd tried and tried and tried again to let those memories push away all the others. To let them overtake the ones of Sarah's last days, spent in this bed, her little body wasted away, her beautiful blond hair gone, with only peach fuzz in its place. He didn't want to think of her that way. He wanted to remember her the way she'd been—happy and healthy and growing—his little girl, living her life, loving every minute of it, with him loving her.

But he couldn't. No matter how hard he tried, he couldn't suppress the memories of what it felt like to sit helplessly by and watch the child he loved and cherished more than his own life, his own soul, suffer and linger, and finally die.

He could never go through that again.

Never.

He didn't even realize he was crying until he heard the floorboards creak.

He looked up to find Bailey standing in the doorway, wearing only her shirt and panties. A troubled look pulled at her features, and sorrow filled her eyes as tears of her own ran down her face.

"Trent?" She hesitated in the doorway, seemingly unsure whether to step inside or leave him alone.

He wanted her to go. She had to.

He couldn't give in to the part of him that longed to take her in his arms and simply let her hold him while he allowed his pain to wash away on a wave of tears.

With the back of his hand, he swiped at his eyes, then rubbed his fingers vigorously against them. "You shouldn't be in here," he said. The words were out before he could stop them. *Hell,* he didn't really want her to go. Somehow, Bailey's presence didn't feel intrusive, the way anyone else's would have. But to admit that meant he needed and wanted her, and it was time he remembered he hadn't planned on feeling that way ever again. He had no choice but to push her away.

"I'm sorry," she said softly. "I woke up and found you gone. I—I wasn't sure if you wanted me to spend the night or just go."

He said nothing, fighting the urge to push himself away from Sarah's bed and cross the room, close the door behind him and simply leave with Bailey.

He couldn't do that. He couldn't care about her, couldn't fall in love with her. Love meant pain, and the very aura that surrounded him in this room was enough to tell him what he had to do. The answers he'd sought in California came clearly to him now.

"It's all right," Trent said. "But you should probably go now."

The look of hurt that flashed across Bailey's face was enough to tear his heart in two. "You're right," she said.

She turned and left without a backward glance.

And he sat staring at the floor, hating himself for letting her go, yet knowing it could be no other way.

CHAPTER FOURTEEN

BAILEY SHUT the door to her office and sank into her desk chair. Exhausted, she closed her eyes and rubbed her forehead. The sight of Sarah's bedroom refused to fade from her memory, as did the look on Trent's face last night when he'd told her to leave.

She'd found sleep all but impossible after going home to her own bed. Thoughts of Trent whirled through her mind, making her toss and turn. That he might never have cleaned out his daughter's room after she died hadn't even occurred to her. Knowing he kept the room just the way it had been when Sarah was alive sent a clear message—one she could not afford to ignore.

Bailey stared at the potted plant on her desk and recalled her past. Losing her parents at an early age and being shuffled from one foster home to another—more than thirty in fourteen years—had been hard.

Some of her foster parents had been nice, and most had treated her decently, but many had not. Whether it was a personal possession—of which she'd had few—or simply being considered a member of the household she lived in, Bailey had constantly battled for what should rightfully have been hers.

You're not my real sister. My parents only take in foster kids for the money social services pays them.

The words of Dottie's eldest son still echoed in her mind. And before that, there'd been the twins she'd shared a room with when she was eight years old, in the tenth of her foster homes.

Go ahead and tell our mother we took your Barbie doll. We'll tell her you're lying, and that you always lie and steal things. Our dad will throw you out on the streets, and you'll be homeless.

She'd only stolen once. Feeling lonely and unwanted, Bailey had longed for something to love and take care of. The twins had a puppy they'd gotten for their ninth birthday, but Bailey was seldom allowed to play with him. While walking home from school, she'd spotted a kitten inside a pet shop window, and when the store clerk had his back turned, she'd lifted the kitten out of its cage, tucked it inside her jacket and taken it home.

Since she slept in the far corner of the room she shared with the twins, she didn't think they'd find the kitten hidden in a box under her bed. But they had, and they'd told on her, and Bailey had gotten the spanking of her life. Her foster parents made her

take the kitten back to the pet store and apologize
to the manager. Bailey never stole anything again,
but just knowing the twins would use the single incident to blackmail her into letting them keep her
Barbie doll was enough to send Bailey looking for
vengeance.

Climbing onto a kitchen chair, she got the pow-
dered packs of Kool-Aid her foster mother kept in
the top cupboard and poured them into a box of
bubble bath in the master bathroom. When the
woman took her bath and found that Kool-Aid, not
Calgon, had taken her away in a sea of pinkish-
purple foam, Bailey had once again been spanked.

Never mind that she'd cleverly planted the evi-
dence of the empty Kool-Aid packets in the pockets
of the twins' jeans in the laundry hamper. Never
mind that she'd pleaded temporary insanity, using
her wildest imagination to come up with a logical
explanation about why she'd done what she had.
Within weeks, Bailey found herself being moved to
yet another foster home.

And each time she was shuffled from one home
to the next, a part of her spirit died. But she'd sur-
vived, and learned to put her past behind her and
move on. She'd chosen a new life for herself here
in Ferguson, the type of life she'd always wanted.
She still planned to have a family, still wanted to
give her children what she'd never had. She was

more than ready to take that step. Obviously, Trent was not.

The look on his face last night had broken her heart. She'd stood in the doorway of Sarah's room, torn between wanting to cross the floor and take Trent into her arms and wanting to turn away and leave him to the privacy of his grief and sorrow. The expression on his face had held her momentarily rooted in place. He, too, had seemed torn.

She'd seen something in his eyes—for the span of a heartbeat—a silent plea that said he needed her and wanted to reach out to her. Then the wall had closed around him once more, and he'd asked her to leave. She could have been more pushy in offering him comfort, could have refused his request that she go. But what would have been the point?

Before work this morning, she'd taken flowers to Sarah's grave. She'd laid them down at the foot of the little blue spruce and stood there for a long time, thinking. She'd known before that she loved Trent, and after last night, there was no doubt in her mind. She loved him more than she'd ever loved anyone. But if he couldn't open his heart up to her and love her back, she couldn't force him to do so. And no amount of wishing things were different could change that.

Bailey had always prided herself in being strong. She'd had to be to live through what she'd experienced as a child and move on. And that was exactly what she would have to do now—stand strong and move on with her life. No matter how much she loved Trent, she couldn't afford to spend a lifetime pining away for a man she could never have.

She'd made up her mind to go to him tonight after work and tell him that they could be nothing more to each other than the friends they'd started out as. She'd rehearsed the speech she would give him so many times that she had it memorized. But now that the time had come to leave work and confront him, the thought of doing so practically made her laugh.

How on earth did one go from making love to a man who felt like her soul mate, to turning her back on him and treating him as a mere acquaintance? It seemed an impossible thing to do, but somehow, she vowed to do it anyway. Pushing away from her desk, Bailey gathered her things and left the bank.

After changing her clothes, she fed the animals. She was too edgy even to think about eating supper. It would be better to go straight over to Trent's house now, before she lost her nerve. The sooner she got it over with, the sooner she could begin the long, painful process of forgetting what they'd shared.

As she left the barn, the sound of a vehicle pulling into the driveway drew her attention. Buddy barked a warning from his post on the porch. The minute Bailey saw Wade Darland's truck, she remembered what she'd forgotten. Days ago, while she and Macy had fed Trent's horses, the little girl had invited her to the 4–H club celebration that marked the end of the show season.

Roundup Days began tomorrow night and lasted through the weekend, and Bailey had promised to take Macy shopping for some new boots and fancy western shirts to wear for the event. Wade had telephoned to make sure she didn't mind and that Macy hadn't sweet-talked her into it. Bailey had assured him she'd be delighted to go shopping with Macy, and Wade had seemed more than happy to turn the very uncowboylike task over to her. He'd agreed to drop Macy off at Bailey's house this evening, but in the wake of all that had happened last night, the shopping expedition had completely slipped her mind.

"Hi, Bailey," Macy said as she climbed out of the truck and slammed the door shut. Excitement laced her voice, and she skipped, rather than walked, toward Bailey. She wore her usual boots, jeans and ball cap and, in one hand, clutched a Breyer collectible horse.

Bailey smiled. She'd been in love with the Breyer horses since she was a kid, and still had the one she'd gotten as a child—a plastic model of Marguerite Henry's Misty of Chincoteague—sitting on a shelf in her living room.

"Are you ready?" she asked Macy, waving to

Wade as he turned his truck around and headed back down the driveway.

"Oh, yeah," Macy said, following Bailey into the yard. She plopped down on the porch step and scratched Buddy behind the ears. "Dad gave me some money, plus I've got my allowance all saved up. I want to get these really cool lace-up boots I saw at the western store."

"I see you brought your Breyer horse."

"Uh-huh." Macy held out the black-and-white Appaloosa. "I wanted to show him to you, since I saw your Misty horse in the living room."

Bailey took the horse and examined him, admiring the lifelike detail that had gone into the workmanship. "He's beautiful."

"He was Sarah's," Macy said.

A spark of sadness jolted through her, clenching Bailey's heart. She saw the horse in a new light.

"Trent gave him to me after Sarah died. He said he knew she'd want me to have the Appaloosa, because it was her favorite. He thought I should have something special to remember her by." Macy smiled sadly. "But even if he didn't give me anything, I'd never forget her."

Bailey swallowed over the lump in her throat. The horse felt warm in her hands. "Of course you wouldn't," she said. She ran her fingertips over the Appaloosa, then handed him back to Macy. "He's

one of the prettiest Breyer horses I've ever seen.''
She smiled, and Macy smiled back.

"I knew you'd say that. He's my favorite, too.
Can I put him on the shelf with your horse for
now?''

"Absolutely.'' Bailey held the screen door wide.

Minutes later, she gathered her purse and a light
jacket, and headed for the door with Macy. Indian
summer continued to fill the days with sunshine and
high temperatures, but the evenings could grow
chilly.

"Shall we take the truck?'' Bailey asked. Macy
loved the old Chevy, and had made Bailey chuckle
at her obsession with pickup trucks, especially ones
from the fifties. Bailey had to admit that she, too,
had become attached to it. Living on the farm, she'd
quickly discovered just how handy having a pickup
could be.

"Sure,'' Macy said. "It's too bad Lester never
got it painted. Are you going to?''

She hadn't really given it much thought, since
she'd planned to sell the truck back to him. Now,
she wasn't so sure that would ever happen. "I probably will. Maybe you can help me decide what
color.''

"Cool!'' Macy grinned at her, and Bailey
laughed.

They climbed into the Chevy and started off for
town. Bailey glanced down at the fuel gauge. It was

near empty. "We'd better stop and get some gas in this thing before we end up stranded somewhere," she said. Within minutes she pulled into the parking lot of the one and only convenience store in town, which also sold gas. Normally, she bought her gas at the Texaco station, but since Lester worked there, it wasn't the best choice now.

Bailey filled up, then leaned in the open driver's window and spoke to Macy. "I'll be right back, kiddo. Want something to drink?"

"Sure," Macy said. "A Mountain Dew?"

Bailey tapped the truck with the palm of her hand. "You've got it."

Inside the convenience store, she waited in line to pay for her gasoline and two Mountain Dews, then went to rejoin Macy. She'd come to enjoy the little girl's company immensely. Being around her made Bailey long all the more for a child of her own. Thoughts of Trent assailed her, and she did her best to ignore them. Her heart ached, knowing she would never have a child with him, when he'd grown to mean so much to her.

She'd never meant to fall in love with a wayward cowboy.

The sound of squealing tires reached her ears a split second before the sight registered. Her truck careering out of the parking lot, Lester Godfrey behind the wheel, Macy still in the passenger seat.

Trent told himself he'd made the right choice. Loving Bailey felt wonderful, but the uncertainties that came with it were too much for him to deal with. Over and over, he recalled his resolution to remain alone for the rest of his life. But his heart argued with his head, waging a constant battle that he felt he was quickly losing.

If nothing else, the least he owed Bailey was an explanation.

He'd promised her they would talk when he returned from California. Instead, he'd sent her away from his home—from his bed—in the middle of the night, as though she'd done something wrong. He felt like a jerk.

Bailey deserved far better. A woman like her should have someone who could love her without holding back, and if Trent couldn't, then he needed to tell her so face-to-face. Pushing her away without an explanation wasn't right. She knew that Sarah's death had devastated him. Yet he'd never bothered to tell her exactly *why* he could never give his heart to anyone again. The risk of loss was so painful.

Would she understand?

Trent climbed through the fence and headed for Bailey's house. Buddy lay stretched out on the porch, and Star grazed contentedly in the pasture. The peacefulness of the farm gave him a warm feeling, stirred a longing to be a part of it. He wished things could be different. How on earth was he sup-

posed to keep his distance from Bailey with her living so close to him? Maybe he should just move
back to California.

As quickly as the thought came, he pushed it
away. He could never do that. He didn't want to live
anywhere remotely close to Amy and her new family, and more important, he could never abandon
Sarah's grave. Who would take care of her tree?

Trent knocked on the door, making Buddy bark.
He spoke to the dog, and the heeler tentatively
sniffed his pant leg. "What's wrong, fella? You
haven't forgotten me already, have you?"

Buddy wagged his tail but jumped out of reach
when Trent reached to pet him. "Yeah, I know the
feeling," he said to the dog. "It's not easy to trust
someone, is it?" He knocked again, then glanced
around the yard, noting Bailey's Mustang in the
driveway. There was no sign of her truck. She must
have gone to town.

Disappointed, Trent walked back home. It had
taken him all day to drum up the courage to face
her.

Climbing behind the wheel of his truck, Trent
headed to town. If Bailey was out and about,
chances were he could find her, since Ferguson
wasn't very big. Unless, of course, she'd gone someplace else.

He drove slowly down Main Street, his gaze
combing the bank parking lot on the off chance she

was working late. He also checked the parking lot of the video store, the feed store and the ice-cream parlor. Nothing. At the edge of town, he approached the convenience store, and his heart skipped a beat when he spotted her truck next to the gas pumps. It pulled away just as he drew near, and Trent saw that it wasn't Bailey behind the wheel.

He had only a moment to register that Lester Godfrey was driving the Chevy and that Macy was in the truck, before he saw Bailey. Futilely, she ran toward the pickup as it sped off, her face hardened in fury, her lips mouthing words at the departing vehicle.

Trent stomped on the gas and swerved into the convenience store parking lot, pulling up next to Bailey. "Get in." He leaned over and threw the passenger door open, and Bailey hopped inside. She tossed her purse and two bottles of pop onto the seat, then clamped a hand to her forehead.

"My God, Trent, Lester's got Macy!"

"I know. I saw him." He reached for his cell phone and thrust it at her. "Call 911 and get them to send the sheriff's department."

Bailey dialed while Trent raced after Lester. The Chevy shot down the two-lane highway at breakneck speed, rapidly putting distance between it and Trent's Ford.

He hoped to God he could catch Lester.

Trent punched the gas pedal. His focus on driving, he was barely aware of Bailey's voice as she gave their location to the dispatcher. She stayed on the line until the surrounding mountains broke up the cell phone's reception.

Bailey turned the phone off and gripped the dashboard. "Oh my God, this is all my fault. I shouldn't have left Macy in the truck while I went inside the store."

"Don't worry about it," Trent said. "We'll catch them." But cold fear had knotted his stomach and refused to unwind. From the way Lester was driving, Trent would safely bet he was drunk, and that, coupled with the high-powered engine under the Chevy's hood, could only spell disaster. If anything happened to Macy, Trent would never forgive himself.

He'd be damned if he'd give up easy.

Only now did he realize how attached he'd become to the little girl. Knowing she'd been close to Sarah was only part of the reason. Macy was a good kid, and he enjoyed being around her. The way she and Bailey had so much fun together gave him a good feeling deep down. He just hadn't wanted to admit it.

He'd kill Lester with his bare hands if harm came to that child.

Up ahead, Lester slowed the pickup truck a bit. Even drunk, he must have known the curves in the road were beginning to tighten. Taking advantage of that, Trent closed the distance between his truck and Bailey's. But the moment he did, he realized his mistake. Spotting the Ford in his rearview mirror, Lester sped up once more, pushing the Chevy to a dangerous rate of speed.

"Lord." Trent clenched his jaw and backed off. Frustration filled him, but an instant later, Lester slowed down again. Was he playing some sort of sick game of cat and mouse with Trent? Trent, too, slowed.

"What are you doing?" Bailey asked.

"I'm hoping to get him to ease up a little," Trent snapped, then regretted his loss of patience. Like him, Bailey was scared. "I can't catch him," he added. "Every time I try, he just speeds up." He glanced at the speedometer. Lester might be driving slower, but he was drunk, and they were still going faster than they should be.

"Where the hell is the sheriff's department?" Bailey's voice shook with fear and anger. "I swear, when I get hold of Lester he's going to wish he'd never met me."

"You'll have to stand in line," Trent said dryly. His mind raced as he tried to come up with a way to safely stop Lester.

In the distance, a siren wailed. Would Lester hear it and pull over? Or would he try to outrun the sheriff's deputies, as well? He might figure he had nothing to lose and drive all the more recklessly. Trent *had* to get him to stop.

At the moment, double solid yellow lines marked the two-lane highway. *Come on, come on!*

The minute the lines turned into a single, broken yellow one once more, he gave the Ford all it had and pulled out to pass Lester.

"Now what are you doing?" Bailey asked, panic lacing her voice.

"If he sees the deputies are after him, he might try to run for it. I have to make him stop."

Trent rounded a corner and nearly collided with the Chevy. Too drunk to accurately gauge his speed, Lester had slowed way down. Trent sped up and moved in front of him, then gradually downshifted the Ford. Lester stepped on the brakes, causing the Chevy to fishtail. In the rearview mirror, Trent could see him shaking his fist, mouthing curses. Macy looked small and helpless in the passenger seat.

Anger filled Trent all over again, and he tapped the brake firmly, slowing the Ford even more.

Lester swerved into the opposite lane and tried to pass Trent, but Trent cranked the steering wheel left, blocking his path. His heart in his throat, he checked the highway for oncoming traffic. He could see only a short distance ahead because the road curved.

Bailey let out an expletive. "We'd better hope no one's coming around the mountain in the other lane."

Trent knew he had to do more than hope. Slamming on the brakes, he angled the Ford sideways to block both lanes. The Chevy's tires squealed as Lester hit the brakes. The pickup swerved left, then right, clipping the Ford's back bumper.

The sound of tearing metal split the air as the pickup slid into the ditch on the side of the road, the fender scraping an outcrop of rock.

Bailey screamed.

Trent's heart all but stopped.

The Chevy shuddered to a halt, and Bailey leaped from the Ford before Trent had even brought it to a complete stop on the shoulder of the road.

He threw open the door and hit the dirt at a dead run.

Lester wasted no time in exiting the vehicle. He staggered into the ditch, then up the other side.

Knowing Bailey would tend to Macy, Trent bounded up the mountain in pursuit. "You sorry SOB," he shouted. "I'm gonna tear you limb from limb!"

A siren pierced the air, and Trent was vaguely aware of the sheriff's deputies as they jumped from their Blazer on the road below and headed up the mountain. Trent reached Lester before they'd barely started to climb, and took solid satisfaction when his fist connected with Lester's face. He yanked him up by the shirtfront and met Lester's frightened gaze, nose to nose.

"Don't hit me, man," Lester said, his voice slurred. "I just wanted my truck back."

"You're going to jail, bud," Trent replied through gritted teeth. "And you'd better thank your lucky stars, because those deputies are going to be a lot friendlier to you than I would've been."

Lester's face paled, and it was all Trent could do not to pummel him to a bloody pulp. Behind him, one of the deputies shouted, "Don't do it, friend."

Trent whirled around, and recognition registered. The officer was a regular at Audrey's Café.

"Hey, Trent. Let him go."

Reluctantly, Trent shoved Lester away. "He's not worth it," he said, looking from Officer Stillwell back to Lester.

Stillwell's partner took hold of Lester, and Stillwell laid his hand on Trent's shoulder. "You okay, Trent?"

He nodded, still breathing hard. Funny thing was, he really did feel okay. Letting out his pent up anger in that one solid punch to Lester's nose had done wonders.

"I'll sue you," Lester threatened, dabbing at his bloody nose.

"I don't think so," Stillwell cut in. He spoke to his partner. "I'm pretty sure I saw ol' Lester here take a swing at Trent. How about you, Davis?"

Davis nodded. "I do believe he did." He turned Lester around none too gently and handcuffed him.

"Come on, Lester, we're going for a little ride. 'You have the right to remain silent...'"

Trent's hands shook with residual anger as he climbed down the mountain and saw Bailey standing beside the Chevy's open door. He prayed Macy wasn't injured. Fear gripped him anew and he hurried forward.

Macy had crawled across the seat and now had her arms wrapped tightly around Bailey's neck as Bailey leaned inside the pickup. "Shh," Bailey crooned. "It's okay now, honey. We'll get the paramedics to give you a ride to the hospital and make sure you're all right." She eased back and brushed a loving hand over Macy's forehead. A blood-caked goose egg had already risen there.

"Is she hurt?" Trent asked.

"She's mostly just shaken up," Bailey said.

"I don't want to go in the ambulance," Macy said. "It scares me."

"There's nothing to be afraid of," Bailey assured her. "Trent and I will follow you in his truck. Okay?"

The ambulance pulled up a moment later, and Macy reluctantly succumbed to the paramedics' ministrations.

Trent drove with Bailey to the hospital. He had no time to think about his previous visits there, as he concentrated on finding out how Macy was doing.

The nurses, who knew Trent well, allowed him and Bailey to sit with Macy while they waited for Wade to arrive. The poor kid had been scared half out of her wits by Lester's drunken stunt, but miraculously, she had only the bump on her head and a few bruises. She clutched Bailey's hand as though she would never let go, while Dr. Bevins checked her over.

"I'm so sorry, honey," Bailey whispered. "I never should have left you alone in the truck."

"It's not your fault," Macy said. Tears streaked her cheeks, but she managed a smile. "My dad leaves me in the truck when he gets gas too."

Bailey was visibly relieved. Trent was glad she realized that she hadn't done anything stupid or out of the ordinary. What had happened truly wasn't her fault. Who could know Lester would pull such a stunt?

Without a second thought, Trent placed his hands on Bailey's shoulders, massaging her taut muscles with his thumbs. She glanced up at him and smiled, and his heart did a flip-flop.

Could he really end their relationship?

Wade arrived minutes later and reassured Bailey over and over that the only person he held responsible for what had happened to Macy was Lester. Stillwell and Davis came to the E.R. and talked to Wade, then spoke to Bailey about having her pickup towed to the auto-body shop in the next town.

But Trent barely listened. Instead, he focused on Wade, who held his daughter tightly in his arms and kissed the top of her head. Macy clung to her father, wearing a brave smile, drawing strength from him.

Longing pulled at Trent.

He remembered how it felt to hold a child who believed you walked on water. To love and protect her. And he remembered how it felt to stand by, powerless to help when it mattered most. Nothing had been able to stop death from taking Sarah away from him.

Nothing.

His father's words echoed in his mind:

You can't crawl into the grave after your daughter.

All this time, he'd somehow felt responsible and guilty for being unable to save his little girl. He'd prayed a million times that God would take him in her place. His prayers had gone unanswered, and he'd blamed himself. If only he'd known about the cancer sooner.

Daddy, my tummy's poking out. Look.

He'd exchanged such harsh words with Amy over it.

Damn it, you're the one who gets her into the shower! Didn't you notice the lump? Didn't you see?

I didn't see, Trent! God, why are you blaming me?

Trent closed his eyes. Why indeed? The doctors

had told him there would have been no stopping the cancer, no matter what. It wasn't Amy's fault, or his.

The conversation they'd had in California came back to him now, Amy's words resounding in his memory: *Why can't you realize that life goes on, with or without us?*

And Macy's:

I don't know why Sarah had to go to heaven. But I know she watches over me and she wants me to keep riding and having fun....

Trent's hands began to shake.

After losing his little girl, he'd never wanted to be a parent again. But now, as he watched Wade and Macy, knowing Wade was all Macy had left after losing her mother, something stirred inside him.

He had nothing left. Nothing.

He couldn't spend the rest of his life this way. Alone, lonely, aching for a child who was no longer here.

Still trembling, he squeezed Bailey's shoulders possessively. He loved her with all his soul. Could he find a way to share his life with her? Dear Lord, was there room in his heart to love another child?

Bailey had stuck by him all this time, in spite of his stubbornness. She'd given herself to him without hesitation, and he'd repaid her by turning her away. A woman like her had a right to be loved wholeheartedly. Bailey should be with a man who was willing to marry her and give her the family she so longed for.

He wanted to be that man.

Uncertainty threatened again, but he batted it down. Taking a deep breath, he looked at Bailey and vowed to give it his best shot.

She stared curiously at him, a puzzled frown creasing her forehead. "What's got you thinking so hard, cowboy?" She reached up to place her hand over his. "I can practically see steam coming through your hat."

He took her hand and pressed a kiss against her palm. "Actually, I've got something pretty serious on my mind."

Concern filled her eyes. "What is it? Is everything all right?"

"I'm not sure, but I hope it will be." He choked back the hot achy feeling that clogged the back of his throat. "I have to talk to you, Bailey."

She stood, and he slipped his arm around her waist.

He took a deep breath. "I have to tell you what happened when Sarah died."

CHAPTER FIFTEEN

THEY DROVE to her house, and Bailey swayed between worry and curiosity the whole way there. She knew Trent must be thinking about Sarah. But there was more to it than that. Something had happened in the E.R. She'd bet her farm on it.

Trent gripped the steering wheel as though he might slide out of the truck if he let go. Sweat beaded his forehead and his jaw muscles worked back and forth. He said nothing on the ride over to the farm. Bailey wanted to ask him why, but better judgment told her not to. He'd said they would talk. She would wait for the right moment.

He parked in her driveway and climbed from the truck, not touching her at all as they made their way to the house. In the living room, Trent sank onto the couch, and Bailey brought him a glass of ice water. He was beginning to scare her. Had his grief finally pushed him over the edge?

Absentmindedly, Trent took the ice water and took a sip. As he set the glass down on a coaster, his gaze found the black-and-white Appaloosa, which sat on the shelf above the television. As though in a trance, he walked over and lifted the horse. He turned to her, a sad smile on his face. The expression in his eyes made Bailey feel like crying.

"This is Macy's," Trent said. "I gave it to her, when—when Sarah..."

She nodded. "I know. She brought it over here tonight to show it to me."

He sat down beside her, running his fingers across the shiny surface of the Appaloosa's body.

"Sarah knew she was dying," he said. His eyes took on a faraway look. "I knew it, too. All the doctors had told us the cancer had spread too far and too fast for there to be any real hope. But Amy wouldn't believe it. She kept insisting that Sarah would get better. That the doctors would be able to save her."

He looked directly at Bailey. "You can't imagine what it's like to sit by and watch your child slowly slip away. To hold her hand while she throws up, sick from the chemo, and see her long pretty hair fall out in clumps."

Tears burned Bailey's eyes, and she reached for Trent's hand. "No," she said. "I can't."

"Sarah begged me to take her home," he said. "She didn't want to die in the hospital. She was afraid..." His voice cracked, and he drew a deep breath. "Afraid that the angels wouldn't find her there. She wanted them to be able to come to her room, where she said her nightly bedtime prayers.

Her dying wish was for me to bring her home. How could I refuse?''

Tears flooded his eyes, and Bailey thought her heart would shatter.

She couldn't speak. She could only squeeze his hand.

''Amy was furious with me. She kept insisting that if I'd just leave Sarah in the hospital she would get well. She didn't believe in hospice care. I provided our daughter with the best home care money could buy, but Amy blamed me as Sarah grew weaker. She said it was all my fault, because I'd brought her home.''

Silent tears flowed down his cheeks.

''Those last few hours it was just me and Sarah. I'd asked the nurse to leave. There was nothing she or anyone else could do. Amy refused to sit by and watch Sarah die. She left. Just like that. I wanted to shake her. At that moment, I hated her for abandoning us.

''But Sarah understood. She'd gotten so weak she could barely even talk. And then, all of a sudden, this awesome energy flowed through her. She squeezed my hand—hard—and when she looked up at me, Bailey, I swear it was the first time in weeks that her eyes looked clear and free of pain.''

His lips trembled, and he had to pause a moment before he was able to continue.

''She said, 'Mommy's just too sad to wait for the

angels with us, Daddy.' I told her that Amy was
tired, and that she'd come back in a little while. But
Sarah knew that wasn't true.'' He gazed down at the
Appaloosa. "She said, 'I'm tired, too, Daddy. Too
tired to stay awake anymore.' Then she fell asleep,
and she never woke up again.''

Trent's eyes locked on hers. Abruptly, he let go
of Bailey's hand and set the Breyer horse down on
the table.

"Damn it!'' he cried, clenching his hands. "Oh,
God, Bailey.'' He reached out to her, and she took
him in her arms and held him as sobs racked him.
"I miss her more than you can ever know. I miss
her so much that sometimes I want to die, too.''

"I know.'' She held him tight, rubbing his back
while he cried. "I know, sweetie. Just let it out.
Lean on me, Trent, and let it out. I'm here for you.''

He cried for a solid hour.

Bailey cried with him, until her throat ached and
her eyes swelled and she could barely breathe.

And then the two of them curled up on the couch
and simply held on to each other.

TRENT FELT MORE DRAINED than he ever had in his
life, more than if he'd spent the entire day doing
hard physical labor.

He lay on the couch with Bailey for a long time,
until darkness claimed the sky and the room. As he
held her, a sense of peace washed over him. It had

felt good to share with her the things that had eaten him up inside for the past year. Things that had kept him from wanting to go on with his life, from wanting to live it fully.

And while they'd lain there, he'd made a decision.

He hoped it was the right one.

Trent sat up, and turned on the lamp beside the couch. He had to see Bailey's face, and he wanted her to see him, too, so that she could look in his eyes and know that he meant every word he was about to tell her.

When the light clicked on, they both blinked against the sudden glow for a moment. Trent reached out to smooth Bailey's hair. Her eyes were red and puffy, but she'd never looked more beautiful to him. She'd cried those tears for him, for the pain he felt…and for the daughter he'd lost.

He loved her with all his might.

Trent easily read the expression in her eyes. The love she held in her heart for him was there, waiting for him to take. Could she read his thoughts, as well? Did she know he'd fallen in love with her, in spite of his fears, in spite of his determination not to?

"Are you going to be okay?" she asked. Sorrow lined her pretty face. He didn't want her to be sad.

He nodded. "Bailey, you have to understand something. Ever since Sarah died and Amy left me, I've been afraid to let myself enjoy life. Afraid ever to open my heart up to that sort of pain again. I felt numb and dead inside, and I told myself that the best way to handle it was to withdraw from everything and everybody. I believed all I needed was my ranch and my horses, and that I didn't deserve to have happiness anyway, with Sarah gone. Why should I be happy—how could I possibly ever be— when my daughter was dead?''

''Trent,'' Bailey whispered. ''Do you really think Sarah would want that? Don't you think she'd be upset, knowing you felt that way?'' She cupped his face gently in her hands. ''If you were the one who'd died and left her behind, then she would be your legacy. Instead, she's gone now, and you are Sarah's legacy. You're all that's left of her. Trent, you have to draw on that and use it as your strength to go on.''

Her words shook him. He knew she was right. Deep down, he'd always known that Sarah would want him to be happy. He just hadn't been able to allow himself to be.

''I know that,'' he said. He took Bailey's hands in his. ''But I didn't give a tinker's damn about my life until you came along.'' He watched the look in her eyes. He saw hope flicker there, and love, followed by worry.

He wanted to erase that worry.

''The first time I laid eyes on you, I thought you were the most beautiful woman I'd ever seen. And the more I got to know you, the more I admired your spunk, your determination. But your love of life and your ability to move past the things that happened to you as a child scared me.''

''I didn't understand how you could just forget about the tragedy you'd suffered, losing your parents and being raised in foster homes all your life, and simply move on. I wanted to turn my back on you and forget I'd ever met you. But I couldn't.'' He ran his hands along her shoulders. ''God help me, I couldn't.''

Bailey slid her arms around his neck. ''Do you know why I was able to move on?'' she asked. ''Because I had no choice. Not any viable one. My parents were gone, and nothing could change that. I spent my life being shuffled from one foster home to another, always hoping someone would love me for who I was. I decided that if no one wanted me, then I would grow up to be my own person. I would make my dreams come true one day, and have a home of my own and children to love.''

''And as I got older, I hoped to find a special man to share it all with. To be my life's partner.'' She gave a dry laugh. ''I never found him in the city, and when I moved here and met you, I certainly didn't plan to take on a stubborn cowboy with a ton of emotional baggage. But I haven't been able to keep my distance from you, Trent. One thing after another seems to always draw us together. I can't help but think there's a reason behind all of it.''

He caught hold of her arms and pulled her close. "There's a reason, all right, Bailey. It just took me a while to figure out what it was." He took a deep breath. "You were sent to me, Bailey, to show me how to live and love again. And maybe I was sent to you, as well, to help you take that final step away from your past, into the life you've always wanted. I don't claim to have all the answers. I'll never understand why I had to lose my little girl, or why the world is often filled with so much sadness. But I do know one thing."

He pressed a kiss against her lips. "There's a lot of joy to be had, also, and if you'll have me, I'd like to share that joy with you. I love you, Bailey, with all my heart and soul. I've never felt for any woman what I feel for you, and tonight, when I saw Wade with Macy, I realized how much I'd been missing out on, not having a family of my own. I finally understood that the things you'd been trying to show me, and the things my dad told me were right. There are no guarantees in life. But I can't crawl into a hole and hide, and I definitely can't go on living my life without you."

He rose from the couch and knelt on the floor at her feet. "Marry me, Bailey. Say you'll be my wife and spend the rest of your life with me."

She clutched her hand to her mouth, smiling

through the tears that filled her eyes. "I love you so much, Trent. Yes, I'll marry you." She stood and tugged him to his feet. "Just try to change your mind, cowboy, and you'll see how wicked this mean old city banker woman can truly be."

Laughing, he held her. "I'll never change my mind about you, city girl. And you can take that to the bank."

Never again would he be afraid to love the woman who'd grown to mean so much to him.

Never again would he be afraid of what life had to offer. He hoped and prayed it offered many happy years with Bailey.

He had a very good feeling that it would.

EPILOGUE

BAILEY MURDOCK SLOWED her Ford Mustang as she reached the entrance to the cemetery. The Christmas tree stood in the late-afternoon sun, its blue-green branches cloaked in a wet spring snow.

Bailey parked and got out of the car. Kneeling beside the tree, she ran her hand over the carved marble headstone. ''You'll always live on in our memories, sweetie,'' she whispered.

And in the children she and Trent would one day have. The children who would be Sarah's brothers and sisters.

She hung the silver wedding bells on the tree, one pair of many that had decorated the church pews a week ago when she and Trent had become husband and wife.

But this pair was special. Engraved on one bell was Trent's name and hers, with the date of their wedding. And on the other bell were the words *We love you, Sarah.*

''What are you doing?''

Bailey swung around and rose to her feet. This

time, the voice behind her was not gruff. This time, the look in Trent's gray eyes was warm and loving.

"She's my daughter now, too." Bailey folded herself into his arms. "I wanted her to have our wedding bells."

He held her for a long moment, then placed a tender kiss on her lips. "I think she would've liked that." He gazed up at the heavens, and Bailey followed his line of sight.

A bald eagle soared high in the sky, its cry ringing across the mountains. For a minute, the bird seemed to look right at them. Then it sailed away on the wind and disappeared above the distant trees.

"Come on," Trent said softly, taking Bailey by the hand. "Let's go home."

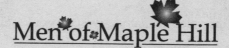

Men of Maple Hill

Muriel Jensen's new trilogy

Meet the men of the small Massachusetts town of Maple Hill—and the women in their lives:

Hank Whitcomb, who's back in Maple Hill, determined to make a new life for himself. It doesn't take long before he discovers he wants his old high school flame, Jackie Bouregois, to be a part of it—until her long-held secret concerning the two of them gets in the way!

Cameron Trent, who's despaired of ever having the family he's wanted, until he meets Mariah Shannon, and love and two lonely children turn their worlds upside down!

Evan Braga, who comes to Beazie Dedham's rescue when a former employer threatens her life. Then Beazie learns the secrets of Evan's past, and now the question is—who's saving whom?

Heartwarming stories with a sense of humor, genuine charm and emotion and lots of family!

On sale starting January 2002

Available wherever Harlequin books are sold.

HARLEQUIN *Super*ROMANCE®

Old friends, best friends...

Girlfriends

Your friends are an important part
of your life. You confide in them,
laugh with them, cry with them....

Girlfriends

Three new novels by Judith Bowen

Zoey Phillips. Charlotte Moore. Lydia Lane.
They've been best friends for ten years, ever
since the summer they all worked together at a
lodge. At their last reunion, they all accepted a
challenge: *look up your first love.* Find out what
happened to him, how he turned out....

Join Zoey, Charlotte and Lydia as they
rediscover old loves and find new ones.

Read all the *Girlfriends* books! Watch for
Zoey Phillips in November, *Charlotte Moore* in
December and *Lydia Lane* in January.

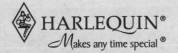

HARLEQUIN®
Makes any time special ®

Visit us at www.eHarlequin.com   HSRG

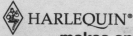

The

ShannonSisters

A Trilogy by C.J. Carmichael

The stories of three sisters from Alberta whose lives and loves are as rocky—and grand—as the mountains they grew up in.

A Second-Chance Proposal

A murder, a bride-to-be left at the altar, a reunion. Is Cathleen Shannon willing to take a second chance on the man involved in these?

A Convenient Proposal

Kelly Shannon feels guilty about what she's done, and Mick Mizzoni feels that he's his brother's keeper—a volatile situation, but maybe one with a convenient way out!

A Lasting Proposal

Maureen Shannon doesn't want risks in her life anymore. Not after everything she's lived through. But Jake Hartman might be proposing a sure thing....

On sale starting February 2002

Available wherever Harlequin books are sold.

HARLEQUIN®
Makes any time special ®

Bestselling Harlequin® author

JUDITH ARNOLD

brings readers a brand-new,
longer-length novel based on her
popular miniseries *The Daddy School*

Somebody's Dad

If any two people should avoid getting
romantically involved with each other, it's
bachelor—and children-phobic!—Brett Stockton
and single mother Sharon Bartell. But neither
can resist the sparks...especially once
The Daddy School is involved.

"Ms. Arnold seasons tender passion with a dusting
of humor to keep us turning those pages."
—*Romantic Times Magazine*

*Look for Somebody's Dad
in February 2002.*

HARLEQUIN®
Makes any time special ®